Wingless Flights

Wingless Flights:
Appalachian Women in Fiction

Danny L. Miller

Bowling Green State University Popular Press
Bowling Green, OH 43403

Copyright © 1996 Bowling Green State University Popular Press

Library of Congress Cataloging-in-Publication Data

Miller, Danny, 1949-
    Wingless flights: Appalachian women in fiction / Danny L. Miller.
      p.   cm.
    Includes bibliographical references (p.).
    ISBN 0-87972-717-9 (clothbound). -- ISBN 0-87972-718-7 (pbk.)
    1. Women and literature--Appalachian Region -- History and criticism.
2. Women and literature--Appalachian Region--History--20th century.
3. American fiction--20th century--History and criticism.
4. Appalachian Region, Southern--In literature. 5. Appalachian Region--In literature. 6. Mountain life in literature. 7. Women in literature.
I. Title.
PS286.A6M55 1996
813.009'9287'0974--dc20   96-30729
                                                                                      CIP

Cover photograph of Belzona Spencer Osborne is from the family. Photographic collection of Danny L. Miller.

Cover design by Laura Darnell-Dumm

Contents

Preface	ix
Introduction, The Spirit of Mountain Women	1
Chapter 1, The Paradox of Appalachia and the Stereotype of the Mountain Woman	15
Chapter 2, Romantic Idealization and the Mountain Woman as Victim: The Works of Mary Noailles Murfree	31
Chapter 3, Mountain Gloom in the Works of Edith Summers Kelley and Anne W. Armstrong	53
Chapter 4, Native Writers and "Authenticity": Emma Bell Miles and Jesse Stuart	78
Chapter 5, James Still's Mountain Women	102
Chapter 6, Harriette Simpson Arnow's Mountain Women: Defeated or Triumphant?	124
Notes	158
Works Cited	172
Selected Bibliography	177
Index	180

Sister, Thou Wast Mild and Lovely

Sister, thou wast mild and lovely,
Gentle as the summer breeze,
Pleasant as the air o' evening
As it floats among the trees.

Peaceful be thy silent slumber,
Peaceful in thy bed so low,
Thou no more will join our number,
Thou no more our song shall know.

Dearest sister, thou hast left us,
Here thy loss we deeply feel,
But if God that hath bereft us
He will all our sorrows heal.

Yet again we hope to meet thee
When the days of life hath fled.
When in heav'n with joy to greet thee
Where no farewell tears are shed.

A Primitive Baptist hymn sung by the women of the church at the death of a sister.

Sarah Jane Miller Yates, a North Carolina mountain woman, circa 1875. From the family photographic collection of Danny L. Miller.

Preface

Several significant studies of Appalachian literature have been written. In the Ford Study published in 1962, W.D. Weatherford and Wilma Dykeman examined "Literature Since 1900." Cratis Williams's monumental dissertation, "The Southern Mountaineer in Fact and Fiction" (New York University, 1961), was printed in *Appalachian Journal* in 1975 (edited by Martha H. Pipes). In 1977 *Appalachian Journal* published the essay "Appalachian Literature" by Jim Wayne Miller, and again in 1990 Miller published an article in *The Cratis Williams Symposium Proceedings* entitled "A People Waking Up: Appalachian Literature Since 1960." While addressing women writers and some of the depictions of women in the literature, these works do not focus specifically on an examination of the images of women in Appalachian literature.

In this book I examine the lives of Appalachian women through a sustained analysis of their presentations in fiction. Literary portrayals of mountain women are certainly not the "whole truth" about them, but a study of their depictions in fiction may help us to understand their lives more fully. Several general articles on Appalachian women in literature have been published in the last twenty-five years. Jack Welch published "Maidens, Mothers, and Grannies: Appalachian Women in Literature" in 1976 in *Appalachian Journal*. In 1978-79 I published a three-part article "The Mountain Woman in Fact and Fiction of the Early Twentieth Century" in *Appalachian Heritage*. Sidney S. Farr published "Appalachian Women in Literature" in 1981 in *Appalachian Heritage*. An indispensable tool for anyone interested in the lives of mountain women in literature, as well as other disciplines, is Farr's *Appalachian Women: An Annotated Bibliography* (1981). In 1986 Carole Ganim discussed Appalachian women in literature in her essay "Herself: Woman and Place in Appalachian Literature" in *Appalachian Journal*. In addition, numerous papers have been presented at the Appalachian Studies Conference on Appalachian women in literature, notably by scholars Nancy Carol Joyner, Sandra Ballard, Beth Harrison, Laurie Lindberg, Betty Krasne, Grace Toney Edwards, and Jane Hill, among others. This study joins their work in trying to define and understand the roles, qualities and experiences of Appalachian mountain women. By no means do I claim that this analysis is exhaustive; there is still much to be said on the subject.

Besides the scholars named above, I am indebted to several people in the production of this book for their encouragement and support: my mentor for this project, Wayne C. Miller; my friends and colleagues, Darrell N. Hovious, Christiana Hopkins, Chris Moore Smith, Beth Harrison, Deborah Overmyer, and Victoria Longino; my departmental colleagues at Northern Kentucky University, especially Susan Kissel and department chair Paul Reichardt; the Steeley Library librarians Rebecca Kelm, Threasa Wesley, Ann Whittle, Allen Ellis and Emily Werrell; and particularly my Appalachian grandmothers, Della Yates Jones and Clyde Adams Miller (who died at the age of 97 in February 1996), and my mother, Mary Leona Jones Miller.

Introduction

The Spirit of Mountain Women

In the last thirty years or so, the "renaissance" in Appalachian studies has produced a considerable body of scholarship on things Appalachian. Numerous books and articles have examined many aspects of Appalachian life, history and culture. There is still, however, no literary history of Appalachia, although such noted scholars as Cratis Williams, Wilma Dykeman and Jim Wayne Miller have produced valuable articles on the subject. The anthology *Appalachia Inside Out* (edited by Robert Higgs, Ambrose Manning and Jim Wayne Miller), containing many literary critical essays, goes a long way in redressing the lack of an Appalachian literary history, but such a history is still sorely needed.

Appalachian women have played a vital role in the literature about the mountain region. They have been at the centers of the novels and stories about the mountains, as they have been at the center of the Appalachian culture itself. By examining the writings of Mary Noailles Murfree, Edith Summers Kelley, Anne W. Armstrong, Emma Bell Miles, Jesse Stuart, James Still and Harriette Arnow, we can identify the paradoxical attitudes toward Appalachia, which have been manifest in descriptions of the women, who, as Cratis Williams affirms, "bore the burden" ("Southern Mountaineer Part IV" 386) of their culture: they are weak yet strong, victims and survivors, noble and courageous though often uncouth and uneducated by others' standards. At different times various of these qualities were emphasized over others, depending in large part on the purposes of the authors and who the authors were— man or woman, Appalachian native or "outsider"—who was doing the looking and what he or she was looking for.

Mary Murfree was a local colorist, emphasizing setting and the peculiarities of the mountain people. She was also essentially an observer of the mountaineers, not one of them. Although she was sympathetic towards them, her understanding of the mountain people's inner lives was nevertheless superficial in many respects. These two aspects of Murfree's life—her literary genre and her limited knowledge of her subject—helped to shape her descriptions of mountain women. Her young, ethereally beautiful heroines are more literary conventions than descriptions of real mountain women. She often uses these heroines, however, to show that the mountaineers shared the "common humanity" of people everywhere. When not romanticizing or sentimentalizing mountain women, she emphasizes the outward conditions and appearances of their lives. Her typical mountain women are pathetic victims, poor, haggard, uncouth, struggling to raise a houseful of children, slaving over a washtub, subservient to and victimized by often drunken and/or violent husbands.

The emphasis on victimization as the chief quality of mountain women's lives was maintained by writers after Murfree. As local color waned in popularity, many writers in the late nineteenth and early twentieth centuries turned to less romantic depictions of the mountain people. In fact, because these works were often geared to reform efforts, they emphasized many of the most negative aspects of mountain life: violence and brutality, lust and immorality, degeneration resulting from inbreeding, incest, illegitimacy and the subjugation of women. Thus, because women were surrounded by such despressing conditions and their lives were often characterized by defeated acceptance, their victimization appeared even greater than in the works of the local colorists. In Edith Summers Kelley's *Weeds* and Anne W. Armstrong's *This Day and Time* women are depicted as pathetic victims of childbearing, toil, poverty and lasciviousness.

Kelley and Armstrong, however, perhaps because they were women and conscious of women's place in society, were sympathetic toward the mountain women and foreshadowed in their novels, however briefly, the enduring mountain women of later fiction. Judith Blackford's submission to the patriarchal/masculine system and her resigned acceptance of the cruel world in which she lives is a bitter defeat, especially insofar as Judith has actively struggled against this submission. But there is a hint of nobility, courage and endurance in Judith's behavior at the end of the novel. And Ivy Ingoldsby withstands all the forces that beset her and emerges in *This Day and Time* as strong and unbroken.

Native Appalachian writers began to write about their own people in the 1930s. In the novels and stories of these native writers, best exemplified by Jesse Stuart, James Still, and Harriette Arnow, mountain women are portrayed as strong, proud, full of life and indomitable spirit. The emphasis is not on women as victims, although certainly many features of their lives are hard to bear and personal sacrifice is a major characteristic of their existence. Rather, the native writers, by focusing on family relationships and the inner lives of women, emphasize the qualities in the lives of Appalachian women that make them admirable rather than pathetic.

Whatever the personal bias or emphasis of the author, however, throughout all of these descriptions several qualities work together to define the nature of Appalachian womanhood. Most of these qualities are affirmative, admirable attributes that delineate a positive characterization of mountain women. They have an affinity with nature and the cyclic patterns of life; they love their land, homes and families; they nurture and sustain community and culture; they find solace in the everyday tasks and pleasures of life; they survive against desperate conditions and hardships although they are often powerless against the forces that victimize them. A few of the features of their lives presented in the writings, however, suggest some of the problems that these women encounter in their personal lives: loneliness, loss, emotional separation from their husbands, and a subservient role in the patriarchal system.

The first and most obvious attribute of women in Appalachian fiction is undoubtedly their close, almost mythic, relationship with the natural world. Almost all of the writers examined in this study evoke the closeness between women and nature, from Murfree's Arcadian nymphs to Harriette Arnow's Gertie Nevels. For example, Murfree's Cynthia Ware responds to the beauty of nature when she returns home to the mountains after her valiant pilgrimage to save Vander Price from prison in "Drifting Down Lost Creek." In this scene Murfree conveys the living spirit of place, of nature, as the mountain verily breathes with life: "There it stood, solemn, majestic, mysterious: masked by its impenetrable growth, and hung about with duskier shadows. . . . The spirit within it was chanting softly, softly . . . here was her [Cynthia's] home and she loved it" (*ITM* 59-60). Likewise, Celia Shaw in "The Star in the Valley" shares a "subtle affinity" with the rest of nature around her, both "fed by the rain and the dew" (*ITM* 131).

Even the works that emphasized the worst conditions of mountain life show women as close to nature. Ivy Ingoldsby, for example, in Armstrong's *This Day and Time*, is most content and at peace when she is at home in the mountains, which she seeks as a refuge from urban life. Ivy's name itself, suggesting the tenacious mountain foliage, is indicative of her closeness to nature. (Significantly, Ivy is also the name of one of Wilma Dykeman's main characters in *The Far Family* and Lee Smith's wonderful heroine in *Fair and Tender Ladies*.) Judith Blackford, in Kelley's *Weeds*, discovers both the freedom and the cruelty of nature as she learns important lessons about life through her closeness to animals and the natural world.

The native writers, Stuart, Still and Arnow, also present strong relationships between nature and the mountain woman. Jesse Stuart's poem for his mother, Martha Hylton Stuart, for example, links her through

4 Wingless Flights

expressive imagery with nature. She is "on the earth" and "would choose the earth in preference to the skies." She has the strength of the oak; her skin is the color of autumn leaves; she has the "courage of the wind," "the rain's cool sympathy," and the strength of the "twisted grape-vine" (29-31). Subrinea Tussie in *Trees of Heaven* is like Stuart's mother in this respect. She ". . . *is* the forest, earth, flowers, water, and everything on the land. Subrinea is made of the earth" (192). She is a "volcanic outburst of Nature" (309). The novel's memorable scene in which Subrinea saves the newborn lambs explicitly affirms her relationship with nature. Still's Alpha Baldridge and Arnow's Milly Ballew and Gertie Nevels—all find in nature a source of sustenance and beauty.

Woman's closeness to nature is certainly not unique to Appalachian literature, but is, as feminist critics in particular have recently shown, a facet of patriarchal Western civilization. Susan Griffin, for example, in *Woman and Nature*, shows that women have been consistently represented in Western culture as closer to nature than men, and that men see themselves as superior to both nature and women: "The fact that man does not consider himself a part of nature, but indeed considers himself superior to matter, seemed to me to gain significance when placed against man's attitude that woman is both inferior to him and closer to nature" (xv). Woman's place in nature, Griffin shows, is evidenced in folklore, fairy tales and mythology, and her description of women in nature is very similar to portrayals of the women in Appalachian literature:

He [man] says that woman speaks with nature. That she hears voices under the earth. That wind blows in her ears and trees whisper to her. That the dead sing through her mouth and the cries of infants are clear to her. But for him the dialogue is over. He says he is not part of this world, that he was set on this world as a stranger. He sets himself apart from woman and nature.

And so it is Goldilocks who goes to the house of the three bears, Little Red Riding Hood who converses with the wolf, Dorothy who befriends a lion, Snow White who talks to the birds, Cinderella with mice as her allies, the Mermaid who is half fish, Thumbelina courted by a mole. . . .

We are the bird's eggs. Bird's eggs, flowers, butterflies, rabbits, cows, sheep, we are the caterpillars, we are leaves of ivy and sprigs of wallflower. We are women. We rise from the waves. We are gazelle and doe, elephant and whale, lillies and roses and peach, we are air, we are flame, we are oysters and pearl, we are girls. We are woman and nature. (1)

Throughout the literature I explore in this study, women are repeatedly associated with eggs, flowers, animals—sheep, cows, deer, rabbits, the flora and fauna of their world, as Griffin suggests of women in this passage.

Whereas woman's impulse is to protect and save nature, of which she is a part, man's is to subdue and conquer it. This attitude is certainly discernible in Stuart's *Trees of Heaven*, wherein Anse Bushman desires to subdue and control the land; Anse feels that he owns the earth only when he has conquered it. Anse is estranged from nature. He is unable to save the newborn lambs during lambing season, for example. Subrinea Tussie, on the other hand, not only saves many of them, but buries the ones Anse has lost. Part of both Anse's and his son Tarvin's "education" in this novel is that they learn to love the land and nature without the need to subdue and conquer it. Anse learns that, like the free-spirited Tussies who are *of* the land without having conquered or owned it, he can own the land without controlling it, and this makes him a kinder, "better" person. And through his union with Subrinea Tussie, Tarvin becomes one with the land and nature also. It is indeed telling that the final section of the novel is a rhapsody to nature and that it comes from Tarvin, who, through Subrinea, has become sensible to nature:

"Goldenrod is bloomin on the lazy pasture fields now," thinks Tarvin, "and Subrinea will go wild when she gits back to the hills. I can see her goin over the bluffs smellin the fingers of the goldenrod. And the farewells-to-summer have started to bloom on the bluffs. Subrinea is heavy with child but she will run out among the flowers like a bumblebee."

Tarvin looks at the goldenrod on the hill slopes. He looks at the farewells-to-summer on the steep bluffs. Their purple tops are intermingled with their white blossoms. Honeybees and bumblebees buzz lazily over their blossoms gathering sweets to make wild honey. . . . Crows fly over from the pine grove on the hill. They wing across the blue air in Ragweed Hollow by rows. Tarvin looks at them as they fly over. . . . (337)

When he contemplates the dead Tussies buried beneath the trees of Heaven, Tarvin thinks of how they loved life and nature, and of how he and Subrinea are now a part of nature:

"and they loved life. . . . They loved the earth and the smells of spring earth—wind, clean and sweet to smell with the flowers of spring. . . . What were laws to them? The laws of Nature were their laws.

. . . and I am married to Subrinea. When I married her in the sheep shanty, I married all of this." (338-39)

One of Jesse Stuart's unrecognized accomplishments, I believe, is that he shows in this novel an almost mythic reconciliation between man and nature through the union of man and woman, not a union based on conquest or control, but a shared recognition of the beauty of nature. Tarvin's sensitivity sets him apart from other mountain men in literature.

Another example of the mountain man's desire to conquer nature is provided by Nunn Ballew in Arnow's *Hunter's Horn*. Nunn's entire being is obsessed with conquering nature in the form of the red fox King Devil. Nunn devotes his every thought and action to hunting down and killing King Devil, who, it turns out, is actually a vixen, once again associating the female with nature. For Nunn, however, there is no such reconciliation with nature as there is for Anse and Tarvin. Nunn is himself defeated by his attempt to conquer nature. Brack Baldridge's desire to dig coal rather than be a farmer in Still's *River of Earth* and Clovis Nevels's preference for machinery and tinkering to farming in Arnow's *The Dollmaker* are other examples of the man's disassociation from the land and nature, in marked contrast to their wives' kinship with nature.

Closely tied to the mountain woman's love of nature is her love of place—land and all it symbolizes for her. This is a second major feature of the lives of mountain women emphasized in the literature.[1] Mountain women long for land as the one sure and abiding reality in their lives. They nurture the land as they nurture their families because the land sustains them both physically and spiritually. For them it represents freedom and independence as well as security. And thus, in story after story, they long for land and the security of place, or they rejoice in their closeness to the land. Ivy Ingoldsby returns to the mountains at the beginning of *This Day and Time* to escape from the nightmarish city to her own land because she knows that on the farm she can be independent and can make a living for herself and her son, even though she knows it will be hard. When he willed her his land, Ivy's father-in-law had advised her, "Whatsomever you do, don't let nobody git hit away from ye. If you've got ye a little patch o' land that's yourn, you've got your bread, an' ef you've got your bread, you kin live. You hain't beholden to no man" (28). As Roberta Teague Roy states:

Her [Ivy's] attitude toward the land is that it sustains and supports her; she does not force it to yield, and it is not fickle. In addition to this utilitarian attitude, however, there exists a deeply sensitive appreciation for the land which Ivy, in her unlettered simplicity, cannot articulate. She looks on her surroundings and comments, "'I don't reckon heaven could be prettier.'" (71)

Alpha Baldridge in *River of Earth* echoes Ivy's sentiments when she tells her husband Brack that she wishes to stay on their farm rather than go back to a dirty coal camp: "I'm a-mind to stay on here . . . it's the nighest heaven I've been on this earth" (176). Alpha longs for the permanence of a home, a farm of her own, not to be forever moving from one coal camp to another.

Millie Ballew, in Harriette Arnow's *Hunter's Horn*, cherishes her land, working with all her strength to preserve and protect it. Owning the farm has been her dream, and she exults in reaping its produce and knowing that she is thus providing for her family. Gertie Nevels in *The Dollmaker* dreams of owning the Tipton Place; Gertie even sees her brother Henley's death during World War II as part of a divine plan "to help set her and her children free so that she might live and be beholden to no man, not even to Clovis" (131). Often, woman's longing for land is a manifestation of her desire to be free of subservience to her husband.

Mountain women love the land and long for the security it provides; land is perhaps nature's chief manifestation, and the mountain woman is almost inseparable from both nature and the earth. On the other hand, mountain men are often estranged from the land.[2] Even though he desires to control the earth, for example, Anse Bushman in *Trees of Heaven* feels no relationship to it, unlike the Tussies. In *River of Earth* Brack Baldridge tells his wife, "I never tuck natural to growing things. . . . A sight of farming I've done, but it allus rubbed the grain" (47). Instead, he prefers to mine coal. Clovis Nevels in *The Dollmaker*, similarly, is not a farmer. Like Vander Price in Mary Murfree's "Drifting Down Lost Creek," both Brack and Clovis desert the land in favor of the machine. The estrangement between man and the land often serves as a metaphor for the estrangement between man and woman in the mountains.

The difference between men's and women's relationship to the land and to nature points to a third aspect of the lives of mountain women which recurs in literature: the emotional and spiritual distance between husbands and wives, so poignantly expressed by Emma Bell Miles in *The Spirit of the Mountains*. It is unfortunate because it is so rare that Jesse Stuart's depiction of the relationship between Tarvin Bushman and Subrinea Tussie is one of the few portrayals of true harmony between a husband and wife in Appalachian literature. More often, we see men and women distanced from each other, unable to communicate or to fully know one another's characters. Although the mountain women love their husbands and stand by them in all conditions, although they share the same daily lives, the same house and bed, and although there does exist between them an unspoken sympathetic understanding, there is often a wide, even unbridgeable, gap between them, a gulf that results in a great sadness and loneliness for the women. It is no wonder that countless descriptions of the mountain women emphasized their "melancholy" and loneliness.

8   Wingless Flights

What accounts for this emotional distance may be a combination of several things. The patriarchal system itself, which sets up in infancy and childhood a separation of the sexes and defines both the man's and woman's roles in society, especially the man's belief that he must provide materially for his family, may be the chief cause. Thus, we often see men like Brack Baldridge, Anse Bushman, Nunn Ballew or Clovis Nevels, who believe that their primary obligation is to make a living to support their families, or, more specifically, to indulge in their own notions of what is important in their lives, often seemingly unaware of alternatives or heedless of their wives' wishes. Women seldom, if ever, question their place in this system or their husbands' prerogative to control and direct their families economically. And the men feel no need to ask their wives' permission or to disclose to them their actions.

When Nunn Ballew sells his wife Milly's prize heifer in *Hunter's Horn*, for example, he does so without her knowledge, and although Milly is heartbroken she does not reproach Nunn. Alpha Baldridge, likewise, though she would wish a different way of life in *River of Earth*, always acquiesces to Brack's desires to seek work in the ever-closing and reopening coal camps. And although Fronnie Bushman begs Anse for new household furniture, she knows it is within his power to provide or withhold it. Significantly, at the end of *Trees of Heaven*, following his spiritual conversion, Anse allows Fronnie to buy the new furnishings. These women recognize their economic subservience to their husbands. It is for this reason that *The Dollmaker*'s Gertie Nevels, for example, saves money for her own place without confiding in Clovis.

Another reason for the distance between husbands and wives in the mountains may be the natural constraints that the people impose upon themselves, many of them certainly as a result of the patriarchal system discussed above. The mountain people are not very communicative and men and women talk little to each other about the significant events in each others' lives. As Emma Bell Miles states, for example, "They are so silent. They know so pathetically little of each other's lives" (70). Her description of the young couple Gid and Mary Burns in *The Spirit of the Mountains* is a perfect example of this silence and lack of knowledge, as is the relationship between Gertie and Clovis Nevels in *The Dollmaker*. Gertie and Clovis do not communicate with each other, and even though their lives are intimately intertwined, they are both silent, keeping their dreams to themselves. Similarly, when Brack's relatives come to live with the Baldridges in *River of Earth* and proceed to eat the family out of house and home, Alpha remains silent until the situation can no longer be tolerated and then takes matters into her own hands.

Introduction 9

A mountain woman from Muriel Earley Sheppard's *Cabins in the Laurel* (1935). Reprinted with the permission of the North Carolina Collection, University of North Carolina at Chapel Hill.

The gulf that exists between men and women in the Appalachian culture is somewhat paradoxical, however, for these women are very close to their families. In fact, her dedication to her family's well-being is a fourth characteristic of the mountain woman in literature. The woman is committed to her husband and children in every way. She constantly sacrifices for them, and her sacrifices are great. Like Alpha Baldridge, for example, she will go without food herself so that her children and her husband might eat. She will go without new clothes or shoes, and certainly without luxuries, so that her children may have them. Milly Ballew, in fact, goes without food and clothes and all luxuries so that Nunn can feed his *hounds* or buy new pedigreed ones in his vendetta against King Devil. The mountain wife will follow her husband on his endless quest for livelihood, like Alpha Baldridge or Gertie Nevels, although she sacrifices her own dearest wishes and dreams along the way.

In virtually all of the novels and stories discussed herein the mountain women are very close to their families, sacrificing in every way for them, and exerting a great influence on them. The children are often painfully aware of their mothers' sacrifices, and frequently as a result resolve to live differently. Tarvin Bushman in *Trees of Heaven* determines that his own wife will not live as harshly as his mother has had to do. The narrator in *River of Earth* resolves that he will never be a coal miner like his father, barely able to support his family. In *The Dollmaker* Reuben Nevels actually leaves home and runs away back to Kentucky and his grandfather's farm rather than witness his mother's constant sacrifices and self-denial. Suse Ballew in *Hunter's Horn* longs to escape from the mountains in order to avoid the life of hardship and sacrifice of her mother.

The role of the mountain woman in relationship to her family is analogous, in fact, to her role in the community and the Appalachian culture itself. She is in many ways the preserver and nourisher of the community, as she is of her family. For example, it is very often the mountain woman who most desires schooling for her children. Alpha Baldridge, for instance, declares at one point in *River of Earth*: "It's a long walking piece. . . . Four miles one way. [To send her children to school.] But I allus wanted my young 'uns to larn to figure and read writing" (80). Gertie Nevels and Corie Calhoun, likewise, believe that their children should have some schooling and support their community schools. As Wilma Dykeman states, the mountain woman's role of leadership in the community has often been overlooked:

> But often in the mountain family there were certain roles, and very often [the women's] was the role of leadership, the women helping establish and keep going the churches, for instance, [and] the schools. Women were very often leaders in the community. That is why I had Lydia McQueen in *The Tall Woman* be the person who was instrumental in the school. What more vital to a society than helping establish and sustaining the schools, the churches, the community sense there? And I think that's been overlooked in looking at part of the [Appalachian] experience, as outsiders have seen it, as sociologists, as literary people, and certainly as journalists have seen it. (Miller interview 51)

Although the mountain woman's role as preserver of and leader in the community life may not be overtly revealed in the examples in this study, that role is implicit.

Her role as preserver, nourisher and sustainer of both family and community life, the cultural if not political life of the community, is perhaps best exemplified in mountain fiction by the recurring connection between woman and the rituals of birth and death. To her mainly fall the tasks of preserving the living and then mourning and burying the dead. At the end of *Trees of Heaven*, for example, Subrinea Tussie is "heavy with child," but she is also mystically connected at this point, and has been throughout the novel, with the dead Tussies buried beneath the trees of Heaven. *River of Earth* ends with a death and a birth, the death of Grandma Middleton and the birth of a new baby for Alpha. Alpha's egg-tree in the novel is a magnificent symbol of her nurturing and life-giving nature, also suggested by her name, and it is she who mourns the most for and insists on a funeral for her baby Green.

Particularly poignant are the scenes in which the young girls, just at the threshold of womanhood, respond to life in a nurturing and preserving way, recoiling from the horrors of the destruction of nature and the taking of life most often perpetrated by the men. It is the women, most often, through imagery connecting them with the processes of life and death, who (not surprisingly) reveal the cyclical nature of life. Euly Baldridge in *River of Earth*, for example, is heartbroken when her younger brother Fletch comes to show her his treasures and reveals a pocketful of broken partridge eggs (24).

Perhaps the greatest attribute of mountain women in the literature examined in this study is their strength, which enables them to survive, and indeed triumph over, the hardships and adversities of their lives. If they are victims, and they are in many ways, they are not defeated ones. They are the true inheritors of the pioneer spirit. As Kathy Kahn states in the preface to her book *Hillbilly Women*:

12   Wingless Flights

Hillbilly women have a history of strength. Their land was first settled by English, Scottish, and Irish immigrants in the nineteenth century, who came to the Southern mountains to escape an oppressive British government. They were proud people and independent. (xxi)

Although the mountain women are often called upon to accept the struggles of life, they do not always, as some critics have suggested, accept these struggles passively. Alpha Baldridge's burning down of the house to insure her family's survival in *River of Earth* is one example of overt control over a painful situation. Alpha is not a passive fatalistic victim—she knows that her family's future depends on her *action*. Although Corie Calhoun in Arnow's *Mountain Path* cannot assert her will in the same active way to make her husband Lee Buck and her nephew Chris stay at home on the night when she knows their enemies are planning to ambush them, she is actively aware of the peril, and she does what she knows she must do—she remains silent, something that is perhaps harder to do than to prevent their going by speaking out. Milly Ballew in *Hunter's Horn* accepts what comes to her as "God's will," but she questions that will at times; she accepts what she cannot change and has no control over, but through this acceptance she survives. And Gertie Nevels makes an active decision at the end of *The Dollmaker* to split her block of wood into usable pieces for assembly-line dolls in order to help her family endure.

Mountain women find their strength in many things: in their land, which they enjoy cultivating; in their families, for whom their sacrifices are willingly made; in their usefulness to their communities. We find in literature many examples of their delight in these pleasures of life, which gives them the strength to face their hardships. Ivy Ingoldsby exclaims in response to the well-intentioned advice of the outsider Senator Timberlake that "God never intended that a woman's hand should be put to the plow": "Law, Senator . . . I hain't never plowed, but I'ud a heap ruther to hoe an' clear the filth off o' new ground as to work in ary factory on earth" (*This Day and Time* 167). Gertie Nevels carefully digs Miz Hull's potatoes while waiting for word from her missing husband. Milly Ballew feels intense satisfaction, accomplishment, and joy when she surveys her wondrous store of canned and dried goods ready for the winter; and Corie Cal takes pride in making candles for the first Christmas tree her valley has ever known. The lives of these women are not dreary and unfulfilled, for they take pride in and derive satisfaction from their abilities. They also find joy in their arts and crafts, often useful as well as decorative—quilting, canning, making a work of art such as an egg-tree or a whittled doll or cookies made from a paper pattern rather than a store-bought cookie cutter.

Introduction   13

Because they are able to find such comfort, satisfaction and pride in the accomplishments of everyday living, and because of their inner resources, mountain women survive and triumph over the great tragedies and trials of their lives. Very few of the women characters in the literature I have examined succumb to the forces that beset them. While madness and suicide are often seen as woman's means of escape from or a means of coping (or being unable to cope) with the world's hostilities, especially in twentieth-century literature about women, few mountain women in literature go "mad" or commit suicide. Aunt Elgie Cal in *Mountain Path* is heartsick about the death of her son Davey and has become slightly deranged; Judith Pippinger Blackford attempts suicide when she becomes pregnant with an unwanted child and faces a grim, loveless future in *Weeds*; Gertie Nevels suffers a mental breakdown after the death of her daughter Cassie in *The Dollmaker*. But Judith learns that suicide is not the answer and she finally accepts her life for what it is, and Gertie quickly discovers that she cannot find peace in pink medicine.[3]

These women do not give up, are not defeated. They are the kind of women extolled in such non-fiction works as Alice Kinder's *Old-Fashioned Mountain Mothers* or Kathy Kahn's *Hillbilly Women*. Kahn, who interviewed women in the late 1960s for her book, writes of them:

> These are the women who are usually pictured in articles and books as mournful creatures, covered with dust and grime, their thin mouths hardened into a grim expression. Typically, the women are seen as hopeless, helpless, and passive. It is true that hillbilly women mourn, and like everybody who lives in a coal camp or mill town, they are covered with coal or cotton dust. And often their facial expressions are grim, like those of the women waiting to claim the bodies of their dead kinfolk at Buffalo Creek, and Hurricane Creek, and Mannington [scenes of mine disasters].
>
> Yet these women have put their lives on the line. They are the women who have blocked the giant bulldozers which still come to strip the land, destroy their mountains and pollute their rivers. They have organized unions and led long and determined strikes. They have sheltered union organizers from company thugs. They have nursed starving children back to health. (xx)

These are indeed women of strength and determination. They and their fictional sisters—Cynthia Ware and Celia Shaw, Ivy Ingoldsby, Fronnie Bushman, Subrinea Tussie, Alpha Baldridge, Grandma Middleton, Corie Calhoun, Milly Ballew, Gertie Nevels—are the strong spirit of the mountains.

14 Wingless Flights

In 1905 Emma Bell Miles referred to mountain women as the "silent, wingless mate[s]" (70) of their husbands and stated that these women's lives were filled with constant sacrifice. However, there is a striking paradox inherent in fictional portrayals of Appalachian mountain women from the writings of Mary Murfree to Harriette Arnow, as Appalachia has been a paradox in the minds of the American public. On the one hand, their lives of victimization overshadow them; they are victims of the patriarchal system, of hard work, of childbearing, and of the loneliness inherent in the often unbridgeable distance between them and their husbands. On the other hand, especially in the works of native writers, but even in the writings of non-natives, the qualities which most consistently define them are admirable and positive ones. Though "wingless," the Appalachian mountain woman often flies to heights of courage, endurance and heroism.

1

The Paradox of Appalachia and the Stereotype of the Mountain Woman

Few American regions and their inhabitants have been the focus of such sustained national attention as the Southern Appalachian Mountain area and its people. The region itself has been praised as one of America's most scenic, and its natural resources have long been recognized. The people of the region, on the other hand, have been defamed more often than praised, mainly because they have been consistently perceived as essentially different from the mainstream of American civilization, "behind the times," strange, ignorant, even barbaric.[1] The subject of the mountain people has been greatly discussed in the past hundred years, particularly by social scientists and historians. Literary critics, though, have found the topic of the mountain people in literature to be one of only minor interest in their discussions of American literature.[2] The aim of this study is to analyze the depictions of Southern Appalachian mountain women in fictional literature through an investigation of their emerging portrait from the first fully dramatized treatment of the mountain people by Mary Noailles Murfree in the mid-1880s through the 1954 novel, *The Dollmaker,* by Harriette Simpson Arnow.

In his 1921 work, *The Southern Highlander and His Homeland,* considered by many scholars the classic study[3] of the Appalachian region, John C. Campbell defines Southern Appalachia geographically as the mountainous territory consisting of the four western counties of Maryland, the Blue Ridge, Valley, and Allegheny Ridge counties of Virginia, all of West Virginia, eastern Kentucky, eastern Tennessee, western North Carolina, the four northwestern counties of South Carolina, northern Georgia, and northeastern Alabama. In total, Campbell says, it is an area of approximately 112,000 square miles (10). The *Harvard Encyclopedia of American Ethnic Groups* says of the region:

The Appalachian Mountains stretch from Quebec to Georgia; the Appalachian Regional Development Act of 1965, as amended, established the boundaries of the Appalachian Region as including 397 counties in 13 states from New York

16   Wingless Flights

to Mississippi, with an estimated population in 1975 of about 19 million people. But only the central and southern highlands, extending more than 600 miles diagonally across Maryland, West Virginia, Virginia, Kentucky, North and South Carolina, Tennessee, Georgia, and Alabama, are commonly meant by the term Appalachia. (Billings and Walls 125)

The exact boundaries of the Appalachian area are not easily defined, particularly for the critic of the region's literature. The peripheral edges of the southern mountains, the hills and knobs that fade into such areas as the Carolina Piedmont or the Kentucky Bluegrass, are not so easily included or excluded from a definition of the region.

H.R. Stoneback suggests that the use of the term *mountaineer* to designate the people of Appalachia is "by now too freighted with misdirection to be useful in historical or critical writing" and invites a "geographical exclusiveness that does not square with the imaginative setting" (6) of much of the literature that deals with "hillfolk," the term Stoneback prefers. Stoneback points out that the works of certain writers, such as Jesse Stuart (in his view), Elizabeth Madox Roberts, T.S. Stribling, and William Faulkner, do not have settings that can rightly be called "mountain" (5-6). Although I agree with Stoneback that there *is* much inherent "misdirection" in the term, I have retained the traditional "mountaineer" to refer to the Appalachian people in this study. "Mountaineer" is the designation most often used to refer to Appalachians and reflects the fact that the majority of the Appalachian people do live in the mountains and have been affected by their isolation and environment there.

The Southern Appalachian mountain people have been called many things throughout the years. In 1899 Berea College president William Goodell Frost referred to them in the title of an essay as "Our Contemporary Ancestors," suggesting the pioneering values possessed by the mountaineers. Horace Kephart, in the title of his 1913 sociological study, called them "Our Southern Highlanders." In 1965 Jack Weller referred to their reputed backwardness when he dubbed them in the title of his study "Yesterday's People." And throughout their history they have generally been referred to by the old standby—"hillbillies." Whatever the label, the stereotype of the mountaineer has long been known and is well established. As H.R. Stoneback aptly states:

Hillbillies, barefoot and guitar strumming, murdering and moonshining, poor and illiterate but proud and independent, are so much with us in our slick fiction, our daily television, our comic strips, and have been with us for such a long time, that the fixed character, the mythical hillbilly, is open neither to question nor accretion. He is as established as the land. (1)

The people of Appalachia have been unable to shed the persistent stereotyping of fiction and nonfiction writers; and they have not escaped a rather ignominious representation in all segments of the popular culture.

Although the stereotype of the "mythical hillbilly" is well fixed, it has, not surprisingly, often been challenged. Indeed, the Appalachian region and the people who live in it have been perceived paradoxically almost from the time of Appalachia's "discovery" by the rest of the nation. There are currently, and historically have been, two opposing concepts of Appalachia—one essentially unsympathetic, the other fundamentally sympathetic. As noted Appalachian poet and scholar Jim Wayne Miller says:

One is the Appalachia of [Jack Weller's] *Yesterday's People*, the place of problems, poverty, and peculiar people. The other is the Appalachia of *Foxfire* [the series of nonfiction books depicting mountain crafts and the mountain way of life which have been appearing since the mid-1970s], the place of promise and the preserve of all those virtues and values that are, or should be, at the heart of our national life. (25)

The former Appalachia has been decried and denounced by those who have seen its people as failures at modernizing and adopting the standards of American "civilization." The latter has been admired and commended for its continued withstanding of those same forces of "civilization," which have been seen as encroaching upon it.

The paradoxical nature of America's conception of Appalachia can be illustrated by a brief discussion of the question of the Appalachian people's origins. There are several theories about where the mountain people came from and the conditions under which they came to America and ended up in Appalachia. The two most conflicting views on the subject are illustrated by the positions held by Harry Caudill and Cratis Williams, two leading writers on Appalachia. According to Caudill, the mountain people were for the most part the dregs of England—pickpockets, thieves, robbers, prostitutes and other criminals. The first chapter of his book *Night Comes to the Cumberlands*, titled "Our Disinherited Forebears," asserts that most of the people who settled in the Appalachian region were English criminals or of the lowest classes, brought to America as bondsmen by the labor-hungry plantation owners in the American South during the last quarter of the seventeenth century and throughout the eighteenth. The English Parliament aided the American plantation owners in procuring this element of the English population, Caudill asserts, because they wanted to get rid of such social outcasts. "And so," says Caudill, "for many decades there flowed from Merry England to the piney coasts of Georgia, Virginia, and the Carolinas a raggle-taggle of humanity" (5). Besides the criminals of England who "were worth more to the Crown on a New World plantation than dangling from a rope" (4), this "raggle-taggle" group consisted of penniless workmen, honest debtors, and a good number of orphaned children who were kidnapped from the streets of London.

Once in America, Caudill maintains, these outcast people were virtually unassimilable into the existing population. They were "cynical, penniless, resentful, and angry" and many "ran away to the interior, to the rolling Piedmont, and thence to the dark foothills on the fringes of the Blue Ridge" (6). These hill-dwellers, asserts Caudill, "living under cliffs or in rude cabins," were "the first to earn for themselves the title of 'Southern mountaineers'" (6). It is with this premise that Caudill begins *Night Comes to the Cumberlands*.

Cratis Williams defends a very different origin for the people of Appalachia. He stresses the Scotch-Irish element in the population of the mountains in his article "The Appalachian Experience." "Hardly anyone who has acquainted himself with the history of the region and its people," writes Williams, "doubt [sic] that the 'character' of Appalachian people was determined by the presence of the Scotch-Irish among the early settlers in the mountain country" (4). He continues:

They [the Scotch-Irish] were more numerous than the considerable number of Germans, Swiss, Hugenots, Welsh, and English. In the process of border acculturation, others surrendered their own language for the old-fashioned Northern English dialect spoken by the Scotch-Irish as they intermarried into the large Scotch-Irish families and accepted their ways. Thus, the Appalachian experience has been a continued chapter in the story of the Scotch-Irish experience. (9)

Williams describes that Scotch-Irish experience, beginning with the Roman invasion of Britain in 55 B.C., which drove many of the native Celts north into the lowlands on the border between present-day Scotland and England.

Williams describes the sojourn of this predominately Celtic people in the Scottish lowlands for several centuries, during which time they were exposed to and became staunch adherents of Calvinism. During the reign of Queen Elizabeth I, many of these lowland Scots were removed from this area and transported to Northern Ireland, where they were given lands confiscated from the Irish Catholics. They took with them their store of popular ballads, music, dance and folklore. In Ireland they prospered until the British merchants became envious of their successful textile industry, forced high taxes on that industry, and virtually reduced the "Scotch-Irish" to poverty.

Potato famines in Ireland added to their dispiriting experience in that country and eventually led to their emigration to America in the early years of the eighteenth century. Williams states: "It has been estimated that as many as 200,000 Scotch-Irish came to America prior to 1775 and that they had increased their numbers to 600,000 by the time the American Revolution began" ("Appalachian Experience" 8). Thousands of these immigrants later moved into the Southern Appalachian mountain region. Williams stresses the thrifty, industrious, religious Scotch-Irish element in Appalachia, a very different emphasis than Caudill's.

America's paradoxical attitudes toward Appalachia have been present since what some have called the "discovery," others the "invention," of Appalachia following the Civil War. Henry D. Shapiro, in *Appalachia on Our Mind: The Southern Mountains and Mountaineers in the American Consciousness, 1870-1900*, asserts the invention theory, that the *idea* of Appalachia rather than its reality is what took hold of the American people at this time. The public's awareness of Appalachia in the late nineteenth century "did not involve the perception of a new reality" (xi), says Shapiro, for Appalachia had been known for some time as a distinctive region in the nation. Rather, Shapiro states,

> it followed from the recognition that the well-known realities of southern mountain life were not consonant with the new notions about the nature of America and American civilization which gained currency during this period: that America was, or was becoming, or ought to be a unified and homogenous national entity, and that what characterized such an entity was a coherent and uniform national culture. . . . It was only in the context of such notions about the nature of America that the southern mountains and mountaineers became Appalachia, a "strange land and peculiar people." (xi)

Shapiro emphasizes the general public's perception of Appalachia as a "strange land and peculiar people" throughout *Appalachia on Our Mind*, a perception that has certainly contributed to the ambivalent attitudes about the region still evidenced today.[4]

The changing perceptions of the nature of American civilization and the relationship between the parts and the whole of the nation that Shapiro discusses were largely a result of the American Civil War, an event which—more than any other in American history—had a profound effect upon the discovery of Appalachia's "otherness." The Civil War drew the nation's attention to the southern mountain region. In the first place, the region called considerable attention to itself because of the way its inhabitants responded to the conflict. Unexpectedly, the mountain areas of the southern states were not wholeheartedly Confederate in their sympathies; in fact, many mountaineers were loyal to the Union cause.[5] William Goodell Frost, for example, pointed out as early as 1899:

> The feeling of toleration and justification of slavery, with all the subtleties of state rights and "South against North," which grew up after the Revolution did not penetrate the mountains. The result was that when the civil war came there was a great surprise for both the North and the South. Appalachian America clave to the old flag. It was this old-fashioned loyalty which held Kentucky in the Union, made West Virginia "secede from secession," and performed prodigies of valor in east Tennessee, and even in the western Carolinas. (314)

Added to the idea that a uniform American civilization could not be achieved until elements outside the mainstream were brought into line, as Shapiro suggests, this "betrayal" by the Appalachian mountaineers of the Confederate cause helped to create an unfavorable attitude toward the mountain region.

But the paradox of the views concerning the nature of Appalachia is that while this negative attitude toward the region was emerging, another attitude was emerging alongside it. If the region was seen as foreign to the idea of a uniform American culture, it was also seen—and for some of the same reasons—as an Edenic preserve of the values of America's founding fathers, untouched by the "blight" of civilization.

The Appalachian region was often written about in fiction and nonfiction in the late nineteenth and early twentieth centuries as an Edenic or Arcadian world or in terms that linked it with a golden age, such as that of Homer. Implicit in these writings is the belief that Appalachia was an "unspoiled" region where the noblest of American values were held as they had been by the country's forefathers. Let us take the example of William Goodell Frost's article "Our Contemporary Ancestors in the Southern Mountains," which appeared in the *Atlantic* in 1899. In this article Frost suggests the paradoxical attitudes toward the region. On the one hand, Frost had an obvious missionary motive for the article, based on his view of the region as in need of "enlightenment." As a result, he outlined an educational plan to put the mountain people "in step with the world" by making them "intelligent without making them sophisticated" (319). On the other hand, Frost saw no need to make the Appalachian people fit a uniform American mold. "As a matter of both taste and of common sense," he wrote, "we should not try to make them conform to the regulation type American; they should be encouraged to retain all that is characteristic and wholesome in their present life" (319). Frost conceived of himself as a "friendly interpreter" (311) of Appalachian life and attempted therefore to foster a positive attitude toward the region by linking the Appalachian culture to that of America's pioneering stock.

The title of Frost's article alone suggests the link between his "contemporary" Appalachians and their "ancestors," the American forebears. Likewise, much of Frost's language in this article emphasizes the golden age simplicity and wholesomeness of the Appalachian region. He speaks of his "sylvan hosts" on his visits to the mountaineers and of their "sylvan life" (312). He makes many comparisons between the life of the mountaineers and a heroic age. For example, he says: "Mountain homicides are not committed for purposes of robbery. They are almost universally performed in the spirit of an Homeric chieftain, and the motive is some 'point of honor'" (316). Throughout the article he admires the "Arcadian simplicity" (319) of the mountain way of life.

There emerged then, as a result of the nation's focused attention on the southern highlands during and in the wake of the Civil War, two distinct, though not necessarily mutually exclusive, attitudes toward the Appalachian region and its people. Before the war the mountain people had not been seen as intrinsically alien to American life. It took new notions about the nature of American civilization to effect that change. Before the war the mountain people had been seen as simply a pioneer stock living in the remote and isolated hollows of the Appalachian Mountains. After the war they became a "peculiar people," out of step with the rest of the nation, although there were opposing views as to whether this peculiarity was positive or negative. Before the war the mountaineers were seen as no more than frontiersmen or pioneers. After the war the myths and stereotypes about them that are still with us today began to emerge. Likewise, as the region became a focus of attention during the last decades of the nineteenth century, historians, social scientists, and fiction writers began to present ambivalent attitudes about the region's relationship to the rest of America in their works.

Depictions of Southern Appalachian mountain women in literature have not escaped the ambivalent attitudes toward the region as described above. Like the stereotype of the "hillbilly" mountain man—as lazy, shiftless, uncouth, feuding and moonshining, among other things, the stereotype of the mountain woman emerged in full bloom in the works of the local colorists and in the historical and sociological writings that began to try to "understand" the mountain people. By the turn of the

22 Wingless Flights

Annie Russell as the typical mountain woman in the theatrical production of *Esmeralda* (1881), based on the local color story by Frances Hodgson Burnett. Reprinted from *A Pictorial History of the American Theatre 1860-1976* by Daniel Blum and John Willis. Courtesy of Crown Publishers, Inc.

century the subject of the "strange land and peculiar people" of Appalachia was of great interest to the nation and many socio-historical essays and books began to attempt thorough analyses of the highland culture. The first and most well-known of these were written by "observers" from outside the region, who, because of their limited knowledge, often misrepresented the mountaineers. All of these writers presented the mountain woman in a typical way: she was pretty in youth, but married young, bore a houseful of "youngens," led a life of endless drudgery often tinged with "unaccountable" melancholy, became old at thirty-five, and ended her life sitting on the front porch of her log cabin with a corncob pipe in her mouth and a black sunbonnet on her head. Despite this basically negative picture of the mountain woman, however, there was often in these writings some degree of ambivalence and always a note of pity.

In "Our Contemporary Ancestors in the Southern Mountains," for example, Frost wrote of mountain women:

A word deserves to be said of the native refinement of many of the mountain women. The staid combination of a black sunbonnet and a cob pipe is not unusual, and the shrill voice that betokens desperation in life's struggles may be heard. Yet there is withal a real kindliness and a certain shy modesty, and often a passionate eagerness to note points of superiority which may be imitated. (315-16)

Frost, though certainly sympathizing with the mountain women and noting the "native refinement" of many of them, pointed out several of the features that were then and afterwards associated with them: the sunbonnet and pipe, the modesty and shyness, the "passionate eagerness" to improve their lives (or at least to imitate "points of superiority"), and the "desperation" of their "life's struggles." This description changed little in essence in subsequent observations.

In 1903 Julian Ralph more fully defined the role of the mountain woman:

The girls are often married at thirteen. Marriages at fourteen and fifteen are very common, and a girl of twenty is considered an old maid and ineligible if she has younger sisters. What I have seen of the girls and whatever I have heard of them and their mothers has roused my pity. The oldest daughter of these almost always large mountain families is almost certain to begin her life of drudging while very young, and as the women are all drudges after marriage and are married in childhood, drudging is their lot until they die.

> They do all the work of cabin and farm, excepting during the few days of harvest-time, when the men help to garner the crops. They bear very many children; they cook, wash, mend, weave, knit, plow, hoe, weed, milk the cows, and do practically all else that is to be done. The men loaf about on horseback along the roads, visit their neighbors, the store, and the nearest village, and have as good and easy a time as they know how. (41)

Ralph saw the mountain women as menial victims of endless toil, early marriage and constant childbearing. They were to be pitied.

Ralph's statement about the mountain woman was echoed by another outsider to the hills, Horace Kephart. Kephart's study, *Our Southern Highlander*, written in 1913, was the first book-length account of the mountain culture. In it, Kephart said about the mountain woman almost exactly what Ralph had said before him—the complete similarity of the two descriptions is in itself revealing of the stereotype held by much of the nation at this time:

> Many of the women are pretty in youth, but hard toil in house and field, early marriage, frequent childbearing with shockingly poor attention, and ignorance or defiance of the plainest necessities of hygiene, soon warp and age them. At thirty-five a mountain woman is apt to have a worn and faded look, with form prematurely bent—and what wonder? Always bending over the hoe and the cornfield, or bending over the hearth as she cooks by an open fire, or bending over her baby, or bending to pick up, for the thousandth time, the wet duds that her lord flings on the floor as he enters from the woods—what wonder that she soon grows short-waisted and round-shouldered?
>
> The voices of the highland women, low toned by habit, often are singularly sweet, being pitched in a sad, musical, minor key. With strangers the women are wont to be shy, but speculative rather than timid, as they glance betimes with "a slow, long look of mild inquiry, or of general listlessness, or of unconscious and unaccountable melancholy." (214-15)

Both Kephart and Ralph noted characteristics of mountain women that were typically associated with them at the time, although both somewhat mitigated their stereotypical descriptions. For both Kephart and Ralph, the mountain woman was a sad, overworked, little-appreciated victim of her culture. For both Kephart and Frost, the very voice of the mountain wife, "pitched in a sad, musical, minor key," or "the shrill voice that betokens desperation in life's struggles," was seen as an indication of the pitiful plight of the mountain woman.

Conspicuously, these statements say nothing about hopes, dreams, or aspirations, implying that the mountain woman had none. Speaking of the young mountain woman, for example, John C. Campbell, echoing Kephart and Ralph, stated that she "matures early into a vigorous blooming girlhood, whose aspirations are too often blunted and coarsened by the bald unrelieved hardness of life. She is alternately suspicious, given to fits of fiery temper, emotional, and sullen—yet again of a delicate, a touching and gentle sweetness that has in it an unconscious pathos" (127). It is the loss of what few aspirations or hopes that she has that excites pity in these observers of the mountain woman, the "unconscious pathos" that they attribute to her.

In addition to her lack of hopes and aspirations, these early descriptions emphasize another feature of the mountain woman's life: her complete subordination to her man, her total subjugation to him. As Kephart states, the mountain woman's husband was "her lord" (215). Speaking of the woman's subservient place in the social organization of the mountains, Kephart states:

"The woman," as every wife is called, has her kingdom within the house, and her man seldom meddles with its administration. . . . At table, if women be seated at all, the dishes are passed first to the men; but generally the wife stands and serves.

There is no conscious discourtesy in such customs; but they betoken an indifference to woman's weakness, a disregard for her finer nature, a denial of her proper rank, that are real and deep-seated in the mountaineer. To him she is little more than a superior domestic animal. (257)

In this passage Kephart betrays his own bias concerning women's nature, not simply as an outsider describing mountain women but as an inheritor of nineteenth-century patriarchal ideology. "And yet," Kephart closes his discussion, "it is seldom that a highland woman complains of her lot. She knows no other" (257).

Again, John C. Campbell reiterates Kephart's statements. The mountain woman knew no other way of life than subservient drudge, states Campbell, because the traditional masculine and feminine roles were instilled in mountain children from infancy:

From babyhood the boy is the favored lord of all he surveys. . . . There is a dignity, a conscious superiority, in his youthful mien that says more clearly than spoken words that womankind are not his equals. Through an old mountain usage, now yielding in places to the new, he is not his own man until he is of age or marries and makes his own home, he enters early into the heritage of the past and holds himself the proud equal of any human creature. As a man, he recognizes from the first man's prerogative to order and be obeyed, and right bravely does he stride in the long steps of his father and older brothers. With them he sits at table while mother and sisters stand to serve his wants, and from them he gathers much that were better unknown. . . . While he thus grows into the ways of mountain manhood his sisters are learning to tread the painful path of mountain womanhood. For them there are few of the child's irrepressible joys. (124, 126)

Thus, like his fellow observers of the mountain culture, Campbell saw the mountain woman as a pathetic victim of patriarchy.

Even as late as the 1960s, Cratis Williams reiterated these earlier views in "The Southern Mountaineer in Fact and Fiction":

in his family organization the mountain man is a patriarch, the lord of the household. When he gives orders they are obeyed. . . . There is a traditional division of work in his household. "There is nothing at which a mountain man or boy balks so positively as doing woman's work. To milk a cow or wash dishes or make a bed is a humiliation not to be borne." The women do all the work in the home and the garden and assist with the crops. ("Southern Mountaineer Part I" 34-35)

The pictures and their captions that accompany the earlier studies are in themselves enough to tell the story. Beneath a drawing of two mountain women in Ralph's article, the caption reads: "They mend, weave, knit." And beneath another showing a woman and two small children: "The women are all drudges after marriage." In Kephart's book a photograph of a gaunt mountain woman is captioned, "At thirty a mountain woman is apt to have a worn and faded look," and another picture of a woman slaving over a washtub is captioned, "Let the women do the work."

It is impossible not to notice that the mountain woman is always much more sympathetically presented in these writings than is the mountain man, with whom she is either explicitly or implicitly contrasted. Mountain women are always depicted as industrious and hardworking (though often slovenly of personal appearance and habits) in contrast to the indolence and shiftlessness of the mountain men. If the mountain man had a "strong aversion to hard labor and cleanliness, and an equally strong proclivity for drink—strong drink" (Higgs 1), the mountain woman certainly could have no aversion to hard work—it was her only possible way of life in her world. Williams argues:

The apparent loyalty of the mountain woman to her husband and family probably grows out of economic and social conditions. She cannot leave her husband, for she would then have no place to go. . . . Her function is basic and simple:

The caption of this photograph in Muriel Earley Sheppard's *Cabins in the Laurel* (1935) reads: "She has time now to sit down and rest." Reprinted courtesy of the North Carolina Collection, University of North Carolina at Chapel Hill.

she bears children, takes care of her house, and raises the garden. ("Southern Mountaineer Part I" 30)

"Marriage," states Campbell, "is her goal. There is little comfort for the spinster" (127). Forever in the shadow of her "lord," the mountain woman who escaped comfortless spinsterhood had been described as early as 1728 by William Byrd II, who wrote that mountain men "just like Indians imposed all the work upon the poor women" (cited in Higgs 3) while the men mainly slept and smoked.

Another aspect of the stereotype of the mountain woman as presented by the early sociological studies is her physical appearance. All women over fifty are described as aged crones, often toothless, wearing black sunbonnets and smoking corncob pipes. Wives and mothers, who married as early as thirteen in many cases, quickly lost all beauty and became faded and worn from their endless bending and working. Particularly in the fiction of the period, the young mountain woman is often depicted as either comely or ethereally beautiful, a kind of romantic wildflower, whose first flush of maidenhood is all too quickly extinguished after marriage. As the stereotype of the older mountain woman is familiar to us even today through such comic strip and television characters as Mammy Yokum and Granny Clampett, so is the younger woman through such characters as Daisy Mae Yokum, Moonbeam McSwine, and Ellie Mae Clampett. In the sociological essays of the period, however, the beauty of the young mountain woman is a subject of much debate.

In 1901, for example, John Fox, Jr., describing a trip through the mountains, observed:

> . . . an artist who rode with me through the Kentucky mountains said that not only were the men finer looking, but that the woman [sic] were far handsomer than elsewhere in the southern Alleghenies. While I am not able to say this, I can say that in the Kentucky mountains the pretty mountain girl is not always, as some people are inclined to believe, pure fiction. Pretty girls are, however, rare; for usually the women are stoop-shouldered and large-waisted from working in the fields and lifting heavy weights; for the same reason their hands are large and so are their feet, for they generally go barefoot. (558)

Clearly, Fox thought that small hands and feet were the distinguishing marks of feminine beauty and measured the mountain women by the prevailing standards of his own culture. Fox does recall having seen one truly beautiful mountain woman:

Pretty girls there are in abundance, but I have seen only one very beautiful mountain girl. . . . She was sitting behind a little cabin with a baby in her lap, and her loveliness was startling. She was slender; her hair was golden-brown; her hands were small, and, for a wonder, beautifully shaped. Her teeth, for a wonder, too, were very white and even. Her features were delicately perfect: her mouth shaped as Cupid's bow never was and never could be, said the artist, who christened her eyes after Trilby's—"twin grey stars"—to which the eyebrows and the long lashes gave an indescribable softness. But I felt more the brooding pathos that lay in them, that came from generations of lonely mothers before her, waiting in lonely cabins for the men to come home. (559)

Even the beauty of this celestial creature, however, was tempered for Fox by the pathetic loneliness he saw in her eyes.

On the other hand, Anne Newport Royall, in her 1826 *Sketches of History, Life, and Manners in the United States*, comments on the beauty of the mountain youth:

The young people of both sexes are very fair and beautiful, and many of them well-formed: the men are stout, active, and among the best marksmen in America. They are, both male and female, extravagantly fond of dress; this, and their beauty, only serves to expose their unpolished manners, and wont of education. They have no expression of countenance, nor do they appear to possess much mind. (cited in Higgs and Manning 73)

For Royall, however, as for many other observers, the fairness of mountain youth was tempered by their total ignorance, another trait of the stereotype. As early as 1784, the women of the mountains had been described as "little better than beautiful savages" (Smyth 61). They were often considered completely devoid of intelligence or the power to communicate. They were reported to be shy and timid around strangers, which also helped to perpetuate this idea.

No discussion of the stereotype of the mountain woman would be complete without considering one other characteristic: she was often considered morally irresponsible, perhaps as a direct result of her lack of intelligence or formal education. The mountain woman's lack of morals contributed, in the public's mind, to the disgraceful condition of widespread illegitimacy in the mountains. Even Campbell appears to have taken this position:

The question of illegitimacy is not absent from the mountains, but the social evil is not marked by enticement or seduction. It is more in the nature of animalism and may be traced in part to the lack of privacy in the home, early acquaintance with the sex relation, and a promiscuous hospitality. There is not, however, the same stigma put upon the "baseborn" child as in other sections. Many times he is known by his father's name or by the name of both father and mother, and the father feels some responsibility for him. The mother quite generally marries—an older man, often, or a "widder man" with children—and her husband provides for the child of her unmarried state as for his own. (132)

By attempting to show that the moral fiber of the mountains more easily condoned illegitimacy than that of other parts of the nation, Campbell surely did much to help strengthen the case against the mountain woman's morality; her animalistic nature, as he referred to it, further reduced her to the level of a mindless creature.

The "promiscuous hospitality" of the young mountain woman was a given assumption of outsiders in the late nineteenth and early twentieth centuries. Merrill Maguire Skaggs devotes considerable space in *The Folk of Southern Fiction* to the stereotype of the promiscuous young mountain woman and concludes that she "flits alluringly in and out of Southern local color fiction; but the local colorists never quite summon the courage to pursue, or even to admit the existence of her" (153). In the writings of the early twentieth century, however, such as Anne W. Armstrong's *This Day and Time*, in which the character Old Mag has had several illegitimate children, with apparently little social stigma, illegitimacy is depicted as a fact of mountain life. Even in Harriette Arnow's *Hunter's Horn*, published in the 1940s, Suse Ballew becomes pregnant out of wedlock.

From the foregoing discussion, then, we can see the basic stereotype of the mountain woman as it was known to the American public at the beginning of the twentieth century. In the following chapters, beginning with the works of Mary Noailles Murfree, images of mountain women will be examined in terms of this stereotype, much of which Murfree, in fact, and other local colorists, helped to establish. As with a great deal of the sociological descriptions of mountain women, there is in Murfree's writings an often paradoxical representation of Appalachian womanhood, partly as a result of Murfree's literary genre of local colorism and partly because of her own limited but sympathetic knowledge of the mountain people.

2

Romantic Idealization and the Mountain Woman as Victim: The Works of Mary Noailles Murfree

In 1884, the year Cratis Williams calls the *"annus, mirabilis* in the history of the mountain people in fiction" ("Southern Mountaineer Part II" 134), the Houghton Mifflin Company published Mary Noailles Murfree's *In the Tennessee Mountains* (under the pseudonym of Charles Egbert Craddock), a collection of eight short stories about the Southern Appalachian mountaineers; all of these had originally appeared in the *Atlantic Monthly*, beginning in 1878 with "The Dancin' Party at Harrison's Cove," one of Murfree's first mountain stories to be published.[1] The publication of *In the Tennessee Mountains* is a significant landmark in the history of the mountain people in literature, for its publication, in Williams's words, "definitely marks the time at which the Southern mountain people had become generally recognized as a people possessing their own idiosyncrasies, not to be confused with other Southern types" ("Southern Mountaineer Part II" 134).

According to Carvel Collins, Mary Noailles Murfree is "the most important writer of Southern mountain fiction during the nineteenth century" (86). Although her reputation declined even during her own lifetime and she is recognized today as only a minor figure in American literature, Murfree's first works, on which her reputation was built and still rests, were a tremendous literary success at the time of their publication. *In the Tennessee Mountains* "captured the entire country" (Cary 45). And her novel, *The Prophet of the Great Smoky Mountains*, originally printed serially in the *Atlantic Monthly* and then published in book form in 1885 (only one year after *In the Tennessee Mountains*) produced a "literary sensation" (Parks 172).[2] These two works reached a large segment of the American population, both in their initial publication in one of the leading middle-class magazines of the day and in book form. *In the Tennessee Mountains* went through twenty-four editions during Murfree's lifetime. The images of the mountain people that Murfree presented in these works—the lazy rail-sitting mountain man, the moonshiner and drunkard, the aged pipe-smoking crone in a sunbonnet, the patient and hard-working wife and mother, the beautiful young woman, and the idiot, for example—became stereotypical within her own works and for almost all later writers of mountain fiction. Her plots and major concerns also became common in much of the fiction about the Appalachian mountains and mountaineers even to the present.

Like the travel writers and outsider "observers" who first described the mountains and mountaineers, the first authors to write about Appalachia in fiction were nonnatives of the region. Murfree, the leading figure in this group, although born in Tennessee, was not a native Appalachian, and thus her view of the mountain people was that of an "outsider." She was essentially an observer of the people of the region, not one of them. Born in 1850 in Murfreesboro (named after her grandfather), southeast of Nashville in central Tennessee, Murfree was from an "aristocratic" family (Williams, "Southern Mountaineer Part II" 134). During most of her girlhood Murfree's family spent their summers vacationing at Beersheba Springs Resort in the Cumberland Mountains of East Tennessee, which "afforded about her only contact with the mountaineers" (Collins 86). This contact was further limited by a slight lameness, the result of a childhood fever, which kept Murfree from venturing far from the hotel to places where she might have become more fully acquainted with different types and classes of mountain people.

Thus Murfree's observations of mountaineers were mainly restricted to the "humbler people who came to the resort to sell produce or stare at life around the Springs" (Collins 86). Fanny N.D. Murfree, in her unpublished biography of her sister, says of Murfree's contact with mountain men and women:

> Often, sad-faced, pallid mountain women in calico or homespun dresses and drooping sun bonnets would come into the big wide hall, and seat themselves in a row on sofas against the wall, or in the swaying cane rockers. Mary would look at them smilingly, and go on with her singing or playing. These impromptu concerts would last for an hour or so without a word being addressed by either party. Gaunt men slid in silently, and effaced themselves against the wall. She would sing her best. I never hear a lovely selection from *L'Etoile du Nord* that I do not see once again before my eyes blue mountains shimmering in the noonday heat and in the shadowy room motionless figures with intent listening faces. Sometimes she sang ballads: Mary of Argyle, Goodbye Sweetheart, and Flee as a Bird. They liked these, and occasionally one was asked for. As the hour waxed late, they would at some hiatus silently stroll out. (cited in Parks 54-55)

Romantic Idealization   33

E.B. Spence, her cousin, gives a further description of Murfree's contact with the mountaineers on these occasions and at other times at Beersheba:

> At times they [the mountaineers] would depart as silently as they came, at others they would linger for a little conversation with Miss Murfree. . . . They willingly expressed their own customs and possessions. One [sic] fine days the sisters [Mary and Fanny] would go foraging among the mountain homes for butter and eggs, chicken, fresh fruits and vegetables, for their table. In this way they met and talked with the women of the region and saw the interiors of their bare little homes. (17)

Thus it can safely be said that Murfree's acquaintance with the mountain people was superficial at best and limited to the humbler type of people with whom she came in contact at Beersheba Springs.

Indicative of Murfree's limited knowledge of the mountain people is the fact that it was only *after* she had written all the stories of *In the Tennessee Mountains* and her novel *The Prophet of the Great Smoky Mountains* that she traveled through the Appalachian backwoods at all. In 1885, she made a trip by horseback with her father and sister into the Smokies. In September of that year Mary and her sister Fanny went to Montvale Springs in East Tennessee, a resort similar to Beersheba Springs. From Montvale Springs, the two sisters, joined by their father, made a trip "far into the mountains" (Parks 130) where

> mountain men and women welcomed her heartily, with the best they had: usually the party stayed in good houses, with prosperous farmers and local officials, but at times the food was pork and potatoes and corn pone. They even made unusual provision for her to the extent of serving butter and milk, two items in little favor among them.
>
> Mary was fascinated. Here was a mountain life ruder, wilder, even more independent, than any she had ever known. (Parks 131)

As Cratis Williams states, "Perhaps [Murfree's] most serious mistake in her preparation for her role as an interpreter of the mountain people was her failure to become intimately acquainted with more mountaineers and with their social history" ("Southern Mountaineer Part II" 135).

Despite these shortcomings, Murfree was genuinely sympathetic toward the mountain people. Beersheba Springs, states her biographer Edd Winfield Parks, "was the scene of Mary's happiest moments. She could not stand it to hear flippant youths mock the uncouth dialect and uncouth ways of the mountain people, however amusing they might seem to city dwellers" (54). Isabella D. Harris also states that although Murfree

> had no more than a summer cottager's acquaintance with [the mountaineers] her knowledge was extensive, more sympathetic, and more enthusiastic than that of the usual traveler who saw little of the region and understood less. Admittedly a summer visitor, she had the advantage of some fifteen seasons in the mountains rather than a few weeks or a few days, as in the case of superficial observers. She was genuinely attracted by the mountaineer whom she described. (97-98)

But, "despite [her] long-range background and sympathetic attitude," Harris concludes, "Murfree could hardly be called a native interpreter" (98).

Murfree's stance toward the mountaineers is comprised of many impulses, some at odds with each other. Her literary footing in local color, for instance, often conflicts with her genuine sympathy for the mountaineers. As Harris states:

> It was not entirely her fault, perhaps, that [Murfree] made of the mountaineer whom she liked and admired just another "uncouth specimen" to add to the growing list of illiterates, ne'er-do-wells, outcasts, unfortunates, and sentimental misfits engendered by Harte, Cable, Page, Allen, and the others. Although she was in sympathy with her characters and wrote alone, independent of purpose and spirit, she was influenced by the demands of her readers as well as by the ephemeral fashions of local color. When the public liked her fragile girls and slothful rail-sitters, considered them representative mountaineers, and read her books avidly (that is, to begin with), she repeated the pattern almost without variation. Too much the Victorian lady to become original, she was also too much the popularizer to become artistic. (102)

Likewise, Murfree's efforts toward realism, in dialect, for example, are often in conflict with her romanticization of certain elements in the mountain culture, notably her characterizations of the young mountain women who are often her heroines.[3]

Murfree's stories in *In the Tennessee Mountains* are particularly important in an examination of the evolution of portrayals and images of mountain women in literature. Women are, in fact, the central characters in these works. One comes away from *In the Tennessee Mountains* remembering first and foremost the heroines of these stories—Cynthia Ware, Clarsie Giles, Celia Shaw or Selina Teake, for example. The older women in these stories, who often serve only minor functions, are also memorable as drudging victims. As with the conflict between realism or romanticism in Murfree's writings, however, a conflict can be seen in her presentations of mountain women.

Murfree's Older Women

On the one hand, many of Murfree's mountain women are portrayed as victims in almost every way. It is especially the older women in her stories who are depicted as the real victims of the patriarchal mountain social system, leading lives of apparently little value and much hardship. They are considered inferior by their fathers, husbands and brothers, who have little, if any, real sympathy for, sensitivity to, or understanding of their womenfolks. This attitude toward women is cogently expressed by the storekeeper in "On Big Injun Mounting" when he describes the family of the pathetic Mrs. Boker: "An' all her chillen is gals,—little gals. Boys, now, mought grow some help, but gals is more no 'count the bigger they gits." The storekeeper's statement suggests that females are of little value in this society.

One can find many examples of the woman as victim, of the pathetic mountain wife and mother, in the stories of *In the Tennessee Mountains*. These women are careworn, haggard, old at thirty-five, drudges and always surrounded by an aura of "hopeless melancholy." Mrs. Johns, for example, in "The Dancin' Party at Harrison's Cove," is in Cratis Williams's words, "the first in Murfree's gallery of pathetic mountain women" ("Southern Mountaineer Part II" 136). Mrs. Johns's age is not specified in the story, but she is presented as

tall and lank, with such a face as one never sees except in these mountains,—elongated, sallow, thin, with pathetic, deeply sunken eyes, and high cheekbones, and so settled an expression of hopeless melancholy that it must be that nought but care and suffering had been her lot; holding out wasted hands to the years as they pass,—holding them out always, and always empty. She wore a shabby, faded calico, and spoke with the peculiar expressionless drawl of the mountaineer. (*ITM* 217)

Of particular importance here is the description of Mrs. Johns's life as "wasted," "empty" and "hopeless": her life has been full of suffering and care. She is described exactly like the mountain women as they were presented by the socio-historical critics of the next twenty to forty years—Frost, Campbell, Ralph, Kephart and Fox, for example—even the "expression of hopeless melancholy" in her eyes. It is apparent that their descriptions owed much to Murfree.

Cynthia Ware's mother in "Drifting Down Lost Creek" and Melinda Price's mother in "Old Sledge at the Settlement" are likewise epitomes of the pathetic mountain wife and mother. Neither of these women is given a first name, and neither has a very well-defined character: in fact, both are pure type. Cynthia's mother is described as one of those old crones of the mountains:

> She was a tall woman, fifty years of age, perhaps, but seemingly much older. So gaunt she was, so toothless, haggard and disheveled, that but for her lazy step and languid interest she might have suggested one of Macbeth's witches, as she hovered about the great cauldron. (*ITM* 3)

Melinda's mother is similarly described. She is a "faded, careworn woman of fifty" (*ITM* 112). Neither Mrs. Ware nor Mrs. Price is very important to the action of the stories; they are memorable simply as faded, careworn, toothless and haggard women, worn out and doomed to lives of endless drudgery and service to their families.

The pathetic mountain women in these stories are usually the victims of sometimes brutal and often drunken husbands (Murfree's mountain men are usually depicted as drunkards operating their moonshine stills). The women are, however, accepting of their lots in life and in most cases either will not or cannot leave their husbands. The wife of Ike Peel in "The Star in the Valley" is a good example. One of the central episodes in this story involves the attempted murder of Ike Peel by his wife's brother, Elijah Burr, and other kin because of the mistreatment to which Peel subjects his wife. "No man," Burr says, "ez treats his wife like that dad-burned scoundrel Ike Peel do oughten be let live." When Reginald Chevis, an outsider to the mountains who is present when Burr makes this remark, suggests, "Wouldn't it be better to persuade her to leave him?" (*ITM* 141) another one of the wife's brothers answers, "Thar's whar all the trouble kem from. She wouldn't leave him, fur all he treated her awful. She said ez how he war mighty good ter her when he warn't drunk. So 'Lijah shot him" (*ITM* 142). The attempt to murder Ike Peel failed, however, due to his wife's interference. Peel's wife is stereotypical in Murfree's fiction. Though her husband is often drunk and abuses her, she continues to defend him and to overlook his faults in favor of his better qualities.

Isaac Boker's wife in "On Big Injun Mounting" is of the same type as Ike Peel's wife. The storekeeper in the Settlement, upon hearing that Isaac Boker is drunk again, says of Mrs. Boker:

> "I'm powerful sorry fur his wife, 'kase he air mighty rough to her when he air drunk; he cut her once a toler'ble bad slash. She hev had ter do all the work fur four year,—plowin', an choppin' wood, an cookin', an washin', an sech. It hev

aged her some. She air a tired woman surely. Isaac is drunk ez a constancy,—dancin' drunk, mos'ly. Nuthin' kin stop him." (*ITM* 166)

Again, in this example, we see a mountain woman abused by her husband when he is drunk. But, like Peel's wife, Boker's wife has taken him for better or worse. "She air his wife," the storekeeper says later, "an' she air powerful tuk up with him. I hev hearn her 'low ez he air better dancin'-drunk than other men sober. She could hev married other men; she didn't suffer with hevin' no ch'ice" (*ITM* 167). Both Peel's wife and Boker's epitomize the abused and patiently suffering mountain wife, whose life is one of continual work and heartache. At some point in their lives, however, these women must have known some happiness and the freedom to make choices, and they seldom seem to regret the hardships they must endure.

Speaking of what she calls the "memorable women characters" (114) in Murfree's stories, Isabella D. Harris describes them as a type of the "tired mountain woman, whose weariness and drab outlook on life outlasted her name and identity in any story" (112). Of this type of woman, however, Harris concludes:

It is entirely possible that Miss Murfree over-emphasized the sadness and hardships of mountain women. E.C. Perrow suggests that "to call [the lives of mountain women] unhappy is a kind of pathetic fallacy. Their lot is simple, but they love their homes and even the monotony of their daily lives." Adelene Moffat insists that the mountain woman, expecting to age under the difficulties of her life, finds solace in tributes to her past beauty and vanishing charms. Yet the mountain woman, as portrayed by Miss Murfree, neither pitied herself nor received sympathy from others. The storekeeper, for example, found it only mildly regrettable that the hardships of a drunkard's wife had "aged her some." (113-14)

Although the picture of the mountain women as hardworking, patient, in many ways subservient, and victims of the mountain social system is accurate in some respects, it seems obvious that Murfree's depictions of the older mountain women over-emphasized the hardships they endured. Perhaps Murfree's genuine sympathy for these women was turned into pity by her observations of them from the height of the "gentle-woman."

Murfree's Young Women Heroines

The tired, careworn melancholy mountain woman is, however, but one of Murfree's portrayals. Murfree's young mountain women are depicted in a much different manner, although they retain certain features of the first type—lives of sadness and servitude, for example, seldom relieved by happiness. Murfree's beautiful, often willful, outspoken and independent younger heroines are overly romanticized and are depicted much differently from their mothers, grandmothers and older sisters. Harris describes the two types of women in Murfree's works: "One unforgettable character was the tired mountain woman, whom Miss Murfree with her ready sympathy probably understood best of all her portrayals. Another recurring picture was the fragile young woman, almost too good for the mountain world, romantic, ethereal, and sentimental" (109). Inevitably, these young women are "diamonds in the rough," real heroines, whose sensibilities appear to be far superior to those of their fellow mountaineers. Harris states that

the young girls in Miss Murfree's fiction were unreal and romantic. . . . Their composite picture resembled that of a Victorian heroine, with eyes like "limpid mountain streams," "dark silken eyebrows, each describing a perfect arc," "tangled yellow hair like skeins of sunshine, an exquisitely fair complexion, and a physique as frail as a slip of willow." (114-15)

She continues: "Perhaps [Murfree] was describing in these fair, fragile, and ethereal creatures not so much a mountain girl as any heroine whom she considered worthy of the name" (115).

In addition to fitting the stereotype of the Victorian heroine, Murfree's young mountain women are often described in terms that link them with the Arcadian or heroic ideal (suggesting that the Appalachian region itself is a place of Edenic, Arcadian simplicity, uncorrupted by the outside world). Cynthia Ware, for example, is presented in "Drifting Down Lost Creek" as the epitome of the ancient heroic ideal. She is first seen nobly pounding her clothes clean, as did Nausicaa, and in the final scene she is left patiently weaving at her loom, reminiscent of the industrious and patient Penelope. Not only does Murfree's description of Cynthia suggest the heroic ideal, but the world around Cynthia is likewise described as an Edenic place, a pastoral preserve:

The wild grapes were blooming. Their fragrance, so delicate yet so pervasive, suggested some exquisite unseen presence—the dryads were surely abroad! The beech-trees stretched down their silver branches and green shadows. Through rifts in the foliage shimmered glimpses of a vast array of sunny parallel mountains, converging and converging, till they seemed to meet far away in one long, level line, so ideally blue that it looked less like earth than heaven. (*ITM* 6-7)

This description of an Arcadian paradise strengthens the suggestions of the heroic ideal as exemplified in Cynthia.

Similarly, Dorinda Cayce is described near the beginning of *The Prophet of the Great Smoky Mountains* as a woman of a golden age: "she might have seemed the type of a young civilization,—so fine a thing in itself, so roughly accoutred" (*PGS* 4). She even wears her hair "drawn back, except for the tendrils about her brow, and coiled, with the aid of a much-prized 'tuckin'-comb,' at the back of her head in a knot discriminated as Grecian in civilization" (*PGS* 223). Dorinda is indeed "the pioneer woman, the Eve of the new world and its 'young civilization,'" as H.R. Stoneback states (115).

It is significant that Murfree associates her young mountain women with both the typical Victorian heroine and the heroic ideal. By doing so, she is revealing her attitude that the life of the mountain people is inherently noble and heroic and that they are capable of refined sentiments. She also does this by her chief plot device involving these romantic heroines.

One of Murfree's major plot complications is the romantic attachment between young mountain women and more "civilized" outland men with whom they come in contact. According to Cratis Williams, the plot motif of the "interest of an outsider of cultural pretensions in a beautiful mountain girl" is first significantly developed in Murfree's works and subsequently becomes the "most overworked motif in mountain fiction" ("Southern Mountaineer Part II" 137).[4] Because it is "one of the unbreakable rules of fiction based on the lives of mountain people that sons and daughters of real mountain folk may never be permitted to marry into genteel families of the settlements, except on rare occasions when the mountain youths are subjected to the influence of distinguished colleges and finishing schools," as Williams states ("Southern Mountaineer Part II" 109), the romantic attachments that most of Murfree's young women entertain come to nought. They are hardly romantic "attachments" at all, in fact, for few of the couples in Murfree's stories ever tell their love and are often mutually unaware of their feelings until it is too late.

Murfree's use of the romantic attachment between idealized young mountain women and "sophisticated" outsiders in her plots is more than a mere convention in her fiction, however. It is obvious that her depictions of these young women differ markedly from those of the older careworn and haggard women, but this paradoxical image of mountain women is the result, I believe, of Murfree's attempt to reveal one of her main attitudes about the Southern Appalachian people, their shared humanity. Ironically, though she depicts, on the one hand, the mountain people as cruel and debased—mountain men are drunkards and wife-beaters, for example—she genuinely believed that they were *not* peculiar people in their inner desires, emotions, and values, and that, in fact, they shared with all humankind the noblest of virtues. As Williams says, Murfree's "insistence that [the mountain people] were children of nature and motivated by the same desires and emotions as people in more complex social organizations led [Murfree] to marvel at times at nobility and self-sacrifice thought to belong only to the tenderly nurtured and refined children of Wealth and culture" ("Southern Mountaineer Part II" 136). Likewise, Carvel Collins states:

Miss Murfree took the view that the mountaineers were of great interest because, despite their ignorance and backwardness, despite their isolation and poverty, in their hearts were the same emotions that were in the hearts of more civilized people. Her discovery of love, hope, hate, courage, and religious yearnings under the highlander's crude exterior gave her the opportunity to point a moral at the end of each story—an opportunity she rarely let slip, the moral tag being one of the chief characteristics of her fiction. (87)

In several of the stories of *In the Tennessee Mountains* this is Murfree's central theme. Her motive is obviously a didactic one: to educate the outside world to the truth of the mountaineers' inner lives.

"The Star in the Valley" is a pointed example of this theme.[5] The story is a tale of unrequited love, heroic self-sacrifice and self-discovery. Because it is a "mountain story," it may seem somewhat surprising to readers of "The Star in the Valley" that the main character is not a mountaineer, but is, in fact, Reginald Chevis, a cultured outsider from the lowlands whose hunting trip in the Cumberland Mountains just happens to involve him in the events of the community, although purely as a spectator. The reason why Chevis is the protagonist of the story becomes clear, however, when one realizes that the point of "The Star in the Valley" is Chevis's education into the true life of the mountain people, his realization that they do share in the "common humanity" of the world no less than do other people. It is through his relationship with the mountain woman Celia Shaw that Chevis's education is achieved.

Reginald Chevis is the typical outsider to the mountains, and he serves Murfree's purpose as a spokesperson for the outside world's attitudes toward the mountain people. When he first arrives, Chevis has little real understanding of the mountaineers, although he does express a romantic interest in them as quaint specimens of a peculiar society, a typical reaction of the mountain outsider. Because he is a romantic, and because he thinks his sensibilities are of a superior sort, Chevis begins to show a sympathetic interest in the mountain culture and to pride himself on his interest. Writes Murfree:

He piqued himself on the readiness with which he became interested in these people, entered into their thoughts and feelings, obtained a comprehensive view of the machinery of life in this wilderness,—more complicated than one could readily believe. . . . They appealed to him from the basis of their common humanity, he thought, and the pleasure of watching the development of the common human attributes of this peculiar and primitive state of society never palled upon him. He regarded with contempt [his friend] Varney's frivolous displeasures and annoyance because of [mountain man] Hi Bates's utter insensibility to the differences in their social position, and the necessity of either acquiescing in the suppositious equality or dispensing with the invaluable services of the proud and independent mountaineers; because of the *patois* of the un-tutored people, to hear which, Varney was wont to declare, set his teeth on edge; because of their narrow prejudices, their mental poverty, their idle shiftlessness, their uncouth dress and appearance. Chevis flattered himself that he entertained a broader view. (*ITM* 134)

However, Chevis's self-congratulation is really egotistical. In truth, his attitude is much the same as Varney's, is just as narrow, although he prides himself on believing otherwise. Following the above passage, Murfree comments on Chevis: "He had not a subacute idea that he looked upon these people and their inner lives as picturesque bits of the mental and moral landscape; that it was an aesthetic and theoretical pleasure their contemplation afforded him; that he was as far as ever from the basis of common humanity" (*ITM* 134-35). Chevis's attitude at the beginning of the story is thus, in essence, that of the sophisticated outsider who feels that because he is sympathetic toward the mountaineers he can know their inner lives, when in reality this understanding is purely superficial, perhaps offering some parallels with Murfree's own.

Chevis does, however, become well acquainted with the mountaineers through his frequent visits to Jerry Shaw's cabin. He is first lured by the sight of Shaw's daughter, Celia. From the first moment he sees her, Chevis thinks of Celia as a beautiful flower perishing unappreciated in the wilderness. Chevis becomes such an accustomed visitor to the Shaw cabin that he is included in a conversation one night when Jerry Shaw, his cousin Elijah Burr, and other kin discuss the marital situation of Elijah's sister, the wife of Ike Peel. The men are planning to attack and murder Peel and his two brothers because of the way the often-drunk Peel has treated his wife. The Burrs have tried more than once to persuade her to leave Peel. She, however, has maintained a kind of truce between her kin and her husband for seven years.

A week prior to the conversation at Jerry Shaw's cabin, the Burrs had tried once more to convince their sister to leave Peel. She stepped between her husband and her brother when Burr tried to shoot Peel and refused to leave him, so the Burrs tried another approach. They kidnapped the Peels' two small children when everyone else was away from home and burned down the house, thus hoping their sister would be forced to come back to her own family. Having lost their home and possessions, however, Ike Peel, his wife and the entire Peel clan decide to leave the area and go to Kentucky. Before their sister can be carried off such a great distance from them, Burr, his brothers and Jerry Shaw plan to try one last time to kill the Peel men.

During the conversation at Jerry Shaw's cabin, to which Chevis listens attentively but with little real sense of involvement, the only person who speaks up in defense of the Peels is Celia:[6]

"I don't see no sense," said Celia Shaw, her singing monotone vibrating in the sudden lull,—"I don't see no sense in shootin' folks down like they war nuthin' better nor bear, nor deer, nor suthin' wild. I don't see no sense in it. An' I never did see none." (*ITM* 146)

Her father and the other mountaineers are astonished by Celia's outcry, and her father tells her to "Shet up!" "Them folks ain't no better nor bear, nor sech," Shaw continues; "They hain't got no right ter live,— them Peels" (*ITM* 146). Heedless of her father's command to be quiet, Celia speaks again:

"They is powerful no 'count critters," I know, replied the little woodland flower, the firelight bright in her opaline eyes and on the flakes of burnished gold gleaming in the dark masses of her hair. "They is always a-hangin' round the still an' a-gittin' drunk; but I don't see no sense in a-huntin' 'em down an' a-killin' 'em off. 'Pears ter me like they air better nor the dumb ones. I don't see no sense in shootin' 'em." (*ITM* 146)

Celia is again ordered to "Shet up!" and she says no more. But Chevis, having witnessed this uncommon act, is "pleased with this indication of her sensibility" (*ITM* 147).

Though Celia does not speak again during the rest of the evening, she formulates a daring plan to warn the Peels of her father's and his kinsmen's intended attack. She passes around the jug of moonshine and encourages the men to drink up. This shocks Chevis, and he begins to wonder at Celia's "sensibility" after all. The menfolks do drink up, and Chevis leaves, disillusioned by Celia's behavior. Shortly after his departure the men become drunk and pass out. This, of course, has been Celia's plan all along. While the men are unconscious and the other women are sleeping, Celia hurries out into the night and walks fifteen miles through the newly-fallen snow to the Peel house. When Jerry Shaw and his cousins finally rouse themselves and ride to the Peel house, they find the Peels gone and only Celia in a feverish swoon on the steps. Celia becomes ill and later dies as a result of her heroic act of bravery in warning the Peels.

When Chevis hears of Celia's self-sacrifice, he experiences a moment of self-discovery and a true glimpse into the real "common humanity" of the mountain people. As Hi Bates recounts the story of Celia's courage, Chevis contemplates:

There had fallen upon Chevis a sense of deep humiliation. Celia Shaw had heard no more of that momentous conversation than he; a wide contrast was suggested.

He began to have a glimmering perception that despite all his culture, his sensibility, his yearning toward humanity, he was not so high a thing in the scale of being; that he had placed a false estimate upon himself. He had looked down at her with a mingled pity for her dense ignorance, her coarse surroundings, her low station, and a dilettante's delight in picturesque effects, and with no recognition of the moral splendors of that star in the valley [Celia]. A realization, too, was upon him that fine feelings are of most avail as the motive power of fine deeds. (*ITM* 152)

Through an understanding of Celia's true bravery and courage, Chevis is educated into the reality of the moral splendors of the mountain people.

Celia Shaw is indeed the vehicle whereby Reginald Chevis recognizes the superficiality of his perceptions of the mountain culture. It is through Celia that Chevis is first drawn to examine the mountain culture, and it is through Celia's actions that Chevis begins to re-examine his romantically shallow and pompously egocentric attitudes about the mountaineers. When Chevis first sees Celia he doesn't really *see* her, but unconsciously thinks of her as a "picturesque bit of the mental and moral landscape" (*ITM* 135). She is for him a romantic diversion in an otherwise bleak environment, and although he endows her in his imagination with sensibilities not shared by her fellow mountaineers, he fails to see her in a sincere way. Murfree's comment on Chevis's first reaction to Celia is telling: "She was hardly more human to Chevis than certain lissome little woodland flowers, the very names of which he did not know"

(*ITM* 131). Throughout the story, until his final awakening, Chevis thinks of Celia as an ethereal creature and is "touched in a highly romantic way" (*ITM* 133) by her. She is never thought of as a real person, but as a plant or animal, a *thing*, albeit an ideal thing. He muses, for example: "It seemed hard that so perfect a thing of its kind should be wasted here, unseen by more appreciative eyes than those of bird, or rabbit, or the equally uncultured beings around her" (*ITM* 133). Just as he does not know the names of the woodland flowers to which he compares Celia, Chevis does not know her name until he has been acquainted with her for some time. She is for him only a "star in the valley" or a creature to be pitied.

During the course of the story Chevis's attitude toward Celia changes, and the reader can see that his feelings toward the mountain people in general have evolved. But Murfree makes the theme of the story explicit when she describes Celia's journey to warn the Peels. As Celia struggles through the snow,

Her prayer—this untaught being!—she had no prayer, except perhaps her life, the life she was ready to imperil. She had no high, cultured sensibilities to sustain her. There was no instinct stirring within her that might have nerved her to save her father's, or her brother's, or a benefactor's life. She held the creatures that she would have died to warn in low estimation, and spoke of them with reprobation and contempt. She had known no religious training, holding up forever the sublimest ideal. The measureless mountain wilds were not more infinite to her than the great mystery. Perhaps, without any philosophy, she stood upon the basis of a common humanity. (*ITM* 150)

This is Murfree's message: despite her lack of cultured sensibilities or religious training or answers to the great mystery, Celia Shaw, and by extension the whole Appalachian culture, shares a common humanity with the rest of the world.

Murfree takes this theme a step further in "The Romance of Sunrise Rock." There are *two* outland men in this story who entertain romantic notions about the heroine, Selina Teake. John Cleaver, a valley man, is much like Reginald Chevis. Cleaver is a young doctor who has been "reduced" to a practice in the hills because he could not get one elsewhere. He feels banished from society in the mountains, as if they have nothing to offer him in the way of civilization or humanity: "He often told himself that there was nothing left but to think of what might have been, and eat out his heart" (*ITM* 185). Like Chevis, Cleaver views the mountain people from a position of superiority and with a clinical cutting attitude (even his name and profession suggest dissecting, cutting).

Romantic Idealization   45

As with Reginald Chevis's attitude toward Celia Shaw, Cleaver is mildly attracted to Selina Teake's natural charm and beauty, but he is horrified to discover that his housemate, another young city man, Fred Trelawney, actually considers marrying Selina. However inappropriate he finds Selina as a wife for Trelawney, Cleaver is nevertheless captivated by something about her. She becomes for him, but only after her death, the same kind of romantic inspiration that Celia was for Chevis. Like Celia, Selina is only a means whereby the real protagonist of the story, in this case Cleaver, comes to a new understanding of life and of the mountain people. Selina loves Cleaver secretly; he never knows of her love until she reveals her feelings through a haunting look on her death bed:

> In her dying eyes John Cleaver had seen the fresh and pure affection that had followed him. In her tones he had heard it. Was she misled by that professional tenderness of manner which speaks so soothingly and touches so softly—as mechanical as the act of drawing off his glove—that she should have been moved to cry out in her huskily pathetic voice, "How good—how good ye air!" and extend to him, amongst all her kindred who stood by, her little sun-burned hand? (*ITM* 206)

Following her death, which has deeply touched him, Cleaver is driven to examine his own feelings for Selina and about himself. Selina's unrequited love and the tragic drama involving himself, Selina and Trelawney haunt Cleaver almost to madness. But out of this emotional turmoil, and an encounter with Selina's ghost, he is able to write a highly successful treatise on the "Derangement of the Nervous Functions," which brings him praise in the medical profession and allows him to return to civilization.

By utilizing her young heroines to help present her morals at the end of several stories in *In the Tennessee Mountains*, Murfree counteracts some of the stereotypical qualities that she often attributes to the mountain women. She suggests that they are not ignorant, although they may be unlearned, have no great "philosophy" or civilized "sensibilities." She shows that they are not weak or cowardly, either physically or morally, as exemplified in Celia's act of heroism. In fact, although her purpose seems to be only to convince her readers to accept the "common humanity" of the mountaineers, she actually shows them to be superior in many ways to others. Throughout her stories she makes many comparisons between mountain women and their more sophisticated city counterparts in which the mountain women are always presented as superior.

In "The Romance of Sunrise Rock," for example, the heroine Selina Teake is explicitly contrasted with the cultured city woman in a speech by Fred Trelawney, a visitor to the mountains. In a scene in which Trelawney is discussing Selina's merits with Cleaver, Trelawney compares Selina with more "educated," more cultured women:

"Education," Trelawney said abruptly, "what does education accomplish for women in our station of life? They learn to write a fashionable hand that nobody can decipher. They take a limited course of reading and remember nothing. Their study of foreign languages goes so far as to enable them to interject commonplace French phrases into their daily conversation. . . . Sometimes they are learned; then they are given over to 'making an impression,' and are prone to discuss, with a fatal tendency to misapply terms, what they call 'philosophy.' . . . What would that girl [Selina]," nodding toward the log-cabin near Sunrise Rock, "think of the girls of our world who pursue 'society' as a man pursues a profession, who shove and jostle each other and pull caps for the great matches, and 'put up' with the others when no one better may be had?
. . . Upon my soul, I think the primitive woman holds her own very finely in comparison with the resultant of feminine culture." (*ITM* 198-99)

In this speech it is Selina, the young mountain woman, who is sincere and unpretentious, unaccomplished in the artifices of cultured society, a "primitive" in the Arcadian sense. For Trelawney, Selina is the "ideal of a modestly delicate young girl," and he says that she "is the only sincere woman [he] ever saw" (*ITM* 199).

The "fashionable" world outside the mountains is again unfavorably contrasted with the mountains in this story when Trelawney's friend Cleaver, like Chevis the real protagonist, returns home after his sojourn in the mountains. He has thought of his existence there as bleak and dreary, but when he returns to the city he finds that he has been changed by his stay in the mountains, and especially by his knowledge of Selina's unrequited love for him:

and so he returned to his accustomed and appropriate sphere. In his absence his world had flattened, narrowed, dulled strangely. People were sordid, and petty, and coarse-minded; and society—his little clique that he called society—possessed a painfully predominating amount of snobs. . . . He was suddenly successful, he had suddenly a certain wealth, he was suddenly bitter. He thought much in these days of his friend Trelawney and the independent, money-scorning aristocrats of the mountains, of the red hills of the Indian summer, and the towering splendors of Sunrise Rock. That high air was perhaps too rare for his lungs, but he was sensible of the density of the denser medium. (*ITM* 211-12)

In this passage we can clearly see that the snobbishness, pettiness, and materialism of the outside world suffers greatly by comparison with the primitive and Edenic world of the mountains and its independent, non-materialistic people.

The same kind of indictment of the superficiality and shallowness of society outside the mountains can be seen in the novelette "Drifting Down Lost Creek," the first story in *In the Tennessee Mountains*. In this instance, as in Trelawney's speech in "The Romance of Sunrise Rock," the contrast is conveyed through a comparison between the mountain woman and the city woman. Vander Price, a mountain man, has left the mountains to live in the lowlands. Having at first been sent to prison for a crime that he didn't commit (but for which he valiantly took the punishment in order to save his idiot brother, the real perpetrator of the crime), Vander is later enticed to remain in the lowlands by the possibilities for indulgence in his love of working in the iron business. In the city Vander is "attracted to a woman far superior to himself in education and social position, although not in this world's goods" (*ITM* 75). Emily is a telegraph operator near the iron works where Vander works, and we are told:

> She had felt that there was a touch of romance and self-abnegation in her fancy for him, and this titillated her more tutored imagination. His genius was held in high repute at the iron works, and she had believed him a rough diamond. She did not realize how she could have appreciated polished facets and a brilliant lustre and a conventional setting until it was too late. Then she began to think this genius of hers uncouth, and she presently doubted if her jewel were genuine. For although of refined instincts, he had been rudely reared, while she was in some sort inured to table manners and toilet etiquette and English grammar. She could not be content with his intrinsic worth, but longed for him to prove his value to the world, that it might not think she had thrown herself away. (*ITM* 75-76)

Emily's eventual coldness toward and disappointment in Vander contrast markedly with the genuine love and sincere abiding faith in Vander felt by Cynthia Ware, his mountain sweetheart and the heroine of the story. Indeed, it is Cynthia's arduous pilgrimage out of the familiar mountains and down into the lowlands to see the state governor that results in Vander's release from prison. Unlike Vander's city wife, Cynthia is not materialistic nor concerned with outward appearances.

Vander, too, is changed dramatically as a result of his stay outside the mountains and of his marriage to a city woman:

> Though he had done much, he had done less than he had expected,—far, far less in financial results than she [his wife] had expected. His ambitions were still hot within him, but they were worldly ambitions now.
>
> He had changed greatly: he had become nervous, anxious, concentrated, yet not less affectionate. He said much about his wife to his friends, and never a word but loyal praise. "Em'ly air school-l'arned fur true, an' kin talk ekal ter the [circuit] rider." (*ITM* 77)

In his final visit back home, after ten years in the outside world, Vander's separation from the mountains is emphasized by Murfree's description:

> [H]e often turned and surveyed the vast landscape with a hard, callous glance of worldly utility. He saw only weather signs. The language of the mountains had become a dead language. Oh, how should he read the poem that the opalescent mist traced in an illuminated text along the dark, gigantic growths of Pine Mountain! (*ITM* 78)

Vander has become a part of the outside world and insensible to the beauty of the mountains. There is in this description an explicit contrast between the Edenic world of the mountains and the materialistic and deadening world beyond.

In significant contrast to the description of Vander's return to the mountains is the description of Cynthia's return following her pilgrimage to save Vander from prison. Whereas Vander is dead to the language of the mountains, Cynthia hears it strongly and is renewed by the song:

> They were weary hours before she came upon Lost Creek, loitering down the sunlit valley to vanish in the grewsome caverns beneath the range. The sumach leaves were crimsoning along its banks. The scarlet-oak emblazoned the mountain side. Above the encompassing heights the sky was blue, and the mountain air tasted like wine. Never a crag or chasm so sombre but flaunted some swaying vine or long tendriled moss, gilded and gleaming yellow. . . .
>
> There it [Pine Mountain] stood, solemn, majestic, mysterious, masked by its impenetrable growth, and hung about with duskier shadows whenever a ravine indented the slope. The spirit within it was chanting softly, softly. For the moment she felt the supreme exultation of the mountains. It lifted her heart. (*ITM* 59-61)

Romantic Idealization 49

Although this is one of those long "purple" descriptions of the mountain scenery that critics tend to feel mars Murfree's writing,[7] this extended description of Pine Mountain serves its function in the total pattern of imagery throughout the story.

This passage also points to another facet of Murfree's descriptions of Appalachian women, one that became a dominant trait throughout the course of fiction: the almost mythic connection between woman and nature.[8] Murfree associates almost all her young mountain women, and some of the older ones, although not nearly as often, with the natural world around them. They are, in fact, often described as manifestations of nature and its beauty.

For example, Celia Shaw in "The Star in the Valley" is described in the following way:

No creature could have been more coarsely habited: a green cotton dress, faded to the faintest hue; rough shoes, just visible beneath her skirts; a dappled gray and brown calico sunbonnet, thrown aside on a moss-covered boulder near at hand. But it seemed as if the wild nature about her had been generous to this being toward whom life and fortune had played the niggard. There were opaline lights in her dreamy eyes which one sees nowhere save in clouds that brood over dark hills; the golden sunbeams, all faded from the landscape, had left a perpetual reflection in her bronze hair; there was a subtle affinity between her and other pliant, swaying, graceful things, waving in the mountain breezes, fed by the rain and the dew. (*ITM* 131)

The description of Selina Teake in "The Romance of Sunrise Rock" is very similar:

[S]he wore a dark blue homespun dress, and despite the coarse texture of her attire there was something in the mingled brilliance and softness of the autumn tints in her humble presence. Her eyes reminded him [John Cleaver] of those deep, limpid mountain streams with golden-brown pebbles at the bottom. (*ITM* 187)

Cynthia Ware is likewise described in imagery that links her to nature in "Drifting Down Lost Creek":

The girl stopped short in her work of pounding the clothes, and, leaning the paddle on the bench, looked up toward the forge with her luminous brown eyes full of grave compassion. Her calico sun-bonnet was thrust half off her head. Its cavernous recesses made a background of many shades of brown for her auburn hair, which was a brilliant, rich tint, highly esteemed of late years in civilization, but in the mountains still accounted a capital defect. There was nothing as gayly colored in all the woods, except perhaps a red-bird, that carried his tufted top-knot so bravely through shade and sheen that he might have been the transmigrated spirit of an Indian, still roaming in the old hunting-ground. (5)[9]

In all of these passages the young mountain woman is presented in imagery clearly associating her with the natural world—birds, autumn leaves, mountain streams, bounteous nature.

Perhaps the most vivid example of a mountain woman's connection with nature is Clarsie Giles in "The 'Harnt' That Walks Chilhowie." In this story Clarsie is constantly described as the benefactor of the animal kingdom. When the old widower Simon Burney, who is interested in Clarsie as a new wife, speaks of her, for example, he says:

"An' she air a merciful critter. She air mighty savin' of the feelin's of everything, from the cow an' the mare down ter the dogs, an' pigs, an' chickens; always a-feedin' of 'em jes' ter the time, an' never draggin', an' clawin', an' beatin' of 'em. Why, that thar Clarsie can't put her foot out'n the door, that every dumb beastis on this hyar place ain't a-runnin' ter git nigh her. I hev seen them pigs mos' climb the fence when she shows her face at the door. 'Pears ter me ez that thar Clarsie could tame a b'ar, ef she looked at him a time or two, she's so savin' o' the critter's feelin's!" (*ITM* 287)

Clarsie is strongly linked with the natural world in Murfree's description of her also:

She was a tall, lithe girl, with that delicately transparent complexion often seen among the women of these mountains. Her lustreless black hair lay along her forehead without a ripple or wave; there was something in the expression of her large eyes that suggested those of a deer—something free, untamable [sic], and yet gentle. "T ain't no wonder ter me ez Clarsie is all tuk up with the wild things, an' critters ginerally," her mother was wont to say. "She sorter looks like 'em, I'm a-thinkin'." (*ITM* 289)[10]

Throughout the story Clarsie is repeatedly described in affinity and likeness to animals.

The explicit connection between nature and the young mountain woman has several ramifications in Murfree's works. First, these associations clearly link the mountain woman with the environment of which she is a part. Not only is she close to the land and the earth, to nature, she is, in fact, inseparable from them. The mountain woman's relationship to nature and the land is a theme that is explored throughout all of this literature, perhaps the most important theme, and it is significant that, although not a major theme in Murfree's sentimental works,[11] it is nevertheless present in her imagery.

Second, in many cases this connection between the mountain woman and the natural world is often utilized by Murfree in her plots to reveal the outside world's lack of understanding of the mountain world. By using outsider men to draw the connections between the mountain woman and her natural environment, Murfree shows that the Appalachian region is misunderstood and alien to the outside world. It is Chevis, for example, who thinks of Celia Shaw as "hardly more human than certain little woodland flowers," and it is Cleaver, likewise, who is reminded by Selina Teake's eyes of "deep, limpid mountain streams."

The men who come into the region from outside the area bring with them prejudices, preconceptions, and cultural pretensions. Ironically, they see the mountain women, representing the whole mountain culture, not as real human beings, but as merely extensions of the natural world, picturesque and charming, perhaps even sublime and inspiring. But they do not see the real connections between these women and their community, their world. They invariably destroy the women, and Murfree thus suggests a destruction of the mountain world itself through contact with the outside world. Murfree posits a spiritual encroachment of the outside world upon the region, foreshadowing the kind of socio-historical "rape" of the mountains by the later writers, as well as the machine-in-the-garden motif that is explored more fully in later mountain fiction.[12]

One other aspect of Murfree's depictions of women, closely associated with their relationship to nature, is their attachment to place and home. Though almost all mountaineers have a deep attachment to place,[13] the women seem to possess the greater closeness, a closeness that is most often expressed in their love of home and the land. Throughout "Drifting Down Lost Creek," for example, Cynthia Ware's relationship to her home is emphasized. Murfree takes great care to describe Cynthia's home, even personifying it: it is an "embowered little house, that itself turned its face upwards, looking as it were to the mountain's summit. How it nestled there in the gorge" (*ITM* 18).[14] Cynthia, in the midst of the activity of this house, "with her bright hair and light figure, with her round arms bare, and her deft hand stirring the batter for bread in a wooden bowl, looked the very genius of home" (*ITM* 19). Cynthia is indeed the emblem of home; she is often shown working in the home, spinning at her loom, cooking, washing clothes. These descriptions are in some ways in contrast to the attitude that women's work is only drudgery for which they are to be pitied. From the first descriptions, and certainly down to the present characterizations, the image of the mountain woman as a drudge or slave within the home and in the fields has dominated ideas about her. Their lives in the home have been seen as valueless and unproductive. Even Murfree often depicts mountain women as faded, worn, overworked and unfulfilled. Yet Murfree also suggests that mountain women find value and worth through work that sustains and nurtures both family and community. Through this connection of women with home and hearth they are associated with the archetypal, matriarchal figure of Hestia, and therefore Murfree clearly implies that a powerful matriarchal force exists in the Appalachian society, however patriarchal it may seem on the surface.

Thus we can see in the writings of Mary Noailles Murfree many of the features of mountain literature that have since been perpetuated in that genre, especially the major issues concerning, attitudes toward, and images of mountain women. First of all, two images of mountain women are portrayed: on the one hand, the woman as victim, drudge and slave, living an unsatisfying life of hardship and care within the traditional patriarchal culture, accepting her lot without complaint; on the other hand, the woman as willful, strong, capable and independent. Indeed, despite the suggestions in Murfree's works that the patriarchal social system of the mountains dominates the lives of women, there is likewise the implication that a sustaining and nurturing principle is at work which, because it is very often through women that she shows it, makes explicit the "common humanity" between the mountaineers and the rest of humankind. Secondly, Murfree shows the relationship between woman and her place, her connection to the land and home, a theme that becomes greatly important in later mountain fiction. Third, the mountain world is often compared with the outside world, the simple, noble virtues, almost always shown through Murfree's female characters, contrasted with the world of complexities, false attitudes and values, such as snobbishness and materialism.

By the late nineteenth century a literary and public reaction against Murfree's sentimentality and romanticization produced a new emphasis in literature on the worst and basest aspects of mountain life. Many of the qualities ascribed by Murfree to mountain women, however, remained the same, with only the style of writing and emphases changing.

3

Mountain Gloom in the Works of Edith Summers Kelley and Anne W. Armstrong

Although Mary Noailles Murfree often depicted the Southern Appalachian mountaineers as unsophisticated, ignorant and lazy, and aspects of mountain life that were distasteful and unpleasant, such as feuding among neighbors and families, moonshine making, revenge, idiocy and the mistreatment of wives by their husbands, she seldom depicted the mountain people as ugly, depraved or evil, and she certainly did not emphasize the negative qualities of mountain life. In the writings of the local colorists, Murfree preeminently,[1] the mountaineers were most often depicted as noble and heroic, bathed in a romantic haze, like the mountains themselves. Murfree's sympathy for her subjects is ever present in her writings about the mountain people. And, although she obviously had as a motive of her fiction a desire to foster sympathetic understanding of the region and its people (a desire that was ironically, perhaps, thwarted[2]), she was not a "reformer" in the literal sense.

Once the Appalachian region became a marketable subject for fiction through the local colorists' stories, however, and in response to other activities that began to affect the mountains, a new type of literature emerged almost immediately. By the 1890s a veritable deluge of fiction (and non-fictional accounts) depicting mountain life as irredeemably horrible and emphasizing the worst conditions and characteristics of mountain people began to appear. As Carvel Collins states:

As the nineteenth century passed, more and more stories treated life in the mountains as squalid and ugly. Between 1824, the year of the beginning of fiction set in the mountains, and 1880 mountain life in stories was often rude and uncultivated but not filthy or cruel. . . . It was not until 1880 that unrelieved ugliness of ordinary mountain life began to be the chief subject of several pieces of fiction. But later, in 1889—with the appearance in one year of several stories of cruelty, drunkenness, and depravity—gloom set in hard. (70)

Thus, 1889 is another landmark year in the depictions of mountain people because it marks an increase in mountain stories depicting the basest elements in the mountaineers' lives (Collins 71).[3] Many of the writers of the "gloomy nineties," as Collins refers to this decade in mountain literature, were, like the local colorists, non-natives of Appalachia. From their pens came a vast outpouring of regional sketches and tales, the majority depicting the horrible conditions of the mountaineers' lives.[4]

There was a growing national interest in general reform in the 1890s—labor conditions, women's rights, educational reforms, among other things. This interest in reform led many writers of mountain stories to show the conditions of mountain life in a harsh, negative light in order to secure reforms in the mountains, to help what many saw as "these poor underprivileged people." In so doing, these writers "reduced" the mountaineers, who had been decidedly different specimens of the American in earlier works, such as those of Murfree, to the same status as the poor whites, an attitude that has persisted since then. Isabella D. Harris, discussing the damaging confusion of all "mountain whites" with all "poor whites" which occurred about this time, states:

> It is a human error to remember a fallacious theory longer than its carefully worded qualifications. In the light of misguided missionary frenzy and of various rash assumptions concerning the trashy origin of the mountaineers and pitiable status, it is no wonder that people unacquainted with the highland area jumped to illogical conclusions. Although ignorance and illiteracy are not necessarily synonymous with stupidity nor poverty with indolence, the feeling that mountaineers are inferior people was established in the 1890s beyond the power of recall. (53)

A great deal of the feeling that the mountaineers were an inferior and degenerate group of people was the result of the Protestant missionary movement Harris alludes to, which was in progress during the last few decades of the nineteenth century.

The Protestant missionary movement into the mountains unfortunately contributed much toward the emerging picture of the mountaineers as sordid, degenerate, squalid, and in need of salvation from these conditions. The missionary movement began gradually, as early as the mid-1870s, but by the mid-1880s it was well under way. The chief aim of this movement, which embraced most of the Protestant denominations in the country, was to "uplift" the "mountain whites" by providing them with schools and churches, "those critical institutions for the socialization of individuals and, by extension, groups of individuals"

(Shapiro 33). Ironically, however, the far-reaching implications of this work did more to damage the reputation of the mountaineers than to help them. In their endeavor to uplift the mountain people out of squalor and ignorance, the missionary societies often resorted to painting pictures of the mountain people that emphasized the ugly and cruel aspects of their lives in order to justify their actions. As Shapiro states: "where the local colorists had been content to see mountain life as quaint and picturesque, and for this reason inherently interesting, the agents of denominational benevolence saw Appalachian otherness as an undesirable condition and viewed the 'peculiarities' of mountain life as social problems in need of remedial action" (60).

Shapiro continues:

The inauguration of denominational work in the southern mountains thus had enormous implications for Americans' understanding of the nature and implications of Appalachian otherness. It meant the institutionalization of a peculiar ambiguity, inherent in the work of the local colorists, by which the mountaineers became at once like us and not like us and the characteristics of mountain life came to seem at once permanent, descriptors of a reality of Appalachian otherness, and temporary, remediable conditions which would yield to systematic social action. It also meant the institutionalization of a particular definition of mountain life as squalid and degenerate, of the mountaineers as those who lived in squalor and degeneracy, and of Appalachian otherness as a social problem. (61)

Certainly, there were many positive effects of the missionary movement, but by and large it appears to have done more damage than good, at least to the reputations of the mountain people.

Among the worst conditions of mountain life emphasized in the writings of this period are "stupidity, filth, starvation, and lack of medical care" (Collins 71). Also shown is the shiftlessness of mountain men and their general brutality—"not the familiar viciousness of feuds, Civil War bushwhackers, or battles with revenue raiders but brutal treatment of women, children, and people in general" (Collins 73). The mountaineers are shown to be abjectly ignorant, and the struggle for education in order to overcome ignorance is also depicted (Collins 75).[5] The mountain people are presented as feeling (that is, presumed to feel) a great aversion to their lives and therefore a longing to escape from them. Particularly horrible for these writers were the lives of mountain women and their constant struggle to endure the brutality, deprivation and ugliness of their lives. It is no wonder these writers felt that mountain women should want to escape from their lives of hardship and thus made this a central plot device in much of their writing. As Collins states: "In the late seventies and in the eighties, writers had described a new character—always a woman—who longed to get out of the mountains into a gay richly-gowned world" (74). The romantic glow that had shone upon mountain women and made their lives seem less cruel and hard during the local color period was gone by the 1890s, and they were enveloped in a dark cloud of misery.

The horrible conditions of the mountain people, particularly the hard lives of women, are exemplified by two novels of this period, Edith Summers Kelley's *Weeds* and Anne W. Armstrong's *This Day and Time*. Both of these novels were written by women who were in some way feminists and reformers, and each novel has a female protagonist. Both works were written near the close of the "gloomy stories" period, *Weeds* in 1923 and *This Day and Time* in 1930, and they are examples of the genre that exploited the worst aspects of the mountain people's lives. Many of the qualities of mountain women and the features of their lives are depicted in these two novels similarly to Murfree's women, but the emphasis on victimization is greater.

Edith Summers Kelley's Weeds

Edith Summers Kelley's *Weeds* received favorable critical reviews when it was first published, but it did not sell well and was virtually forgotten until it was rediscovered by critics, especially feminist critics, in the 1970s.[6] It is easy to see in *Weeds* Kelley's concern with women's status and the nature of their lives in American society. Thus, it is not surprising that her rediscovery has been championed by women. In fact, *Weeds* is more of a feminist novel than an Appalachian novel, although the setting is rural Appalachian Kentucky; everything in the novel is subordinate to the unsuccessful struggle of the heroine, Judith Pippinger Blackford, to achieve selfhood and happiness in the face of constant repression, restriction, servitude and self-denial. However, *Weeds* does reveal some of the essential attitudes about Appalachian life that were common during this period. It also points out some of the serious concerns of later mountain fiction, such as the relationship between men and women, for example, or the ways of achieving selfhood open to women in this society. The Appalachian woman was a "natural" for Kelley's novel because the Appalachian woman had traditionally been depicted as a victim of backbreaking and dehumanizing labor and a patriarchal double-standard social system.

Kelley depicts Appalachian women in general in a very unflattering manner. "Most of these women," she writes, "were stolid-faced, ungainly, flat-footed, even the young ones wearing a heavy, settled expression, as though they realized in a dim way that life held nothing further in store for them" (180). One woman is described as "faded, harassed, probably in the late twenties, although she looked much older" (178). This derogatory picture of the women is further presented in a scene describing a neighborhood party:

The women and girls and small children of both sexes were sitting or standing self-consciously about the walls. For the most part they sat bolt upright and stared straight ahead of them. Now and then they eyed each other covertly. Sometimes a woman would speak to her neighbor in a hushed voice and thus start up a small whispered conversation; but of general talk there was none. Almost all of them, daughters and mothers alike, were painfully thin, with pinched, angular features and peculiarly dead expressionless eyes. The faces of the girls wore already an old, patient, settled look, as though a black dress and a few gray hairs would make them sisters instead of daughters of the older women. (85)

These descriptions emphasize not only the bleakness of the mountain women's hopeless lives, but a physical ugliness and unhealthiness as well.[7]

Likewise, the women's utter hopelessness, with their lack of joy or comfort, their listlessness and passivity, is suggested by Kelley's description of Judith Pippinger Blackford's daughter as seen through Judith's eyes:

When she turned from the boys [her sons] to the little girl she felt a more poignant sting. Annie was the kind of little girl one sees often in country places and very rarely in towns. She had a puny, colorless, young-old face, drab hair thin and fine, a mouth scarcely different in color from the rest of her face, and blank, slate-colored eyes. There was neither depth nor clearness in the little eyes, no play of light and shade, no sparkle of mirth or mischief, no flash of anger, nothing but a dead, even slate color. They were always the same. In their blank, impenetrable gaze they held the accumulated patience of centuries. (280)

Quite tellingly, Kelley's emphasis on the worst aspects of Appalachian women's lives can be seen in her descriptions of their eyes, which are dead, expressionless, blank, and have no sparkle of emotion, no depth, in marked contrast to Mary Murfree's romantic and sympathetic picture of the younger women. Murfree's heroines have eyes that are smiling, lustrous, and deep (*PSM* 4), "bright" (*PSM* 10), "shining" (*PSM* 236), full of expression, with "dark clear depths" (*PSM* 135).[8]

As with many of the women in Murfree's stories, the lives of mountain women in *Weeds* age them prematurely and are filled with little but drabness. Aunt Annie Pippinger, the mother of the heroine, Judith, for example, is described as "a small, inconsequential woman in the early forties who was all one color, like an old faded daguerreotype. She may have had some claim to prettiness in the days when Bill courted her; but they had long since gone, leaving her a bit of drab insignificance" (6). Annie dies young, and at her funeral she is described in similar terms: "The long coffin stood on a trestle in the middle of the room. It seemed tremendously large and imposing. The mouse-like little woman was claiming more attention now than she had ever done in all the forty-odd years of her drab existence" (50). Early death claims many of these women; Aunt Annie's own mother had died young, leaving many children.

Kelley attributes much of the unhealthy and sallow appearance of the mountain women (and all mountain people in general) to the practice of inbreeding, which she feels has produced a sickly race of people. She explains the unwholesome appearance of the mountaineers this way:

In backwoods corners of America, where the people have been poor and benighted for several generations and where for as many generations no new blood has entered, where everybody is cousin, first, second, or third, to everybody else for miles around, the children are mostly dull of mind and scrawny of body. Not infrequently, however, there will be born a child of clear features and strong, straight body, as a reminder of earlier pioneer days when clear features and strong, straight bodies were the rule rather than the exception. (13)

Kelley describes the young people of the community as the products of this degeneration by inbreeding. The children of Bill and Annie Pippinger, for example, are presented:

Crawford, the oldest boy, was surprisingly handsome and quite as surprisingly indolent of mind and body. The twins, Luella and Lizzie May, were thin, sickly-looking little girls. Lizzie May was pretty in a pale, blond, small-featured way. Luella had a long, pale face, drab hair and dull gray eyes; and her mouth hung open as though she had adenoids. (6)

The children at the local school are likewise depicted:

[The teacher's] pupils were mostly inbred and undernourished children, brought up from infancy on skim milk, sowbelly, and cornmeal cakes, and living on lonely farms where they had no chance to develop infantile mob spirit. They were pallid, long-faced adenoidal little creatures, who were too tired after the long walk to school to give the teacher much trouble. (12)

From Kelley's perspective as an outsider looking in, inbreeding and undernourishment had created a race of sickly, pale, long-featured people, with little spirit even in childhood, certainly a dismal picture. Unfortunately, this portrait of the mountaineers remains even today, having been perpetuated in such works as James Dickey's *Deliverance*.

Another aspect of Appalachian life that Kelley over-emphasizes in a negative way is the patriarchal social structure. Her indictment of the male-dominated society of Appalachia is obviously employed in order to throw into stark relief the lives of women. In *Weeds* the men are described as the lords of their lives, possessing above all the *freedom* that is denied women. Women are tied to their men and to their children, to their chores and their housework. Sexual roles are established in childhood, and boys and girls, men and women, are expected to conform to these roles. Men would never do "women's work"—anything having to do with the house; their domain is the tobacco field or the social courthouse square. When Judith asks why her brother Craw doesn't take his turn washing dishes, like the girls, for example, her sister Luella states "in a tone of dead finality": "Craw's a boy. Boys don't do dishes" (27). Craw, "the subject of this conversation, engaged in his favorite occupation of doing nothing in a rocking chair by the stove, looked at his sisters with a mild, impartial eye and said nothing. He was safe and aloof in his masculinity" (27). Women, on the other hand, are expected to be passive and obedient. Judith's sisters Luella and Lizzie May were "good, right-minded, docile girls [who] felt it was their duty to try to make [Judith] as good, right-minded and docile as themselves" (28). Women are victims with nothing but childbearing and drudgery to look forward to.

In a scene that presents the man's world from the perspective of an Appalachian woman, Hat Wolf, Judith's neighbor, says:

"The men sholy do have it easy compared with us wimmin, Judy. . . . Here all this summer I worked like a dawg in the terbaccer a-settin' an' a-toppin' an' a-hoein' an' a-wormin' an' a-cuttin'; an' all the fore part o' the winter I'll spend a-strippin'. An' then along about Christmas Luke'll haul the terbaccer off to Lexington an' sell it an' put the money in his pocket an' I won't never see a dollar of it. An' if I ever want a few cents to buy me calico for a sunbonnet, I gotta most go daown on my knees an' beg for it. An' then what does he do while I cook an' wash dishes an' clean the house an' do his washin' an' tend the chickens an' turkeys? He feeds an' tends his hosses. That's what he's got to do outside of his crop. I'm jes sick an' tired of slavin' like a mule an' gittin' nothin' for it." (144-45)

Luke, Hat's husband, spends his free time fox hunting and drinking. And while the women are working and receiving little satisfaction, either spiritually or monetarily, for it, the men are free to socialize with each other and travel to other places, something the women are either denied or have to plead to be allowed to do. Judith, for example, must beg her husband Jerry to take her with him on a trip to Georgetown.

Jerry informs Judith that he plans to go to the next Court Day, and when Judith suggests that they both go, the following conversation ensues:

"But haow about the baby?"
"Luelly'll take care of him. Or we kin take him over to your mammy."
"I was countin' on ridin' over with Joe Barnaby. If you go we'll have to drive the cart an' let Joe ride by hisse'f. Why do you want to go, Judy?"
"For the same reason you wanta go," she flashed angrily. "Because I'm sick o' doin' allus the same thing every day."
Jerry tried to assume an expression of male dignity and importance. "I'm goin' fer to see haow hosses is a-sellin'," he said. "As if you need to go fer that! You know well nuf you kin ast anybody that's bin there. An' anyway you don't need to know; you hain't a-buyin' no hosses. Why don't you tell the truth? You wanta go fer a holiday; an' I wanta go fer a holiday. So we'll both go."
"All right. Have it yer own way," said Jerry.
He had the air of making a concession, and he looked disturbed and annoyed. (168)

The men have more opportunities to escape their work and they exercise this prerogative based on their superior position as money-handlers. Women work just as hard as the men but enjoy few of their pleasures or rewards.

It is not, however, the "typical" Appalachian woman—passively accepting her life of hard work in the home and the fields—that Kelley focuses on directly in her novel. *Weeds* is the story of Judith Blackford, a woman both similar to and yet remarkably different from other women in the novel. Judith is similar to the stereotypical Appalachian women in that she is a victim no less than they. In fact, in a letter to Sinclair Lewis at the time she was writing *Weeds*, Kelley suggested that the heroine of her novel was a tragic character, part of a "worn-out, in-bred, soil-trodden race," trapped by the "hideousness" and "hopelessness" of her fate.[9]

But Judith is likewise very different from the other women of the community Kelley describes. Unlike them, Judith does not passively accept her fate; her whole life is a battle against her victimization and women's denial of self-hood by the inexorable forces that conspire against her. Through an analysis of Judith's character and a comparison of Judith with the other women we can see some of the major features of Appalachian women's lives as depicted by Kelley.

Judith is different in physical appearance and behavior from other women in her community. Even as a child, she is presented as being dissimilar to her peers. Others are slow and unhealthy, spiritless and adenoidal. Judith is quick, blooming and full of life. She is considered by her teacher to be a troublesome student partly because she is better fed than her fellow schoolmates (13). She also has an artistic inclination, which further separates her from the others, and which she must abandon in order to survive on a daily basis all the demands upon her time and energy. But what makes Judith the most different from the other girls is her "masculineness"; her sisters are docile and passive, but Judith possesses a conventionally masculine spirit. In girlhood she is described as a tomboy who "liked her father's company and her father's occupations better than those of her sisters" (30). She is repeatedly referred to by others in the novel as being masculine in nature. Her father says of her to a neighbor, for example: "All my gals is handsome. But this one here [Judith] is more a boy'n a gal. She's her dad's hired hand, she is. She helps me shoe the mules, she does" (34). Similarly, the old farmer Jabez Moore says of Judith to Jerry Blackford, when Jerry begins to court her: "She seems more like a boy. It's on'y lately she's begun to know she's a gal an' not a boy. Too bad she hain't a boy" (99). Obviously, Judith has a man's spirit; even the language of men is more appealing to her than the prim language of women. Men's language to her is an "expression of something real, vital and fluid"; she believes that it is "of natural and spontaneous growth, that it turn[s] with its surroundings, that it [is] part of the life that offer[s] itself to her" (57). She feels that the language of women, on the other hand, is stunted, not allowed to grow naturally and spontaneously, like the lives of women themselves.

What Judith admires most in the language of men is its freedom and naturalness; true freedom is denied women, as Judith grows to learn. In young womanhood, before she has been completely denied this freedom, Judith is described, again very differently from other women of her society:

Judith in red and white shone in her dark loveliness like a poppy among weeds. Something more than her beauty set her apart from the others: an ease and naturalness of movement, a freedom from constraint, a completeness of abandon to the fun and merrymaking, to which those daughters of toil in their most hectic moments could never attain. Somehow, in spite of her ancestry, she had escaped the curse of the soil, else she could never have known how to be free, so glad, so careless and joyous. (88)

Judith is a "poppy among weeds" (perhaps the other Appalachian women are the "weeds" in the novel's title). The other women are, for the most part, victims of the curse of the soil, and it is this fate that Judith struggles against throughout the novel. In fact, Judith's vivaciousness and freedom all too quickly fade into a life of drudgery and victimhood after her marriage to Jerry Blackford. Marriage, it seems, is the inevitable first step toward complete self-annihilation for these women. After her marriage Judith becomes another "daughter of toil."

The life imposed upon Judith—and indeed all of these farm women—by marriage is one of servitude and subjugation. Judith, like her sisters, becomes a slave to housework and motherhood. But the difference between them and Judith is that she longs for something more than wife- and motherhood, while they appear to be content or complacent. Kelley makes an explicit comparison between Judith's attitudes towards marriage and motherhood and her sister Lizzie May's. Judith, for example, realizes that Lizzie May is a better mother than she is:

Lizzie May had two children now. . . . Motherhood had improved Lizzie May. She had taken on flesh and seemed to have discovered some source of strength and vitality inaccessible to Judith. She beamed with maternal pride and satisfaction on her children. . . . As a mother . . . Lizzie May was better than she. She hardly ever slapped her children or fell into a rage with them. They did not seem to annoy her. (214-15)

Lizzie May also does not seem to mind housework as Judith does. Her pride in her housekeeping is described:

She kept [her children's] clothes and her own dresses and aprons washed and starched and fastidiously ironed; and she was always busy scrubbing, dusting, polishing, never tiring apparently of the endless cleaning of things just to have them dirty again, a species of well doing of which Judith constantly experienced weariness . . . . Judith often wondered why it was that Lizzie May got on so much better than herself. It was not hard to see why she was a better housekeeper. She had always liked housework and taken an interest in it. Besides, she did nothing else, never even venturing as far as the barnyard. Dan [Lizzie May's husband] did all the outside chores and when he needed help in the field he called on one of his younger brothers. (214-15)

Not only is Lizzie May a better mother and housekeeper than Judith, she is also a better wife to her husband, as Judith contemplates:

... she was a better wife, too, for just what reason Judith did not know, though she was beginning to have some vague thoughts on the subject. There seemed to be between her and Dan a settled, comfortable intimacy based on as perfect an understanding as can exist between a man and a woman. She bullied and nagged him a good deal about various things: his habits of drinking and fox hunting, his muddy shoes, his carelessness of her company table cloth. But she did not mean a great deal of the scoldings and he took them complacently. He on his side, though decidedly selfish in personal matters like most husbands, adored his family and considered his wife the sum of all perfections. . . . She [Judith] saw quite clearly that Lizzie May and Dan got on much better than she and Jerry. (215)

Judith, in comparison with Lizzie May, sees herself as a failure and her life as one of servitude and victimhood.

With regard to her children, for example, in spite of the fact that "she cared for them more than for anything else in her life" (216), and "in spite of her anxiety about [their] health and comfort . . . she felt more and more that she begrudged them something. She did not serve them wholeheartedly, joyfully, like Lizzie May" (216-17). The language in which she thinks about her children is telling of Judith's attitude: "More and more she chafed against the never relaxing strain of being always in bondage to them, always a victim of their infantile caprices, always at their beck and call seven days a week through weeks that were always the same" (217). She concludes, "If only she could have been a willing victim, like Lizzie May. But she could not" (217). Judith actually dreads being pregnant and sees pregnancy as part of a cruel fate. When she discovers that she is expecting her second child, for example, she feels an "utter helplessness against her fate" and "her flesh cringed at the thought and her spirit faltered" (240). As much as she is an Appalachian woman, Judith is also a "new" kind of woman who doesn't much care for wife- and motherhood.

Likewise, Judith feels that she is a slave to housework: "She had always disliked housework. Now she loathed it as the galley slave loathes the oar" (216). Judith actually feels that she is a prisoner of housework and despises it most precisely because it *is* "woman's work."

64 Wingless Flights

She even enjoys doing outside work in the fields because it allows her an escape from the prison of the house; working out of doors revives her:

> Judith spent all the time that she could spare from the babies and the house working in her garden. . . . She liked this work. She liked the feel of the hot sun on her back and shoulders, the smell of the damp warm earth. Some magic healing qualities in sun and earth seemed to give her back health, vigor, and poise . . . . [S]he was refreshed and in a way invigorated, more able to cope with the washtub and the churn, with the baby when he cried. (212)

In comparison with Lizzie May as a housekeeper, Judith again sees herself as a failure.

As a wife, Judith is unable to thrive as does Lizzie May. There does not exist between Judith and Jerry the kind of understanding (based as it is on a complete acceptance of the assigned feminine and masculine roles, female passivity and male subjugation) that exists between Lizzie May and Dan. A great deal of the novel focuses on Judith and Jerry's marriage. Sadly foreshadowing the estrangement between them, before they are married both Jerry and Judith express their resentment and near-hatred of the other sex. Jerry says to Judith at one point:

> "The ugly thing about wimmin is they never say a thing right out an' have done with it, like a man does. They jes set with their hands in their laps an' say a little bit an' leave the rest to the other woman's dirty 'magination. An' my own mammy herse'f hain't much better'n the rest. I don't like wimmin, Judy. There's sumpin' small an' mean an' underhand an' foul about most all of 'em. Uncle Jabez was purty nigh right when he told me they was all harlots. You're the on'y woman I know that's got a man's ways, Judy. You hain't spiled." (103)

Ironically, it is Judith's masculine ways and her free spirit that attract Jerry to her in the first place, and it is through marriage and its attendant cares that Judith loses her freedom.

If Jerry doesn't like women very much, Judith is likewise resentful of men. She tells Jerry when they are first courting, for instance, as they watch a flock of turkeys:

> "Do you know what them young Toms reminds me of?" said Judith, looking at Jerry with an eye not entirely free from the self-consciousness of sex. "They make me think of a pack o' fellers a-standin' raound the street corner in Clayton or Sadieville of a Sunday afternoon dressed in their good clothes, a-swellin' up their chests an' a-cranin' their necks after every gal that goes by, an' then a-

blabbin' together about her after she's gone past. They otta think shame to theirselves for bein' so vain an' idle." (68)

It is no wonder that there is constant tension between Judith and Jerry, for each has a negative attitude toward the other sex, and for Judith there is the added envy and resentment of men's freedom.

There is a gulf between Judith and Jerry in their sexual lives as well. Even though their marriage has been based largely on physical attraction and sexual passion, Judith soon grows resentful of the sexual relationship with Jerry because it is so closely allied with her unwanted pregnancies. Following the births of her three children closely after each other, Judith is so fearful of another pregnancy that she will no longer have a physical relationship with Jerry. During this period, however, Judith's sexual nature is not repressed for she has an extramarital affair with the visiting evangelist, which, ironically, also results in her becoming pregnant.

When Judith becomes pregnant, she at first attempts to abort the pregnancy, but when this fails she resorts to suicide. Her attempted suicide is unsuccessful, but she does lose the baby. Because of a feeling of guilt and pity for Jerry, or for some inexplicable reason, Judith finally renews their sexual relationship, but at a great cost to her own selfhood. The scene is painfully described:

When she came beside him to put more fried meat on his plate, she let her hand rest upon his shoulder with a caressing touch. He looked up at her quickly, his features suddenly brightened by a smile of surprised pleasure at this unexpected token of her affection. Something about the smile smote her cruelly, something pitiful and heartrending. She felt that she could not bear it. She made haste to go to the smokehouse for another piece of meat; and there amid the hanging sides and shoulders she shuddered convulsively, clenched her hands, and bit into her upper lip, struggling against tears. (280-81)

Judith and Jerry sleep together once more. Afterwards, Jerry sleeps soundly, but Judith lies awake, feeling the complete emptiness of her life:

Lying between her husband and child, she felt alone, cold and dismal, alone yet inextricably bound to them by something stronger than their bonds of common misery. Their future lives stretched before her dull, drab and dreary, and there was nothing at the end but the grave. She began to cry into the pillow. (281)

In language suggesting her almost complete spiritual death as a result of this act of self-denial, Judith is described at dawn as "pale from tears and bitter thoughts; and when the ghostlike dawn peered into the little window it saw them all three lying stretched out stark and pallid like corpses" (281).[10] Even in the most intimate aspect of marriage, her sexual life, Judith fails to achieve comfort, fulfillment or a feeling of selfhood; instead she feels that her selfhood itself is totally annihilated. By reconciling herself to a sexual relationship with Jerry, she resigns herself to the bleakness and drudgery of the lives of all the women in her community.

Sex, in fact, seems to be presented in an ugly way in *Weeds*. Lechery, lust and promiscuous sex are also presented as a major part of the mountain people's lives in *Weeds*. Kelley implies that premarital sex is the normal course of things. Judith and Jerry, for example, engage in premarital sexual relations. Extramarital lust and sex are also a part of the mountain people's lives, for women as well as for men. When Judith and Jerry are grading tobacco with their neighbors Hat and Luke Wolf, for example, lust often seems to fill the air. Hat is described: "Sometimes she lifted her black eyes to Jerry and saw that he was strong, healthy and handsome, then forgot him the next moment in thoughts of some imaginary lover" (151).

While Hat is dreaming of Jerry or some imaginary lover, Luke has designs upon Judith: "Not infrequently his mind wandered from these thoughts to dally with meditations more vague and attractive. Sometimes when Judith lifted her head she met his little blue eyes fixed upon her with a look, the meaning of which was unmistakable. Instantly he would withdraw his eyes and work furiously at his task" (151). Judith, because she is a beautiful woman, perhaps because of her difference from many of the other women in the community, and perhaps even more because of the gossip circulated among the male community about her sexual relationship with Jerry before they are married—as a result of Jerry's "blabbin'" to his friends—is often the subject of lustful desires. Besides Luke Wolf, for example, Bob Crupper has designs on Judith. He comes to see her one day on the pretext of selling some of his crop to Jerry, who is not at home on this occasion. Bob is drunk and speaks boldly to Judith and gives her a "meaningful" look. She is indignant and throws him out of the house, but "[h]er neck and right shoulder were still warmly conscious of the bold glance of his eyes" (164). And later, when he is leaving the community, Judith responds to Bob's good-bye kiss. Judith also has an affair with the visiting evangelist. Jerry, too, has an affair with Hat Wolf. Judith's final surrender to sex with Jerry near the novel's end is devoid of passion and love and is part of her final defeat.

It is ironic in light of her constant struggles against the bonds imprisoning her that Judith attains a tragic stature in the final pages of the book through resignation to a life that she has strived to avoid. Like the other Appalachian women around her, whose lives she has looked upon with fear and loathing, Judith becomes at last the accepting and passive victim:

Since her reconciliation with Jerry in the joyful moment of their baby's triumph over death a new spirit had entered into her. Melting in that moment she had known by what strong ties she was bound to him. Convincingly she had realized the uselessness of struggle. . . . Like a dog tied by a strong chain, what had she to gain by continually pulling at the leash? What hope was there in rebellion for her or hers? . . . She had grown timid about many things since the days of her forthright girlhood. Peace was better than struggle, peace and a decent acquiescence before the things which had to be. At the thought her sunken chest rose a little and the shoulders fell into less drooping lines; and there was a certain dignity in the movement with which she threw a long wrung sheet over her shoulder and stalking with it to the line spread it out to flap in the March winds. Henceforth she would accept what her life had to offer, carrying her burden with what patience and fortitude she could summon. (330-31)

Judith envisions her future days as full of bearing, nursing, and rearing children, working in the fields, becoming "Aunt Judy," and growing old with Jerry. Judith's real tragedy is that so much has been taken away from her in order for her to achieve this "victory" in reconciliation.

In a climactic scene near the end of *Weeds*, Judith watches as her little daughter Annie lies near death with flu and considers the futility and suffering of women's lives and the endless cycle of women's victimization:

Of what use after all that this baby should live? She would only live to endure, to be patient, to work, to suffer; and at last, when she had gone through all these things, to die without knowing that she had never lived. Judith had seen grow up in the families of the neighbors and among her own kin dozens of just such little girls as this one that had come out of her own body: skimpy little young-old girls, with blank eyes and expressionless faces, who grew into prim, gawky, old-maidish girlhood and passed quickly from that into dull spinsterhood as Luella had done, or to the sordid burdens of too frequent maternity. Little Annie was just such a one. In every way she was a product of the life that had brought her into being, and that life would claim her in the end. (321)

This seems to sum up Kelley's attitudes toward the lives of mountain women (and, in fact, *all* women—for Judith is obviously her spokeswoman throughout the novel): "to endure, to be patient, to work, to suffer; and at last to die without ever knowing that [they] had never lived."

Anne W. Armstrong's This Day and Time

Anne W. Armstrong's *This Day and Time* (1930) is another novel that presents many of the cruel and harsh aspects of mountain women's lives.[11] Set in southwestern Sullivan County, Tennessee, *This Day and Time* shares with *Weeds* many of the same character types and depicts many of the same negative features of life in the mountains, although Armstrong is essentially less gloomy and pessimistic than Kelley, showing some positive aspects of mountain life. As in *Weeds*, the major character in *This Day and Time* is a woman, and the novel focuses on her struggle for survival and a measure of autonomy in her life.

The novel begins with Ivy Ingoldsby's return from a nearby town to her "home" in the mountains to try to make a better life for herself and her son. We learn that Ivy was born and reared in the mountains, the seventh of twelve children. She was "born when the laurel was in flower, so that her mother had named her for the rosy cloud of bloom she had looked out on through the little window beside her bed: for the 'ivy' that came each May to lighten the deep shadows of Rocky Hollow" (20). But there has been little brightness in Ivy's life up to this point. She was married at sixteen to Jim Ingoldsby and was deserted by him shortly after they were married, just before the birth of their son Enoch. After Jim abandoned her, Ivy lived with his parents, Uncle Jake and Aunt Jane, but left to try her luck in the nearby town. She held several jobs in the town, including working in a jeans factory, a shirt factory and a poultry farm, and doing domestic work for a snobbish lady. Just before the action of the novel begins, Ivy has decided to return to the mountains and the small farm that Uncle Jake and Aunt Jane, now dead, have left her. The novel chronicles Ivy's bleak existence on this mountain farm.

As in *Weeds*, and in Murfree's stories, many of the women in *This Day and Time* lead lives of continual work and drudgery that age them prematurely and often result in early deaths. Whatever youthfulness and prettiness these women possess is quickly lost. Ivy, for example, is described at the beginning of the novel: "Her regular features indicated that she had once been pleasing to look at, perhaps pretty, but her face was thin and worn at present, deep lines, almost furrows, replacing what a few years before had been dimples" (3). Ivy's neighbor, Old Mag Rider, is also a stereotypical mountain woman in appearance. Mag is presented in a scene in which she visits Ivy just after Ivy's return to the mountains:

"Hain't no use lightin' no lamp fer jest me an' Gid," the older woman protested, lurching from side to side. "We hain't no company, mercy me, I hope not!" With her powerful raw-boned frame, her awkward unpremeditated movements, Old Mag seemed to fill the cabin, almost to imperil it. "You kin save your lamp oil, Ivy. Hit's plenty light with the fire. I hain't so pretty, nohow, me—" and she broke off with a boisterous laugh that disclosed two or three discolored snaggle-teeth with yawning spaces between. Seating herself in one of the splint-bottom chairs close to the hearth, she threw her hat—a shabby, rowdy-looking man's hat—on the floor, smoothed her apron, and ran her big-knuckled hand over a few broken strands of hair that were skinned back to a knot no larger than a walnut. (15)

Old Mag is a prime example of the aged mountain crone.

The life of Ivy's mother, shown through Ivy's reminiscences of her, is a poignant example of the cares and hardships, childbearing and child-rearing, and early death that characterize the lives of women in the novel:

Ivy's thoughts dwelt softly on her mother, a kindly, dragged-out woman, often sick, but always struggling for a semblance of decency and order in the swarming cabin. Her mother would plant a few flower seeds every spring, zinnias or marigolds, touch-me-nots, and bleeding-hearts. "Seems like," she could hear her mother saying, "flowers keeps a body from bein' so lonesome." Ivy could see her mother squatting beside the branch that tumbled down past the cabin, straightening her back from time to time, trying to get enough clothes together so that some of the children could go to Sunday-school two or three times at least in the course of a year. (20-21)

Ivy's mother endured her own ill health, yet struggled to make her home decent and orderly. She knew great tragedies, such as the deaths of one son and a daughter, the son killed by a falling tree, the daughter burned to death while trying to start a fire in the cabin. And she has known *loneliness*, finding in her flowers some solace. She has also endured occasional physical abuse. Ivy thinks, for example: "Her father, if high-tempered, had not been brutal, or only occasionally, when he was drunk and might beat her mother or kick one of the boys" (21). And after having twelve children, probably by the time she was in her early forties, Ivy's mother died, "leaving [Ivy], the oldest girl at home, to mother the family till her father had married again, within the year" (22).[12]

Many of the women in *This Day and Time* are depicted as admirable, long-suffering victims who strive to make the most of their lives. Ivy, for example, is the epitome of industry, thrift and self-sufficiency. Although she and her son Enoch are often hungry, they never despair, and Ivy always seems to be optimistic. She chops wood, cans vegetables, gardens, tends her animals, and finally takes a job as a cook in a logging camp. Many of the women, in fact, must be self-sufficient. They have to make their own livings, because they have been deserted by their husbands, as in Ivy's case, or because they have had children out of wedlock and have never married, as in the case of Old Mag Rider, or because their husbands are serving prison terms (usually for moonshining), as in the case of Mrs. Philips. Most often, Armstrong displays admirable qualities in these women—industriousness, kindness, neighborliness, self-sufficiency, and she likewise shows their uncomplaining endurance of brutality, poverty and loneliness.

However, Armstrong certainly does not romanticize the mountain women as picturesque or saintly. As well as showing the many positive and admirable qualities of these women, she also presents many negative characteristics. In contrast to the caring, hardworking wives and mothers, like Ivy, for example, Armstrong also depicts some of the mountain women as indolent, lazy and slatternly. One of Ivy's neighbors, Leola Odum, for example, allows her children to run wild, heads full of lice, and her home to become a pigsty while she reads "confession magazines." At one point, just after Leola has had a new baby, Ivy takes her some soup and discovers "the young mother, lying back on a dirty pillow, the few days' old babe at her breast, and in one hand a soiled and tattered magazine from which she had been reading, while other tattered magazines were scattered around on the dirty patchwork quilt that covered the bed" (63). The "squalid cabin" is repugnant to Ivy: "Its stench almost took her breath away." Ivy, herself so clean and industrious, is puzzled by Leola's "inert unresponsive ways" (64).

There is also the "new" kind of young woman appearing in the mountains, as a product, Armstrong clearly suggests, of contact with corrupt "city" ways. Nova Philips epitomizes this new woman. Unwilling to do any kind of work, Nova is waited on by her own mother. Nova is spoiled and selfish. She smokes cigarettes, wears make-up, and hankers for Ford cars and a Victrola. Even the otherwise demure Bertha Jane Dillard has succumbed to many of the "town" ways. Greeting the neighbors who have come to help her out at the death of her mother, Bertha Jane appears at the cabin door "mincing on high heels. Her hair was bobbed and her skirt, town-fashion, was knee length" (46).

Mountain Gloom   71

In addition to the kind of personal filth, indolence and squalor exemplified by Leola, and the "corruption" of the city, exemplified by Nova and Bertha Jane, Armstrong indicts many of the mountain women as sexually promiscuous. Premarital sex appears common and several young women become pregnant before marriage, such as Pernie Botts and Nova Philips. Mis' Doss, a neighbor of Ivy's, tells her about how Pernie Botts and Shell Henson "fit till they was down, till they was bloody as hogs" (67) because Pernie is pregnant with Shell's child. When he won't marry her, she calls him a son of a bitch, which results in a bloody fist fight between them. Later, we learn that Pernie has killed her baby in a grisly way. Molly Diggs tells Ivy:

"Pernie were in the bed an' she felt the baby a-comin' so she jumped up an' down right hard on the floor. She busted hit's skull."
"The Lord have mercy!" Ivy screamed.
"Pernie, she mashed hit's face till you couldn't tell hit were nothin' human."
"Law, Molly, I hain't never heern nothin' to beat hit'n all the days o' my life!"
"Well, Shell, he bigged Pernie, an' Shell, he denied her when Pernie 'lowed they otter marry."
"Don't make no difference—I don't see how no woman a livin' kin kill a little baby, hit hern, an' them so sweet!" (145)[14]

Horrible brutality and death also result from Nova Philips's sexual immorality. Nova and Old Mag Rider's son Gid fall in love and have an affair. Nova, however, is smitten by Buck Byrd (who owns a Ford car), and she has an affair with Buck, even though she is carrying Gid's child. In a brutal scene, Gid kills Nova and Buck when he discovers them having sex together.

Even many of the older women in the community had been sexually loose or immoral in their younger days. Warmhearted, kind, and hardworking Mag Rider has had nine children, "all born out of wedlock" (14). The respectably married Mrs. Philips, Nova's mother, and her neighbor Mrs. Byrd, the mother of Buck Byrd, have both had children by men other than their husbands. As Ivy contemplates Nova Philips and Essie Byrd, she thinks, "Well, they otter favor. Ef what folks says is true, old Andy Weaver's the daddy of 'em both!" As she looks at their mothers, Ivy thinks "[b]oth had been wild in their younger days . . ." (196). Armstrong describes many of the mountain women as promiscuous; while presenting this picture of mountain women, however, Armstrong clearly condemns men instead of women for women's behavior. In a nonfiction article entitled "The Southern Mountains," which appeared in 1935 in *The Yale Review*, Armstrong reiterated this point of view: "Anything more than the most superficial acquaintance with mountain life must convince one . . . that mountain women, in respect to chastity, have, in general, been easily violable, and this not so much from any overpowering animalism in their natures as from their complete subjection to the authority of the male" (546). If there are many women of this character in *This Day and Time*, however, there are also those who, like Ivy, are not promiscuous.

Constantly, throughout the novel, Ivy is assailed by would-be seducers. Old Andy Weaver is the first to make advances towards her. When Ivy asks him how much she owes him for the wagon ride back to the mountains, Andy replies: "Not a God-blessed cent, Ivy, if you won't be so everlasting prickly. . . . If you won't deny me!" (8-9). Later, Uncle Abel Dillard proposes to Ivy within days of his wife's death. Old Mag's son-in-law Rat Bunts, with whose family Ivy lived for a few weeks in town, "had constantly tried to see [Ivy] alone" (31). And Doke Odum, husband of the slattern Leola, also tries to seduce Ivy. Through all of these lecherous assaults, Ivy remains unscathed and prides herself that she is not a promiscuous woman. After old Mr. Weaver's lascivious remark, for example, Ivy says to her son Enoch: "The old fool, a-stickin' his face up in mine! He knows good an' well I've allays kep' to myself. I hain't trafficked with men" (11). Among the mountain men, as Armstrong presents them in *This Day and Time*, lechery appears to be a dominant characteristic. As the above discussion shows, almost all of them—young and old, married, single or widower—attempt to seduce Ivy. And many of the other women in the community have been seduced.

Sexual brutality in the form of incest is also presented in the novel. After old Uncle Abel Dillard's wife dies, he is left a "widdy" man with an invalid daughter, Bertha Jane. At first he seems to have his eyes on Ivy as a new wife, but she will have nothing to do with him. Later, it is discovered that he has forced himself upon Bertha Jane, and that she is with child by him. Bertha Jane dies of tuberculosis, the same disease that killed her mother, three days after giving birth to her child. With this subplot of the novel, Armstrong presents one of the most persistent negative qualities associated with the mountain people during most of the twentieth century: incest. Cratis Williams sums it up when he says:

The Tennessee mountaineers have been reduced to misery and moral bankruptcy in Anne W. Armstrong's *This Day and Time* (1930), an honest tale of lechery, fornication, incest, murder, and betrayal as they touch the life of Ivy

Ingoldsby and her son. After Ivy, abandoned by an irresponsible husband, starves out of a textile town, she returns to a miserable shack on a rocky scrap of a farm in a socially disintegrating mountain community to contend with poverty and the hacking lechery of the passion-ridden men who live around her. ("Southern Mountaineer Part II" 349)

Their lechery and sexual brutality are the most negative features of Armstrong's mountain men.

The mountain men, in fact, are in general portrayed very negatively by Armstrong. Besides being depicted as lechers, they are also moonshiners and drunkards. As Ivy nears the settlement store, on one occasion, for example: "she saw some men sitting on the river-bank. . . . A smell of the strong raw mountain liquor assailed her nostrils as she passed the men. 'They're filthy as hogs. They've been a-wallerin' around a still. . . .'" (87). Drunkenness often leads to violence. Young Wash Byrd, for example, murders Godfrey Tipton one night when he is in a drunken rage, something he would probably not have done if sober. Drunken brawls are also common, even among friends.[13] Physical brutality, often liquor-induced, is typical.

Armstrong believed that Prohibition was responsible for a great deal of the moonshining and concomitant drunkenness in the mountains:

over and above any such natural forces as were working slowly for their [the mountain people's] ultimate undoing, was a situation imposed upon them from the outside world that in less than two decades worked them incalculably greater harm than natural forces had done in nearly two centuries. This was Prohibition. . . . There have been moonshiners, I suppose, as long as there have been Southern mountaineers. But where there was one before Prohibition, fifty grew under it. One of the minor evils resulting from 'the changes that Prohibition wrought' has been the mountaineer's growing indifference to such little farming as he had done immemorially, and his ceasing completely to plant the fruit trees and orchards which previously had added much to the pastoral charm of his simple existence. . . . But far more striking than all this, with the enormously increased outside demand for the moonshine liquor, drunkenness among the mountaineers themselves has grown proportionately, for in proofing his raw and potent product by the crude method of repeated tasting, the mountaineer can hardly avoid getting drunk with every run he makes. ("The Southern Mountaineers" 543-45)

Even women, Armstrong contends, were involved in the moonshining business and sometimes drank liquor. In *This Day and Time*, for example, Mrs. Philips is a bootlegger while her husband is in prison for moonshining. And Armstrong states in "The Southern Mountaineers" that "[m]others may even be found who are willing to sell away from their families the last jar of canned vegetables or fruit in order to satisfy their own thirst" (545).

Ivy begins to recognize the brutality of mountain men and their treatment of women when she meets and becomes friends with Shirley Pemberton, the daughter of Ivy's employer at the logging camp where she works. Shirley is not a woman of the mountains. In one scene she discusses the behavior of mountain men with Ivy:

"Ivy, there are a great many women in the mountains whose husbands have deserted them."
"Law, I reckon.—There's several."
"These men in the mountains don't respect women."
"Ay, Lord, they don't think nothin' of 'em."
"Whipping their wives—think of it!"
"The most of 'em," Ivy murmured, "don't hit their wives with nothin' on'y their fists."
"Fists!—Ivy, I hope you'll bring Enoch up to have different ideas about women and to help you all he can."
Though she had tried not to betray the fact, Ivy had been startled. After all, men were men. Some of them might treat their women badly, but men's ways in general were hardly more to be questioned than the ways of God. Nevertheless, Shirley's words had set her thinking.
Yes, mountain women had borne too much. (117-18)

In this scene Ivy shows the general attitude of mountain women toward their men whose ways, however brutal or demeaning, are not to be questioned.

Armstrong paints a very unpleasant picture of mountain life in general in *This Day and Time*. It is a world where men are lechers, drunkards, brutes, and women are subjugated to and victimized by them. It is a world where women's values and ethics have, in many cases, deteriorated from exposure to the harshness of their world or through contact with the more corrupt outside world. Yet the picture Armstrong paints is not entirely gloomy and certainly not as pessimistic as Kelley's in *Weeds*.

There are redemptive qualities in the mountain life as portrayed by Armstrong. As in Murfree's writings, for example, there is a strong city-country contrast in *This Day and Time* and the city is always shown to be a far worse place than the mountains. When Ivy is in town, for example, in flashback scenes in the novel, her life is a hellish nightmare. At one

Mountain Gloom 75

point she reflects, "I reckon I've died an' went to torment" (33). At first she lives with Old Mag's daughter Odie and her husband Rat Bunts, in conditions of true squalor: ". . . it had been almost impossible for her to eat amidst such squalor, the house reeking with unclean smells, and Odie's children dipping their filthy little hands into the potato-dish and the gravy-bowl" (31).

The people in town are also unfriendly and unsociable; Ivy finds that she has no one to talk to, whereas in the mountains she has Old Mag and many other close genial neighbors. The townspeople are also snobbish. When she goes to work for a lady as her housekeeper, the first night Ivy fixes supper and expects that she and Enoch will eat with the lady of the house. Instead, she is told that she must eat in the kitchen. By contrast, the mountains offer security, friendship, and independence. The city's encroachment into the mountains is also felt through the corruption of mountain youths, like Nova Philips and Gid Rider, a generation obviously deteriorating through contact with high-heeled shoes, lipstick, Victrolas, and Ford cars.

In contrast to the condescension of city people, the mountaineers, especially the women, are hospitable and neighborly. When Mrs. Dillard dies, for instance, all of the community women converge at the Dillards to help the family out, to feed them, clean up the cabin, and dress and ready Mrs. Dillard for burial. On another occasion, when Ivy is visiting her neighbor Mrs. Byrd, the latter, knowing that Ivy is without livestock and having a hard time making ends meet, insists that she take a hen and some setting eggs:

"You pack her with ye, honey, an' the partridge rock over yon—she's one o' yourn, an' she's a-wantin' to set, too."

"Law, Mis' Byrd—" Tears stood in Ivy's eyes. "Law, Mis' Byrd, I'ull pay ye!"

"You take you two settin' o' eggs when you go, an don't name hit no more about no pay!" (76)

The neighbor women are always ready to help one another in time of sickness and childbirth or any other trouble.

The more positive picture of mountain life in *This Day and Time* than in *Weeds* is perhaps best symbolized by the life of Ivy Ingoldsby in comparison with that of Judith Blackford. Although Judith endures in *Weeds*, she endures in defeat—Judith is completely broken in spirit. Ivy, on the other hand, endures in triumph. No matter what obstacles beset her, she conquers them. And Ivy endures without the aid of a man. She is independent from the start, making her own way, caring for herself and her son, and freely helping her neighbors. At the end of the novel, Ivy remains alone yet unbroken.

In the climactic scene of the novel, Ivy has a physical fight with Doke Odum because he has lied about her virtue to her husband Jim. Jim had returned to the mountains but leaves after hearing Doke's lies without even seeing Ivy to give her a chance to speak for herself. Following this fist fight, Ivy feels cheap and defeated:

> She was no better now than old Teresa Boardwine, who spat tobacco juice into the men's faces at the store when they enraged her. No better than Pernie Botts. . . .
> "What's hit gained me," she thought bitterly, "me a-tryin' to git above my raisin'? I hain't nothin' but jest a old mountain woman where 'ull fight same as a man ef she flies mad, same as ary old drunken sot." (267)

She then thinks that she and Enoch will go away, back to the town where she will try piece-work again. But when Enoch finds her crying, he says to her, "Mammy, I wouldn't grieve so—I reckon me an' you is better off without him [Jim]. He ain't no 'count, or he wouldn't 'a let no man blackguard ye that-a-way, like Doke done" (268).

But it is not her own loss of Jim that Ivy is most concerned about, although she has longed for him to return. "Hit hain't that," she says to Enoch, "Hit's what I've laid afore ye" (268). She feels that Enoch has lost respect for her and that they will continue to have to eke out their existence. Enoch, however, is proud of his mother:

> "Ef all the women in these here mountains, Mammy, was good as you are,"—the little boy pulled her fingers apart, kissing her on her swollen lips— . . . there wouldn't be no need to build no church-house, an fer no preacher." (269)

Enoch then tells Ivy that the Stringfellows, distant neighbors, have brought them a load of wood as a Christmas present. It is another example of the kindness of her mountain neighbors, and the novel ends with Ivy's recognition of the goodness of people: "Law, Enoch, people is so good, hain't they?" (269).[14] The reader is left with the undeniable impression of Ivy's victory, both morally and emotionally, and the conviction that she will continue to endure. Thus *This Day and Time* ends on a note of triumph and optimism, unlike *Weeds*, which ends in despair and resignation.

Very little in the gloomy novels and stories of the late-nineteenth and early-twentieth centuries was actually new. In Murfree's writings, for example, there had been portrayed many of the less desirable qualities of the mountain people and the mountain way of Life: the patriarchal system that seemed to oppress women in almost every way; the debilitating effects of hard work and hard lives, filled with loneliness and melancholy, on mountain women, who aged quickly and often died young, reared housefuls of children, and were quickly replaced when they died; the brutality of husbands towards their wives, and drunkenness as an almost habitual state among mountain men. But over it all there was a kind of shimmering halo, a romantic haze; the mountains presented an heroic world in the shadows of sublime mountains. What was new in the gloomy writings of the nineties and for several decades following was the pervasive atmosphere of degradation, an emphasis on the negative features of mountain life.

4

Native Writers and "Authenticity": Emma Bell Miles and Jesse Stuart

In the 1920s and 1930s, particularly the latter decade, a significant new development occurred in the literature depicting the Appalachian mountain people: native mountaineers themselves began to write about their region from an insider's viewpoint. At the same time that many writers were still imitating Mary Murfree and writing picturesque tales of local color and others were writing stories emphasizing the worst conditions of mountain life, mountain literature was revived and propelled in new directions by writers who were natives of the region. These authors wrote with a deeper understanding of the Appalachian culture and people than any writers had hitherto exhibited in fiction. As Cratis Williams says of these writers:

By the mid-thirties, as new writers turned toward the mountaineers, they tended to see less of the folk quality in him and, possibly because many of them were mountaineers themselves, became less concerned with romantic and sentimental aspects of his history. Having known his poverty personally during their own youth, the writers who gave direction to mountain fiction as the decade came to a close were those whose voices spoke for him rather than of him. ("Southern Mountaineer Part II" 334)[1]

As Jesse Stuart, one of the leading figures among the newly-emerging native writers, wrote in poem "36" of his *Man With a Bull-Tongue Plow*:

>These are my people and I sing of them.
>I know these people I am singing of.
>I live with them and I was born of them.

The 1920s and 1930s were a time of a second discovery of Appalachia, somewhat like the first "discovery" of the mountains and mountaineers by the local colorists following the Civil War. But this time it was a discovery by native writers themselves.

This new development occurred in the "school" of the native writers, a group who shared similar backgrounds and artistic goals, and most importantly the fact that they were natives of the Appalachian region. Speaking of the native writers' voice of "authenticity" as exemplified by Jesse Stuart and James Still, Dayton Kohler in 1942 said of the new directions in Appalachian literature:

A generation of local color writers from Miss Murfree to Maristan Chapman exploited only the picturesque and sentimental in the lives of the mountain characters; their stories failed to reveal the essential humanity of the people themselves. Jesse Stuart and James Still have an advantage over these earlier writers in having been born into the life they write about. They use the materials of the local colorists, but it is clear that much of their freshness and gusto derives from a sense of identity with a place and its people. No writer's notebook, filled with tourist observations of dress, weather, sayings, manners, crops, could give the casual yet familiar picture of a way of life which we find in Stuart's and Still's best work. Even their language has emotional roots in the common experience, for it takes its color and rhythm from the speech of the people who have lived a long time in one place. Their writing has value quite apart from its importance as regional documentation. (523-24)

Likewise, in speaking of the new directions in mountain literature in the 1930s, H.R. Stoneback discusses what he calls the "renascence" at Lincoln Memorial Institute (now University) at Harrogate, Tennessee.

This "renascence," says Stoneback, was "a hitherto unacknowledged awakening which occurred, appropriately enough, at a tiny college at Cumberland Gap on the Kentucky-Tennessee border" (162). Stoneback further states in defense of his term "renascence":

"Renascence" is not an inappropriate word for the events which transpired at Lincoln Memorial in the late nineteen twenties. Still and Stuart were there; Harry Harrison Kroll, successful writer of hill fiction (first novel: *The Mountainy Singer*, 1928) was there; another who deserves mention is Don L. West, whose slim volume of poetry of the hills, *crab-grass*, was published in 1931. . . . Kroll wrote his hill novels from what Donald Davidson called the "insider's" viewpoint. We may assume that there was much talk in this vein at Lincoln Memorial, since all three—Still, Stuart, and West—were natives of hill country and aspiring writers. (178)

That these three writers, Stuart, Still and West, cultivated a "stance of authenticity—the writer writing of his own people" (178), Stoneback goes further to explain:

When Stuart wrote an introduction to West's *crab-grass*, in 1931, the facts and qualifications which Stuart chose to emphasize were that West was "a hillsman flesh and bone," and that "All Don's ancestors are sturdy mountaineers." Even Still has not been immune to the native bard syndrome; the "autobiographical notes" on the dust jacket of *Hounds on the Mountain* [Still's first volume of poetry] begin: "I was born on Double Creek in the hills of Alabama twenty-nine years ago." Whatever excesses of the authenticists of Lincoln Memorial, the awakening which occurred there could have had only a salutary effect on a stagnated hillfolk tradition which had been at a dead-end since the work of John Fox, Jr., and remained so in the work of hundreds of "picnic" regionalists and local colorists; and it did produce very real results, happily, in the work of Still and Stuart. Thus it is not too much to claim that, along with the publication of three hillfolk novels by three major authors in 1926, the awakening at Lincoln Memorial to native materials constituted a redirection and rejuvenation of the hillfolk tradition that might well be called a "renascence." (178-79)

The mountain world as described by the native writers actually differs little in outward characteristics from that depicted by the local colorists and the "reformers." Many of the same features of this world that were presented in previous literature are still found in works by the native writers: the patriarchal society; the mountain woman's hard life of work, her many children and subservience to her husband; moonshining, feuding, and shiftlessness, for example. However, native writers perceived this world in a markedly different way. Their perceptions are "truer," more than one-dimensional, and provide a needed balance to the excesses of the writers who emphasized the worst aspects of mountain life and to the romanticization of the local colorists.

Not the least of the native writers' accomplishments is their clearer perceptions and depictions of the lives of mountain women. They do not romanticize or glamorize Appalachian women, nor do they revile them. Instead, they describe honestly and uncondescendingly both the joys and strengths and the heartaches and weaknesses of wives and mothers in Appalachia. They give faithful portraits of mountain women, whose influence is so strongly felt in the daily lives of the mountain people.

The year 1940 is a landmark in native Appalachian literature, for in this year both Jesse Stuart's first novel, *Trees of Heaven*, and James Still's first novel, *River of Earth,* were published. But the works of Stuart and Still and other native writers had been preceded over a quarter of a century earlier by the nonfiction writer Emma Bell Miles and her book *The Spirit of the Mountains* (1905). Miles was undoubtedly one of the first to write about the mountaineers from an insider's point of view.

Ironically and unfortunately, however, even though her work preceded the widely-known studies of Horace Kephart and John C. Campbell, it was (and still is) little known.[2] A look at Miles's descriptions of mountain women will serve as an excellent introduction to the portrayals of women by native fiction writers.

Emma Bell Miles and The Spirit of the Mountains

Emma Bell Miles wrote from a close personal perspective. Although she was born in Evansville, Indiana, and lived from about the age of two until she was nine at Rabbit Hash, Kentucky, close to Cincinnati, she moved with her family to Red Bank, at the foot of Walden's Ridge near Chattanooga, Tennessee, when she was nine years old and spent her adolescence there. Through the aid of some wealthy patrons who noticed her artistic talents, Emma studied art in St. Louis for two years; following this stay in the city she returned to the mountains of Walden's Ridge. Just before her twenty-second birthday she married G. Frank Miles, a mountain man who was descended from one of the earliest families to settle on Walden's Ridge. As a result of this marriage, she began a life lived between cultures, partly in the mountains of Tennessee and partly in the more cultured society of Chattanooga.[3] Perhaps as a result of the ambivalence in her personal and professional life, Miles was able to attain an insightful balance in her descriptions of the people and the "spirit" of the mountains. As David Whisnant states: "Although it was first published in 1905, *The Spirit of the Mountains* remains one of the few books about Appalachia that neither romanticizes nor condescends, and which does not depend for its analysis upon unconscious acceptance of middle-class, mainstream American values" (xv). This is what sets *The Spirit of the Mountains* apart from the sociological studies of those like Kephart and Campbell.

In her descriptions of the lives of mountain women especially, Miles captures a balanced portrait, showing the range of their experiences. Wilma Dykeman, herself a noted writer of fiction and nonfiction about the Appalachian region, considers *The Spirit of the Mountains* "one of the best books ever written about Appalachia," (Miller interview 49) particularly as it presents mountain women. States Dykeman:

This is the thing that really startles you in the book: the simplicity of the prose and yet the depth of the insight. So she gave, I think, a special perspective on women's experience in Appalachia. She saw the younger women who were exploited, who were mistreated; she saw the older women who gathered such strength; and she saw all the variations on these too. She saw weaknesses and strengths; she saw hardships; she saw beauty. It was the richness of that experience that she saw that I think makes her own life a testimonial to women's experience in Appalachia, and in America, really. (Miller interview 49)

Through her own life's experiences and her close personal contact with mountain women, Miles was able to understand the subtleties and paradoxes in their lives, not the superficialities.

In one of the most beautifully written and insightful chapters in the book, entitled "Grandmothers and Sons," Miles describes going to visit an old woman, Aunt Geneva Rogers, to learn how to weave. Through this chapter, which sometimes reads like a *Foxfire* article on the art of weaving, Miles threads minute particular descriptions of "Aunt Genevy" and of the young couple Gid and Mary Burns. Aunt Genevy is described as one of the grand matriarchs of the mountains: "I have seen a bust of a Roman matron, mother of an emperor, which, with the addition of a few lines deeply graven by suffering meekly borne, would pass for a portrait of Geneva Rogers" (46). Aunt Genevy has the dignity of a Patrician woman. She capably runs her household, and she is a true artist at the loom as she instructs Emma in the technique of weaving, particularly the difficult part of setting up the loom. But most striking, perhaps, is her "suffering meekly borne," which has nevertheless added to her grandeur as a mountain matriarch.

Aunt Genevy has known a hard life, and yet she has learned from it the lessons of endurance:

She has had her share of crosses. For all her gentleness and courtesy, there is something terrible about old Geneva Rogers, a fascination, as of the stern and awful patience of some grand, stubborn slave. At an age when the mothers of any but a wolf-race become lace-capped and felt-shod pets of the household, relegated to the safety of cushioned nooks in favorite rooms, she is yet able to toil almost as severely as ever. She takes wearisome journeys afoot, and is ready to do battle upon occasion to defend her own. Her strength and endurance are beyond imagination to women of the sheltered life. (54)

"Patience," "strength," and "endurance" are the key words here; the paradoxical description of Aunt Genevy as both empress and slave is a fitting one.

While Miles is visiting Aunt Genevy she also becomes acquainted with young Mary Burns, a woman whom she has never met before, whose husband Gideon is helping Aunt Genevy's husband and his oldest son cut logs. Throughout the chapter, Miles presents a portrait of Mary and Gid's marriage, revealing as she does so a great deal about the relationships between men and women in the mountains. Mary is shortly to

Native Writers and "Authenticity" 83

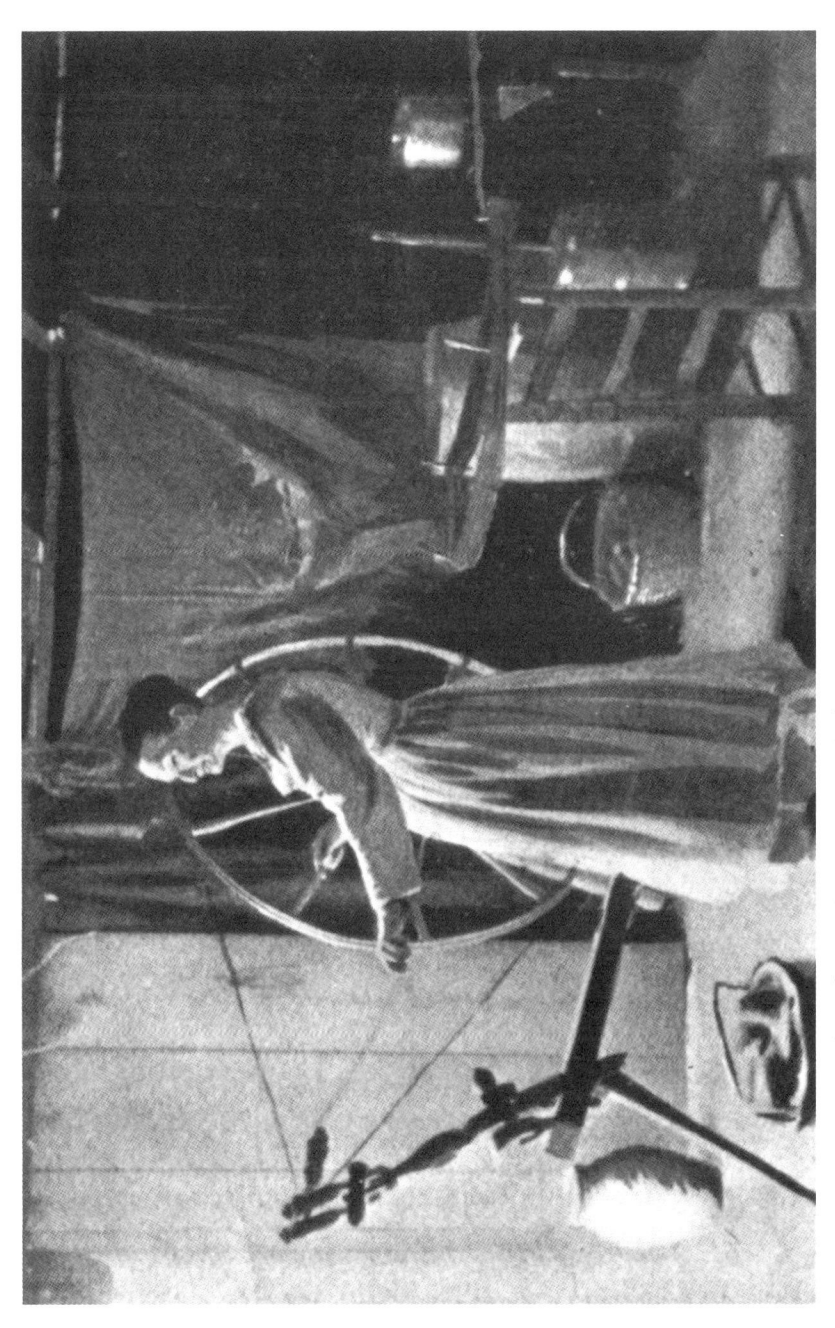

Emma Bell Miles's painting of Aunt Geneva Rogers is from *The Spirit of the Mountains* (1905).

be delivered of a child, which in fact is born at the end of the chapter. Gideon is, we are told, an indifferent, even cruel husband up to this point in their marriage. Aunt Genevy says to Mary, "Law, I know all about children, Mary, and work, too. Mine was never more'n two year apart. Don't you lose heart, Mary; there's better days a-comin' for ye whenever this is over [the birth of her child]" (42). Miles comments:

> She meant, as I discovered later, more than she said in the last sentence. It was known in the neighborhood that Gideon Burns, although not a pronounced drunkard or villain, was cruel to his wife beyond what is usual to mountain men. He never struck her, or, if he did, it was not known; and Mary never complained. But the sympathy of the neighbor women was with her, and the more experienced hoped that the coming of the child could work a change. (42-43)

Miles's sympathy goes out to Mary from the first.

As Aunt Genevy prepares the loom, Miles helps Mary comb out her hair:

> What a web, what a cloak it spread over her shoulders! So matted was it that at first one could not be sure of its texture. But its color was chestnut, glinting gold, and its length and weight were extraordinary. I soon saw that she could not untangle it alone, and went to her assistance. Her pain must have been excruciating; in spite of care, handfuls came away by the roots. But she did not complain, and by patient persistence we straightened out the mouse-nests and witch-bridles lock by lock, until at last the whole mass flowed smoothly, waving around her beautiful face. (45-46)

This description of Mary's uncomplaining acceptance of the pain involved in having her hair combed seems to echo Miles's earlier statement that Mary never complained about the way Gid treated her. In both instances the mountain woman's strength and stoic acceptance is revealed.

When Miles describes Mary, she does so with the same ambivalence she used in her description of Aunt Genevy:

> I have never seen anything greatly resembling Mary Burns. A certain maid once of the village of Nazareth may have had the same pure, modest sweetness, but her loveliness was of a type belonging to another race. For this Mary's hair, as I have said, was rich chestnut, and her eyes were blue—such a blue, softened by lashes a length one notices on the lids of children. There was little light of intelligence in those eyes, but one felt that Mary's capacity for doglike devotion was unlimited. Excepting its innocence, the rich coloring of her face was its most

striking feature. She had such a complexion as the first masters, knowing the effect of southern sun, painted without stint of olive and golden velvet and perfect rose. Gentleness and simplicity are characteristic of the faces of mountain girls. (46-47)

While praising the purity, modesty, gentleness, simplicity, and sweetness of Mary Burns, Miles also points to her "doglike devotion" and the "little light of intelligence in [her] eyes." Despite the fact that she is a woman about to have a child, Mary's is "a child's face, with a child's ignorance behind its lovely mask" (47). There is in Miles's description of Mary a paradoxical mingling of the child and the adult, of innocence and experience.

During the course of this chapter, Miles reveals much about the marital relationship between Mary and Gid. At one point, for example, Miles makes a strong comment on Gid's selfish and uncomprehending attitude toward Mary. On the night that Emma spends with Aunt Genevy Rogers, the local church is holding a camp meeting. Because Mary has no shoes to wear and would be ashamed to be seen barefooted in public, she stays at home; but Gid proudly attends the meeting, where he sings in his "rich and powerful untrained tenor voice" (57). He is "very attentive to the sermon" (57). As Miles states: "The incompatibility of Gid Burns' religious pretensions with his habit of living struck nobody" (57), except Miles herself, of course.

Miles can be objective enough in describing Gid: "His strong teeth flashed, his eyes gleamed as he talked. There was undeniably a certain charm about him. He was simply a young savage with an over-abundance of energy" (59). But with his religious hypocrisy (as Miles sees it) and the conflict between it and his treatment of his wife, Miles has little sympathy:

Gid prated on of righteousness, temperance and judgment to come, without a thought of his own selfishness, since the victim of it was only a woman, and his wife at that. The adolescent male of the human species has, even under civilization, an inborn contempt for girls. And this feeling in the mountaineer's maturity is superseded by a sort of wondering, half-amused pity. In Gideon's mind the pity had not yet arrived. (58-59)

When Gid is dropped off at his house by Uncle Zach, Aunt Genevy's husband, Emma catches a glimpse of "poor Mary, stooping painfully over her fire of gathered chips, sick, overheated, and probably suffering in ways of which we did not know" (59). A few hours later Mary sends for Aunt Genevy to help with the birth of her child. For Miles, the disparity between Gid's exuberant and thoughtless involvement in the church meeting and his openly professed but unlived religious sentiments and Mary's silent suffering, left alone in the house in the hours just before the delivery of her child, is an obviously poignant expression of the relationship between this husband and wife.

Perhaps as the older women of the community have hoped, the birth of the baby, a boy, appears to bring about at least a little change in Gid. Indifferent to his wife's condition for most of the chapter, by the end, after the baby's birth, Gid appears to have some compassion and concern for her. Ashamed that the baby has nothing decent to wear, for example, Gid plans to go to the store to buy his "big man a suit o' clothes" (63). He also asks Mary if there is anything she would like. She asks for a tuckin'-comb for her hair, some crackers, and a pair of shoes, which Gid says he will get, as well as "some dinner besides" (64-65). Aunt Genevy is so surprised that she whispers "Praise God!" Miles looks at Mary Burns and gives a final description of her: "Her face had taken the expression of a happy child's, and she was gazing at the little elevation of the blanket beside her. Then, because it was imperative I should go home that morning, I left them there together, the old woman and the young; the one with her hardships and suffering like a lesson learned and mastered, the other with her eyes just opened on its meaning" (64). Thus Miles ends her descriptions of Aunt Geneva Rogers and Mary Burns.

Miles is, as David Whisnant observes, "at her best . . . in discussing the relationships between men and women in the mountains" (xxix), and particularly in describing the great gulf that divides them from one another. States Miles, "I have never seen Gideon Burns nor his wife since that hour. But I have seen hundreds like them in the mountains, hundreds robbed of life's sweetest gift by the continual failure of well-meant efforts to bridge the gulf fixed by the mountaineers between woman and man" (64). She devotes the remainder of the chapter "Grandmothers and Sons" to differentiating between the experiences of mountain men and women and to defining the nature of the distance that exists between them.

Miles describes the mountain woman's life in a beautiful passage:

At twenty the mountain woman is old in all that makes a woman old—toil, sorrow, childbearing, loneliness and pitiful want. She knows the weight not only of her own years; she has dwelt since childhood in the shadows of centuries gone. The house she lives in is nearly always old—that is to say, a house with a history, a house thronged with memories of other lives. . . . Into her pretty patchwork she puts her babies' outgrown frocks, mingling their bright hues

Native Writers and "Authenticity"   87

with the garments of a dead mother or sister, setting the pattern together finally with the white in which she was married, or the calico she wore to play-parties when a girl. . . .

Thus it comes that early in childhood she grows into dim consciousness of the vastness of human experience and the nobility of it. She learns to look upon the common human lot as a high calling. She gains the courage of the fatalist; the surety that nothing can happen which has not happened before; that, whatever she may be called upon to endure, she will yet know that others have undergone its like over and over. Her lot is inevitably one of service and of suffering, and refines only as it is meekly and sweetly borne. For this reason she is never quite commonplace. . . . (64-68)

The mountain woman's life is one of dignity, nobility, courage, suffering, service, meekness, endurance, patience and an awareness of the "immanent supernatural" that brings her into close contact with the world around her. It is a life of knowledge lived in harmony with the "vastness of human experience."

The man's life, on the other hand, is lived differently from the woman's:

Men do not live in the house. They commonly come in to eat and sleep, but their life is outdoors, foot-loose in the new forest or on the farm that renews itself crop by crop. His is the high daring and merciless recklessness of youth and the characteristic grim humor of the American, these though he live to be a hundred. Heartily, then, he conquers his chosen bit of wilderness, and heartily begets and rules his tribe, fighting and praying alike fearlessly and exultantly. Let the woman's part be to preserve tradition. His are the adventures of which ballads will be sung. He is tempted to eagle flights across the valleys. For him is the excitement of fighting and journeying, trading, drinking and hunting, of wild rides and nights of danger. To the woman, in place of these, are long nights of anxious watching by the sick, or of waiting in dreary discomfort the uncertain result of an expedition in search of provender or game. (68-69)

Miles compares the types of songs sung by the mountain men and women: "The woman belongs to the race, to the *old people*. He is a part of the young nation. His first songs are yodels. Then he learns dance tunes, and songs of hunting and fighting and drinking, and couplets of terse, quaint fun. It is over the loom and the knitting that old ballads are dreamily, endlessly crooned. . . ." The woman's role is that of preserver. Though the man plays a more active role in the conquering of the wilderness, it is the woman who preserves tradition. So much of what Miles says here about the lives of men and women in the mountains is depicted in the novels and stories of the native writers, like Stuart, Still, and Harriette Arnow.

Thus, with great personal insight into the lives of mountain men and women, Miles emphasizes the lack of understanding between them based on their different perspectives and experiences of life. In concluding the chapter, she emphasizes the silence between them, and woman's greater sacrifice:

> Thus a rift is set between the sexes at babyhood that widens with the passing of the years, a rift that is never closed even by the daily interdependence of a poor man's partnership with his wife. . . . The difference is one of mental training and standpoint rather than the more serious one of unlike character, or marriage would be impossible. Man and woman, although they be twenty years married—although in twenty years there has not been one hour in which one has not been immediately necessary to the welfare of the other—still must needs regard each other wonderingly, with a prejudice that takes the form of a mild, half-amused contempt for one another's opinions and desires. The pathos of the situation is none the less terrible because unconscious. They are so silent. They know so pathetically little of each other's lives.
>
> Of course, the woman's experience is the deeper; the man's gain is in the breadth of outlook. His ambition leads him to make drain after drain on the strength of his silent, wingless mate. Her position means sacrifice, sacrifice and ever sacrifice, for her man first, and then for her sons. (69-70)

What is so remarkable in Miles's insights into the nature of mountain womanhood is that, despite the great division that exists between men and women and the harsh realities of the woman's life of constant sacrifice, Miles is above all else optimistic in her attitude towards the mountain woman. As one critic has stated, Miles was "a proud person giving testimony to the positive, if harsh, qualities of daily existence in the mountains" (dust jacket *The Spirit of the Mountains*). In her treatment of the "spirit" of the mountains, Miles anticipated in many ways the works of the native fiction writers.

Jesse Stuart and Trees of Heaven

When he first began to publish his poems, short stories and novels, Jesse Stuart was hailed as one of the most notable voices writing about the Appalachian mountain region. In fact, he can be said to have inaugurated "Appalachian" literature. As Ruel E. Foster states:

> It is significant indeed that Stuart's writing has been the catalyst for the current Appalachian renaissance in literature. The life of the southern Appalachians has

been in American literature for a long time . . ., but it has not been classified as "Appalachian." Either it floated in a kind of critical limbo or was vaguely and obscurely thought of as "southern." Stuart has never felt he was properly classified as a southern writer. He is happy that the critics have now discovered "Appalachian literature." The body of his work, of which his short stories are the finest portion, represents the most significant work of any Appalachian writer. (52)

Stuart wrote from the stance of "authenticity," a native writer writing about his own people. Because he was a native bard writing about the common people, and often in verse, Stuart has been called an "American Robert Burns."[4]

Stuart's canon is markedly masculine; almost all of his critics at one time or another have pointed to the "masculinity" of his writings.[5] He often employs the technique of a young boy narrator, such as Shan in many of his short stories or the boy narrator in *Taps for Private Tussie*, and the initiation of these boys into manhood is often his theme. Likewise, men are often the major characters in his works. Perhaps for this reason very little has been said about Stuart's women characters.[7]

It is evident, as revealed in many of the poems in his first collection, *Man with a Bull-Tongue Plow* (1934), and his first novel, *Trees of Heaven* (1940), that Stuart had a deep respect and admiration for mountain women. These women retain some of the qualities that had characterized them in earlier works, but there is also a new vitality, a greater wholeness and reality in these women. They are not one-dimensional characters, nor merely victims. Rather, they *share* in the life of the mountains and are often bulwarks of the Appalachian culture. His poem for his mother in *Man with a Bull-Tongue Plow* shows this complexity:

Martha Hylton Stuart
(1)

> I shall not speak soft words for her—my mother.
> I shall not praise her to the lofty skies,
> But I shall leave her on the earth—my mother
> Would choose the earth in preference to the skies.
> I say the strength of oak is in my mother;
> Color of autumn leaves is in her skin.
> The solidness of hills is in my mother
> And in her is the courage of the wind.
> And in her is the rain's cool sympathy.
> I hope she gives me strength of the oak tree;

Martha Hylton Stuart, mother of Jesse Stuart. Photograph courtesy of the Jesse Stuart Foundation.

I hope she gives me solidness of hills—
This with the strength of twisted grape-vine will.
I hope she gives me courage of the wind
And backbone that is hard as stone to bend—
I need these things to serve me to the end.

(2)

I shall not speak soft words with stilted phrase
To one who has worked all her live-long days
In furrowed fields and in the open spaces,
But I shall sing of her in plowman's phrase.
The blood that flows in her now flows in me,
Like sap, two seasons, flows in the same tree.
And I am proud to have her blood in me.
I pray for more of her solidness in me.
I pray for more of her philosophy.
I want a heart as free as hers to give,
I want a love like hers to see men live
And women live—her love to help the sick.
I want her meekness—never wanting praise,
And for this rugged mother of the hills—
I sing for her in rugged plowman phrase.

(3)

And you, my mother, who will stack by you?
In beauty—yes—others are beautiful
And you are not in flesh and fancy guise.
But you have lived a life so rich and full,
Few worldly beauties stack beside of you.
If they'd gone through with all you have gone through,
Their eyes would blear and blue fade from the blue,
Their flesh would be as rugged as yours too.
You've asked no man the odds of work to do,
You've done your share—you've done it with a will,
You've done it with the solidness of hill.
And unafraid you've met your life, my mother—
Now unafraid, I say there is no other
That after all can stack beside of you—
The tree in you, flower in you, the hill,
Color of autumn leaf, the twisted grape-vine will.

(4)
The hills are dear to you, my mountain mother.
Corn-fields are dear to you—green in the sun,
The touch of wind is dear to you, my mother,
The rock ribs of the hills are dear to you.
White rain that falls on leaves is dear to you.
The lightning-storm will make no fear to you.
One of the elements, you surely are,
With power to love, a child, a stone, a star,
A will to work—one unafraid of life—
One that loves life and gave her seven life.
An autumn tree, my mother, now you are.
The gold of age is hanging to your boughs.
And unafraid you stand to meet new life,
Beneath white glistening beauty of a star. (29-31)[4]

Reprinted with the permission of the Jesse Stuart Foundation

A companion piece to his poem for his father, "For Mitchell Stuart," this poem speaks with the deepest admiration and love for his mother, a woman of the elements, but it also reveals striking facets of mountain womanhood as perceived by Stuart: women have great strength and will; women work hard and do what has to be done; and, most importantly, women in the mountains lead full, satisfactory lives. Certainly, there is no hint here that Stuart feels his mother has lived a melancholy, unhappy existence. On the contrary, hers has been a life full of love and living, *unafraid*.

Trees of Heaven, Stuart's first novel, is dominated by the presence of two strong men, Anse Bushman and Boliver Tussie, two opposing forces in the novel. Anse is a land-owning farmer who believes in the work ethic and the ownership of land, a powerful patriarch, respected by the community. Boliver is a "squatter," living a poor but carefree existence with his ragged family on the Bushman property. It is around these two men and the feelings that each embodies for the land itself that the novel revolves.[8] However, women play prominent roles in the novel, and Stuart's admiration and respect for them is revealed, particularly in his description of the major female character, Subrinea Tussie. There is perhaps more pathos and stereotype than admiration and originality in his descriptions of the older mountain women, Fronnie Bushman, Anse's wife, and Crissie Tussie, wife of Boliver.

Fronnie Bushman is representative in many ways of the stereotypical older mountain woman. She has borne and reared eleven children; all but Tarvin, the youngest son, have left home, run off by the hard work and constant demands of their father Anse. She has endured Anse's hard work ethic and has grown old with him. The description of Fronnie at the beginning of the novel is similar to Mary Murfree's descriptions of like women:

Fronnie is a tall mountain woman, her once crow-wing black hair is streaked with silvery streaks of gray; her eagle-gray eyes are being dimmed by time. Time, hard work, on the farm and in the house, and childbirth have not bent her tall body. She stands straight as a poplar sapling in the kitchen door and watches Tarvin. Her long arms hang limp at her side. With the calloused long slim fingers of her left hand she fingers at her apron pocket. She is crumbling the homegrown bright burley leaf into finer tobacco crumbs to put in her long-stemmed clay pipe. (12)

As with the descriptions of many mountain women, Stuart's portrait of Fronnie is dominated by her life of hard work, which, although it has not "bent her tall body," has broken her spirit in many ways.

Fronnie's life had been defined by her hard labor alongside Anse. When Tarvin complains that his father is working him too hard in his greed to subdue and own land, Fronnie says to him: "I've worked this way all my life . . . to have what we have. The people here that makes a little more than the rest air old long before their time to git old and they die before their time to die" (55). And later she says to Tarvin, "If you ever marry, Tarvin, don't you ever let your wife work like I haf to work. I've had to work like this and carry you youngins. I've worked like this up to a week before one of you was born" (56). As Frank H. Leavell states: "Fronnie . . . is the most pathetic witness to the brutality of her husband's work drive" (60).[9]

Fronnie is not only a victim of back- and spirit-breaking labor but of the traditional patriarchal social system of the mountains. As John Howard Spurlock states, regarding the Appalachian culture as depicted by Stuart: "The Appalachian family is patriarchal, and masculinity symbols [in Stuart's work] reinforce the concept of the male as a creature to be respected and even feared" (88).[10] Anse Bushman is indeed such a commanding patriarch. At a community gathering, for example, Anse and Fronnie are described:

Fronnie is dressed in a new gingham dress. She wears a neatly ironed apron with a pocket on the corner to hold her pipe, matches and tobacco. Her apron is tied behind with a neat little bow. Fronnie is tall, thin and handsome despite the years of hard labor, dancing and childbearing. Her graying hair gives her the dignity of a woman for her years. She is commanding among other women in the neighborhood, but she is not commanding with her husband. He is the patriarch, the man whose words everybody must listen to; the man whose big farm and whose reputation for hard work and thrift have earned him an enviable place in the community. (66)

That Anse has been a hard taskmaster is evidenced by the fact that all his children but Tarvin have left home, and Fronnie likewise is afraid of him in some ways. She is afraid to ask him for money for "house plunder" (furniture), for example (138).

Anse has traditional male opinions about masculinity and the man's place. Tarvin, for example, says of his father: "Pa likes the out-of-doors. He says a man that will wash dishes aint no good. Pa allus told me to watch that sort of men. Said they warn't good providers fer their families. Pa got mad when he talked about men that would wash dishes and wouldn't git out and do a day of work" (138). Anse believes that a man should be "tough," a good provider and a hard worker. As Fronnie tells Tarvin:

"Anse ust to make the boys wash in ice water in the winter. He said it made 'em tough. I've seen Anse come in and wash in a pan filled with mush ice. I've seen 'im wash his face, throw the pan of water into the air and it would be ice before it hit the ground. . . . Anse had the strength then of a hoss. He didn't know his strength. He was a hard man fer a women to live with. You don't know, Son, what I've had to go through with in my life-time, bearin' children fer Anse, cookin grub to feed a family of gluttons and doin all the housework and helpin with the work outside when Anse was crowded in the crop seasons." (138-39)

Fronnie has indeed endured a great deal as Anse's wife.

Tarvin, however, unlike his father, is sympathetic throughout the novel to his mother's hardships, as he shows in the following speech:

"A woman must have a strong backbone, nerves solid as a rock cliff, and muscles strong as wild grape-vines to go through with all my mother has gone through. . . . There ain't many wimmen that could do it. I just look at Ma going around in shoes without stockins on her legs. I see the big clumps of blood showin under the skin in the broken veins. I see the strain of toil on her face. I just wonder if life is worth livin when a woman hast to work like Ma has had to work. Ma is still workin and Pa is still workin. They have had to pay the price to git a little ahead." (113)

This description of Fronnie is very similar to Stuart's description of his own mother in the preceding poem. Like Stuart's realization of his mother's character, Tarvin realizes—something that Anse appears unaware of throughout most of the novel—that his mother has worked as hard as, or perhaps harder than, his father and that together they have "worked shoulder to shoulder to turn the hard wheel of life" (143-44). The realization of the equality of women's work is an important aspect of *Trees of Heaven*.

Anse eventually seems to come to this understanding of the value of women's work when, at the end of the novel, he allows Fronnie to buy her new furniture, as a way of acknowledging her contribution to their prosperity. Until this point, Anse has believed that Fronnie "ain't never wanted fer nothin'" (210) because he has "allus kep [her] plenty to eat and a good home" (210). He does not realize that Fronnie needs more than these material things from him, that she is spiritually starved for understanding and acknowledgment. The spiritual gulf between Fronnie and Anse is like that described by Emma Bell Miles between the mountain man and woman.

Fronnie is representative of the land-owning farmer class of mountain people; she is neat and respectable, clean and hardworking. Crissie Tussie, the wife of Boliver Tussie, on the other hand, is one of the squatter class of women, many of whom are described by Stuart as lazy and shiftless slatterns. Stuart's presentation of the squatter class in general, in fact, bears some similarity to the description of the mountain people in Kelley's *Weeds*. Like Kelley, Stuart blames many of the ugly features of the squatters' lives on in-breeding. As Crissie says to Boliver at one point:

"Look at the Tussies! They couldn't find squatters to marry and they've married one another. Uncles have married nieces and first cousins have married first cousins, and grandpas have married granddaughters. I don't know what it does to people but I know what it does to hogs. I know the stock in hogs will run out when you breed cousins to cousins and uncles to nieces and aunts to nephews and grandpas to granddaughters. And I know the stock has about run out'n the Tussies." (27)

The squatters likewise live in the kind of squalor as some of the families in Anne W. Armstrong's *This Day and Time*. They leave the doors wide open and dirty dishes and food piled on the table. They lift their hands to do the merest of work and spend most of their time sitting lazily on the porch fanning flies. "The squatters air a dirty lot and they air a triflin lot. They live like hogs" (22), says Tarvin at one point. Nevertheless, these people are not unredeemed by positive qualities. They find great joy in their carefree lives, unencumbered by the obsession to subdue and control their environment. They love singing and dancing. This aspect of their lives is contrasted in the novel to the apparently joyless life of the Bushmans.

Despite the difference in lifestyle between Fronnie Bushman and Crissie Tussie, however, they do share their victimization by male domination. Like Fronnie's in many ways, Crissie's life appears to be a miserable one, one that she finds terrible and hates. Her husband, unlike Anse Bushman, is a drunkard, and Crissie has obviously abandoned all her finer sentiments as a result of the inescapable squalor of her life. Perhaps her most poignant speech comes near the beginning of the novel when she describes her doleful life and the way that people snub her because she is of a lower class:

"Sometimes I think I'll take the ax," says Crissie, "when Boliver gits on his week-end drunk, and take the double bitt and split his goddam head wide open. I git so tired of this life. I've allus wanted to escape it and live as other people live. I see how other people live. I see 'em laughin and talkin and havin a good time. I see 'em walkin from painted houses and drivin fine cars. They pass me when I come from town carryin a load of grub fer my children big enough to break my back. I think back to my family of seven dirty-faced youngins and my shack allus in the head of Cat's Fork without a wagon road leadin to it. Jest a fox path, a hunter's path or a road the oxen made is the way you'll allus walk to my shack." (24)

Although the Tussies are characterized by their carefree lack of responsibility and laziness, Crissie feels a sense of shame for her poverty and knows that there is a better way of living than the squalor that is imposed upon her.

Crissie's victimization seems greater than Fronnie's, in fact, for her husband is a lazy drunkard and they live in abject poverty. Although the squatters are generally described as lazy, Crissie works no less hard than Fronnie both in the house and in the fields, as the two women struggle to raise their large families and meet the needs of their men. Crissie seems to have more to struggle against and therefore her accomplishments are less. And Fronnie and Crissie share a common need for understanding from and communion with their husbands, something of which they are usually deprived. Like Fronnie's, much of the best in Crissie's life has been taken away from her through subservience to her husband. Stuart obviously recognizes this aspect of their lives and admires them for their endurance and survival. At one point, Anse denigrates the squatter women by saying "[t]he squatter wimmen have legs, arms, eyes, hair like all other wimmen—but their skins air tough. I say their skins air tough. They air thick and tough"; yet Fronnie acknowledges the common sisterhood of herself and Crissie when she replies, "We air all tough wimmen through these parts" (133).

Fronnie and Crissie represent one type of mountain woman in Stuart's novel—the hardworking, patient subservient woman, victimized by the patriarchal system, who is nevertheless noble and admirable in her endurance. Subrinea Tussie, the daughter of Boliver and Crissie and the sweetheart of Tarvin Bushman, however, is very differently presented from her mother and Fronnie. In his description of Subrinea, Stuart evokes all that is most positive in mountain womanhood, and thus presents a striking contrast to the lives of the older women. Through Subrinea, Stuart shows that there is more to the lives of mountain women than unacknowledged and unappreciated labor.

First and foremost, Subrinea is vital and healthy, even though she is a product of the extensive intermarriages among the squatter families. This vitality and health are apparent in Stuart's first description of her:

. . . a tall barefooted girl running down the hot dry path to meet Tarvin. A golden shock of long hair falls over her shoulders. It is not combed any more than a patch of love-vines growing among briars and sprouts. Her long brown arms are flung in the air as she runs down the path toward Tarvin. Her strong brown muscular arms move like pistons in perfect rhythm and her thin blue-checked gingham dress is caught above her knees as she runs. (18-19)

When Tarvin looks at her he sees her cat-green eyes and admires her beauty: "her strong shapely body, the outlines of her full bosom beneath her thin dress and her strong brown muscular legs. She is a wild phlox in beauty for him to look at, and she is the ripe fruit ready to be plucked" (22-23). And after she leaves him, Tarvin remembers "the sweet clean smell of her hair, sweet-smelling as Autumn corn tassels streaming in the wind" and "her strong legs brown as a pawpaw leaf in September" (36-37). Subrinea is hearty, full of life and energy. Like her mother, Subrinea has a longing to escape the miserable life of the squatters:

Tarvin walks up the path and these thoughts flash through his mind. All he can see is Subrinea. He can feel her in his arms. She will not go away. She has knocked at the door of his brain and she has entered. The pounding of his heart against the panels of his ribs is Subrinea knocking, knocking to escape the life in the dirty shack, the insults from the lumberjacks, her drunken father—trying to escape from a world of squatters that have intermarried their own blood kin for years, trying to escape the doomed living for the happiness Tarvin can offer her. (37)

Because she is of the squatter class, Subrinea is considered by many of the other mountaineers, even some of her own kinfolks, to be of a lower standing where her sexual conduct is concerned. Like many of the other squatter women, it is believed that Subrinea is "easy" (many of the other Tussie women are considered—and indeed are—common whores). Bollie Beaver, her cousin who has his eyes on Subrinea, for example, has offered her five dollars to have sex with him.

But Subrinea is not sexually promiscuous, although she is not sexually inhibited either. Stuart celebrates Subrinea's natural sexuality. She does have premarital sexual relations with Tarvin, but it is explicit in the novel that both she and Tarvin consider their actions to be a "natural" consummation of their "marriage" in the spirit. In their first sexual encounter, both Tarvin and Subrinea are obviously virgins. Thus Subrinea's sexuality is presented as natural and unspoiled. Even though some readers might believe, like some of the characters in the novel, that Subrinea is sexually immoral because she has sex with Tarvin before their marriage, this is undeniably not Stuart's view.

When Anse discovers that Subrinea is pregnant, he tells Tarvin that he can get four men to swear that they have been with Subrinea, thus making her a common whore (296), but Tarvin quickly defends Subrinea. She is not that kind of girl, he says, and adds, "I am already married. We've been married a long time. We've got to have a weddin ceremony yet. That's all. . . . Goin to a preacher and havin 'im say something aint goin to marry us any more than we've been married fer the past year" (296-97).

Affirming her love for Tarvin and also showing her desire to escape the kind of life she has lived, Subrinea says:

"Like a rock, Tarvin, I will stand by you. I know your people don't like squatters. Squatters don't like themselves. They have to be squatters. They would rather be somebody else. But I can't forsake my people and run away. I've often prayed that my name wasn't Tussie. That don't do no good, fer my name *is* Tussie. If I had a baby by you it would be a Bushman . . . and not a Tussie. I'd be havin my babies by somebody out'n the family. That aint happened among the Tussie wimmen. I know they have had their babies by Tussie men 'r Beaver men. We air all a-kin! That is what's the matter with us. We have married one another." (114-15)

In this passage Subrinea reveals several attitudes. Although she longs to escape the conditions of the squatters' lives, particularly the constant intermarriage among them (which Stuart seems to dwell on and perhaps over-emphasize), Subrinea is deeply committed to her family; she cannot leave or deny them but must work to find a way to live within the context of her family.

As well as feeling a loyalty to her family and kin, Subrinea is industrious, a good worker. She is not lazy like her brothers and father. She works hard with and for her family, and she seems to enjoy her work. Even Tarvin's parents, both Anse and Fronnie, recognize Subrinea's industriousness. Anse, somewhat begrudgingly because he does not want his son to marry a squatter, admits of Subrinea: "'That gal is a good worker,' thinks Anse. 'Fronnie's done a lot of hard work but she ain't no account with the ax. Fronnie can't use the ax like a man. She's [Subrinea] a good gal to get out and work that way with a man [with Tarvin]'" (84). And Fronnie says of Subrinea, "She 'pears to be smart and good to work" (132).

In one of the most beautiful scenes in the novel, a scene that serves to prelude the "marriage" scene between Tarvin and Subrinea in which they first make love, Subrinea works through the night to save Anse's lambs during a winter storm. Many of Anse's lambs have perished from exposure to the freezing weather, and Anse has been unsuccessful in saving very many of them. At evening he sends Tarvin to replace him at the shanty where the lambing is being supervised to watch the ewes and save as many of the lambs as he can. Tarvin is lost in the snowy blizzard and will surely die himself if he cannot find the shanty. Out of the storm he hears a voice—Subrinea's voice—guiding him to the lambing shanty. Subrinea knew that Tarvin would be coming to the shanty that night because she had overheard Anse tell her father, and she slipped out of her own cabin to be with him. She has been there for some time before she rescues Tarvin, and during this time she has saved all of the newborn lambs by putting them in milk-warm water just after their birth. Later, Tarvin and Subrinea make love. Subrinea has worked hard all night to save the lambs, but it has been a labor of love and a life-affirming conviction. Like Fronnie and Crissie, Subrinea knows the difficulty of work, but her work is a joy to her, and, far more importantly, Tarvin acknowledges and appreciates it; he admires and is amazed at her skills in saving the lambs.

Not only is Subrinea a hard worker and one who strives to nurture and sustain life, but she takes joy in life. Like Fronnie, she loves to dance.[12] All of the Tussies enjoy dancing (considered part of their laziness by many), but Subrinea's love of dancing, like Fronnie's, shows her pleasure in and healthy appreciation of life. At a dance, for example, Subrinea calls the dances: "'First couple out and circle,' Subrinea says. Her voice is musical as a mocking bird's singing" (71). Subrinea's dancing is admired by everyone: "Subrinea's long lithe body is graceful on the dance floor. Other women envy her skill on the dance floor and the young men envy Tarvin because he dances with her" (72). In the dancing, Boliver Tussie outdoes Anse in clicking his heels together, perhaps significant in that it shows Boliver enjoys life more fully than Anse. But Subrinea equals Boliver. "I can do it as many times as you, Pa," she says (79), and then she clicks her shoes together three times in the air before putting her feet down. Subrinea's love of dancing shows how much she enjoys life.

One of Subrinea's most important attributes in the novel is her affinity with the earth and nature. She is constantly described as a part of the earth, the land. Tarvin thinks, for example: "Subrinea is the forest, earth, flowers, water, everything on the land. Subrinea is made of the earth" (192). Elsewhere he compares her to nature: "tall as a sapling, swift as a ground sparrow, and timid as a wild rabbit" (37). And in a scene describing the cemetery beneath the trees of Heaven where the Tussies are buried, Subrinea is described:

Subrinea carries the empty basket on her arm. Tarvin carries the gooseneck hoe. They walk down Cat's Fork toward Ragweed Hollow. The April World about them is filled with wild bird calls. It is filled with blossom and song. The earth is alive. It is breathing. It holds Subrinea's dead. It holds their dreams beneath the trees of Heaven. It will hold them eternally there . . . many generations will be born and many will die away; but Subrinea's people are of the earth; Subrinea is a part of the earth and she and her people will live forever enfolded in the rich cover of earth under the trees of Heaven on Cat's Fork. (232-33)

By the end of the novel, Tarvin feels that he too has become the earth that is Subrinea: "He has become part of the wild flower that Subrinea is. He has learned to laugh, to work and play from Subrinea—that volcanic outburst of Nature that she is" (309).

Throughout his description of Subrinea Tussie, Stuart celebrates her as a mountain woman. She is of the earth and akin to nature. She is life-affirming and nurturing. She knows the joys and sorrows of life. By the end of the novel, even old Anse Bushman, opposed to his son's marriage to Subrinea from the beginning, realizes her excellence of character and says to Tarvin: "Son I think you air getting a real gal. She'll be good to stick by you in the time of need. Subrinea belongs to the hills. She can work in the fields. She can hep you with the lambs in lambin time. She's a real gal" (336).

Writing from the perspective of the insider, Jesse Stuart emphasizes the positive and affirmative aspects of the lives of mountain women, rather than the negative ones. Certainly he depicts their subservience in many ways, their labor—the lack of recognition for which, not the work itself, results in their spiritual and physical deterioration, and the hardships of their lives as wives and mothers. But he likewise shows another side to their lives—not hopeless and wretched, but rewarding and meaningful.

The focus in Stuart's portrayal of Subrinea Tussie is not on the harsh and cruel aspects of her life. One senses that she, like her mother and mother-in-law, may lead a life of hard work, but Stuart emphasizes, as in his poem for his mother, that her work is meaningful to her, not merely drudgery. Likewise, Subrinea is depicted as a life-affirming part of nature, vital and alive. Through his spiritual and physical consummation with Subrinea, Tarvin becomes one with the earth and the elements. Stuart also emphasizes Subrinea's equality with Tarvin; they are joined together as equals in mutual love and respect. This is one of the rare instances in mountain literature in which a husband and wife appear bound together by more than a bond of female subservience and male domination. The gulf between men and women, based on traditional gender roles, does not appear to exist between them. Indeed, this may be an idealization of romantic love on Stuart's part, but nevertheless it betokens a mountain writer's understanding of woman's status and a recognition of her equality in the Appalachian culture. Thus, Stuart helps to balance the scale in portrayals of mountain women. Even though Stuart's world is patriarchal and he presents women who are victims of this system, like Fronnie and Crissie, he also shows that the lives of women can be full and joyful, and that women can share the burdens of rough mountain life without being broken by them. Most importantly, as a native Appalachian writer Stuart looks beneath the outward appearances to the inner lives of mountain women.

5

James Still's Mountain Women

In 1940, the same year Jesse Stuart published *Trees of Heaven*, James Still also published his first novel, *River of Earth*, a poetic and evocative work about the lives of Kentucky mountain people that is today recognized as one of the finest novels about the Appalachian region. Still's reputation has grown slowly. As Shirley Williams stated in 1978: "until about four years ago Still feels he was virtually unknown (or at least, unread) in his own adopted state [Kentucky]" (23). In 1970, however, H.R. Stoneback called Still's novel *River of Earth* "one of the finest novels about hillfolk" (193) and stated that Cratis Williams "is on the right track in his discussion of Still whom he judges to be the most successful mountain novelist since Mary Murfree" (180 n 74). Despite its regionalism, even the earliest reviewers recognized the *universal* qualities of *River of Earth*. For example, William Jay Gold stated:

Too many recent regional novelists have ardently rung changes on the note of "how quaint!" and have succeeded only in giving us indigestible wads of dialect. Expounding the group peculiarities of an isolated people, they give us warped characters completely unable to evoke our sympathy or understanding. "River of Earth" has avoided this pitfall. True, its setting is individualized in every detail, the language of the Kentucky mountains is rendered as faithfully as it can be without recourse to phonetics, and the daily lives of the people are described with vividness. But in presenting his Kentucky mountaineers as products of their heredity and environment, living within their own traditions, Mr. Still has not forgotten that first of all they are simply people, suffering the heartaches and rejoicing in the delights common to all of us. Thus his characters are endowed with vigor and stature, and their lives with importance for us. (6)

Likewise, Dayton Kohler, in his 1942 essay comparing Still and Stuart, said: "If Jesse Stuart has escaped from strict localism by a renewal of frontier types and themes, James Still has gone beyond local emotions through the working of a poetic imagination which finds in regional experience the feelings common to very simply people everywhere" (528). And Stephen Vincent Benet, describing *River of Earth* in 1940, said: "It is rich with sights, sounds, and smells, with the feel and taste of things. And it is rich, as well, with salty and earthy speech, the soil of ballad and legend and tall story. . . . You can call it regional writing if you like—but to say so is merely to say that all America is not cut off the same piece" (4).

Stuart and Still share many similarities in their lives and literary careers, although there are certainly some basic differences in their artistic and literary productions. Pointing to the striking similarities between the backgrounds of the two writers, H.R. Stoneback states:

> Still was born in Chambers County, Alabama, in 1906; it is an area of low hills, ridges, and hollows which flattens out to the milltowns—West Point, Lanett—in the Chattahoochee River Valley. Stuart was born a year later in similar country; his slightly steeper hill country gives out in the industrial towns—Ashland, Ironton—of the Ohio Valley. Both spent their entire undergraduate careers at Lincoln Memorial [University, and then both did graduate work at Vanderbilt]. . . . After leaving Vanderbilt, both Still and Stuart were associated with rural schools in the hill counties of eastern Kentucky. Both published a volume of poetry first; both saw their first novel appear in 1940. Perhaps more striking, however, is the extreme disparity of their literary careers, in terms of artistic method, productivity, and recognition. (177)

Stuart produced a voluminous amount during his writing career—more than 50 books, novels, autobiographies, and nonfiction, 2100 poems, 460 short stories, and 400 articles (Spurlock 1). Still's production has been much sparer, with only two novels, several hundred poems, two collections of short stories, several juvenile books, and a personal Notebook. In style, too, Still is much sparer and more economical than Stuart. And, although Stuart started out with the greater recognition, his reputation suffered during the 1960s and is still somewhat tarnished, while Still's reputation has steadily increased.

Like Stuart's canon, much of Still's writing is dominated by male characters. In his collection of short stories *Pattern of a Man & Other Stories*, for example, almost all of the stories are told in the first person by a male narrator and many of the stories involve men in their central incidents, such as "A Ride on the Short Dog," "Pattern of a Man" and "Brother to Methuselem." Likewise, the narrator of his two novels, *River of Earth* and *Sporty Creek*, are young boys (perhaps the same young boy). As Cratis Williams says, "Adopting the technique of the primitivists, Still tells most of his stories from the point of view of the uncomprehending boy, who might range in age from six or seven to his early teens" ("Southern Mountaineer Part II" 367).

Yet, despite Still's emphasis on the masculine through many of his male-dominated plots and masculine narrators, the feminine is still very much a part of his works. Sidney S. Farr writes: "While he has never written from a woman's point of view, the woman plays an important role in most of his short stories and in his novel, *River of Earth*" ("The Appalachian Woman" 55). As Farr states further:

> James Still's picture of the mountain woman goes beyond the careful recording of unusual words and phrases; it goes beyond the accurate descriptions of the women and the girls. Still seems to have an unusually deep understanding of the little facets, the subtleties, the secret yearnings of the mountain woman, and he has presented her as she really is in his works. ("The Appalachian Woman" 56)

Like Stuart, Still probes the inner lives of mountain women—their psychology and feelings, rather than depicting merely the outward superficialities of their lives. Still's understanding of the lives of mountain women and his sure artistry in depicting them make a discussion of women as presented in his works, particularly *River of Earth*, especially rewarding for this study.

Let us first look at two short stories from *Pattern of a Man & Other Stories*, "Mrs. Razor" and "The Nest," which reveal Still's insight into the lives of mountain women. Each of these stories focuses on a little girl, already familiar, however, with the hardships, limitations, and concerns of their older counterparts in the Appalachian culture. "Mrs. Razor"[1] is the story of six-year-old Elvy, told by her brother, another of Still's unnamed boy narrators. The story opens with Elvy crying brokenheartedly behind the Cincinnati stove because in her imagination she has been deserted by her "lazy shuck of a husband who cared not a mite for his own and left his family [wife Elvy and three children] to live upon her kin" (1). Elvy is adamantly convinced that she is an abandoned wife and mother, and the story centers on the family's, particularly the father's, attempts to dissuade her of this "foolish notion." At the end of the story, after first trying to tease Elvy out of her delusion and finally growing angry, Father loads the whole family into the wagon after supper and they head off for the mythical Biggety Creek in search of Elvy's three children, whom Razor has kidnapped and whom Elvy fears will be sold to the gypsies. As Elvy falls asleep, Father turns the wagon for home.

Elvy's fantasy life as Mrs. Razor reveals much about the realities of marriage and the role of the wife in the mountains. As the narrator tells us of Elvy's "marriage":

She spoke hard of her husband and was a shrew of a wife who thought only of her children; she was as busy with her young as a hen with diddles. It was a dog's life she led, washing rags of clothes, sewing with a straw for needle, singing by the hour to cradled arms, and keeping an eye sharp for gypsies. She jerked at loose garments and fastened and pinned, as Mother did to us. (2)

Razor is the epitome of meanness and laziness. Elvy says of him, "My man's the meanest critter ever was" (2). And later she says, "I ought never to a-took him for a husband. . . . When first I married he was smart as ants. Now he's turned so lazy he won't even fasten his gallus buckles. He's slouchy and no 'count" (5). Elvy's fantasy life is indeed a compound of many things, from her father's stories of the mythical and fanciful Biggety Creek to inherent fears of children being stolen by gypsies. But there must also be some grain of realization of the woman's lot in life in Elvy's descriptions of her make-believe married life. Elvy as Mrs. Razor voices many of the realities of the lives of mountain wives and mothers: their deep maternal concern for the welfare of their children, particularly their fear of losing them; frequent cruelty and indifference by husbands to their wives and families; and the laziness often associated with mountain men, which throws a greater burden on the mountain women.

Yet it is also of interest in "Mrs. Razor" that Elvy's father provides a balancing contrast with the imaginary Mr. Razor. Though itching for a hickory switch and beyond exasperation with his child, Elvy's father nevertheless tries sympathetically to resolve the situation by taking her to Biggety Creek to find her lost children. Father's actions in the story are in direct contrast to Razor's. He is providing as best he can for *his* three children, unlike the rascally Razor. Thus, although Elvy's fantasy world may suggest many of the darker elements of marriage and wifehood for Appalachian women, the real world of her own family reveals more positive aspects: a close family unit; a caring father. In "Mrs. Razor" we can see both negative and positive aspects of the mountain woman's life.

"The Nest" is a terrifying story. Like Elvy in "Mrs. Razor," the main character in "The Nest" is another six-year-old girl, Nezzie Hargis. At the beginning of the story, Nezzie is sent by her father and Mam, "the woman her father had brought to live with them after her [Nezzie's] mother went away" (51), to spend the night with her Aunt Clissa while the father, Mam, and the family's new baby go to visit Nezzie's ailing grandfather. Nezzie loses her way in the dark and cold and eventually freezes to death. The main emphasis of the story is on Nezzie's thoughts as she wanders in the freezing cold.

There are several elements of the fairy tale in "The Nest."² Like Cinderella in the Grimms' tale, for example, Nezzie has been separated from her mother, the maternal figure. We are only told that the mother has "gone away," but it becomes apparent in the story that, like Cinderella's mother, Nezzie's mother has died, and Nezzie seeks reunion with her. Her last thoughts before she dies are of her mother:

Her memory danced. She heard her father singing to quiet the baby's fret. "Up, little horse, let's hie to mill." She roved in vision, beyond her father, beyond the baby, to one whose countenance was seen as through a mist. It was her mother's face, cherished as a good dream is cherished—she who had held her in the warm, safe nest of her arms. Nezzie slept at last, laboring in sleep toward waking. (51)

As in the fairy tale also, Nezzie's real mother has been replaced by a stepmother, and Nezzie's father's "new woman" is the archetypal cruel stepmother who is constantly scolding Nezzie and putting her own child, the new baby, first. Like Cinderella, Nezzie also seeks refuge in nature, Nezzie finding comfort and security in the brooding house with the newly-hatched chicks. As in fairy tales, many of the archetypal qualities of life, especially the lives of women, are revealed in "The Nest," through the simple thoughts of a child.

Not only has Nezzie's mother been replaced in her father's new life, but Nezzie herself has been replaced in the family by a new baby. Although Nezzie does not resent the baby, and, in fact, loves him dearly and thinks of him throughout her wandering on the night before her death, the new baby has obviously taken her place in the family. Nezzie has been shut out by the new woman and the new baby. It is perhaps significant that the new baby is a boy, obviously the "chosen one" of Nezzie's father, who voices the traditional attitude of the Appalachian toward the male child: "A master boy, this little'un is. Aye, he's going somewhere in the world, I'd bet my thumb" (48). Later he reiterates, "I figure he'll do better in life than hoist an ax. A master boy, smart as a wasper. Make his living and not raise a sweat. He'll amount to something, I tell you" (48). The baby boy is the father's hope for his old age, as he tells Mam: "Let this chub grow up and he'll be somebody. Old woman, you can paint yore toe-nails and hang 'em over the banisters, for there'll be hired girls to do the work. Aye, he'll see we're tuck care of" (49). It is obvious that Nezzie's father values the masculine child more than his daughter, which Nezzie cannot fail to internalize, and he actually becomes blind to her needs, sending her off alone on a cold night without any apparent thought of her safety. Thus we can see that in the patriarchal system in the mountains, as indeed in other patriarchal societies, the feminine is undervalued in preference for the masculine. Nevertheless, Nezzie's feminine instincts are praised throughout the story.

Like Elvy, Nezzie's maternal instincts, her feminine nature, are intrinsic throughout the story. Far from hating her baby brother as a competitor for her father's affections, for example, she appears throughout the story to love the baby deeply. She kisses and holds the baby, and as she struggles to reach warmth and safety, she dreams of holding him safe in her own arms. Her father had promised her that if she went without a fuss to Aunt Clissa's he would bring her a "pretty," anything she wanted. She had not been able to think of anything. Yet, just before her final thought in which *she* is held warm and safe in her own mother's arms, she thinks of two things. First, she remembers her grandfather and his age, a thought that shows her insight into youth and age, life and death: "And seeing her grandfather she thought of his years, and she thought suddenly of the baby growing old, time perishing its cheeks, hands withering and palsying. The hateful wisdom caught at her heart and choked her throat" (50-51). She thinks almost simultaneously of her grandfather and her baby brother. Then she thinks of her father's promise—"I'll bring you a pretty. . . . Just name a thing you want" (51)—and her first thought is of the baby: "She trembled and her teeth chattered. She saw herself sitting with the baby on her lap. It lay with its fair head against her breast" (51). There is here, I believe, an obvious allusion to Nezzie's own children, which she will never have, as well as her feelings of love and nurturing for her little brother. There is also revealed here a thematic concern for the cyclical nature of life and death, a theme that Still utilizes also in *River of Earth*.

Throughout the story Nezzie is described in terms and scenes that link her to the world of birth and nurturing. She has found refuge in the brooder house, for example, with the newly-hatched chicks: "Her memory spun in a haste like pages off a thumb. She saw herself yesterday hiding in the brooder house to play with newly hatched diddles, the brooder warm and tight, barely fitting her, and the diddles moist from the egg, scrambling to her lap, walking her spread palms, beaks chirping, 'Peep, peep'" (45). The womb-like brooder house provides warmth and security, just as Nezzie's mother's arms had, and Nezzie's own arms would for her children. All of these are the warm, safe nest, the safety that nourishes life. The cultural roles of men and women, the nurturing aspect of womanhood, the hopes and aspirations for manhood, youth and age, life and death—these are the underlying issues of "The Nest." It is a story with many levels of meaning, much like Katherine Anne Porter's

"The Grave." And, like Porter's story, "The Nest" shows woman's archetypal quality of nurturing.

In both "Mrs. Razor" and "The Nest," James Still probes the psychology of Appalachian mountain women, albeit through the eyes of little girls just beginning to awaken to their feminine natures. The deep love of children, the nurturing quality of womanhood, the struggles inherent in being female and inferior in the social and cultural scheme of the mountain society, the woman's early awareness of the cyclical nature of life—birth, age and death, are all present in these stories. And, assuredly, Still goes beyond the particular in these stories to reveal the universal and archetypal in woman's experience.

Still gives a much fuller and deeper description of the lives of mountain women in his masterpiece, *River of Earth*. *River of Earth* is narrated by the oldest son of Brack and Alpha Baldridge. He is seven years old, and the reader never learns his Christian name. The novel centers on the family's attempts to secure a livelihood, with the father constantly moving from one coal camp to another in order to feed his family, with intervals spent on a rented farm in the hills. The story is that of the boy's maturation, as he comes to recognize his place within the family and in his world. As Rebecca L. Briley states: "'How fellers git growed' is the question of the narrator that 'grabs the reins' in *River of Earth*. His life becomes a questing journey with the task of determining who he is and what his purpose in relation to his heritage is to be" (66).[3] Although the narrator and main character of the novel is a boy, however, two of the major characters in the novel are women, and their relationships with the boy and their importance in his maturation process are of pivotal significance in the novel.

The boy's mother and grandmother are, in fact, the central characters, the focal actors, in the drama of *River of Earth*. His mother and grandmother exert a tremendous influence on the boy's maturation. It is this aspect of the mountain woman's life—the preserving, sustaining and nurturing role of mountain women as they instill values and serve as role models for their children, that is particularly important in Still's depictions of women. It would be hard to determine who is the major female character in *River of Earth*: Alpha Baldridge, the young narrator's mother, or Alpha's own mother, Grandma Middleton. Alpha dominates the first and third sections of the three-part novel, while Grandma Middleton is the chief character of the second part. Both women play a major role, and they are very much alike, particularly in their dominant characteristic of strength and perseverance in the face of hardship and tragedy, difficulty, loss and poverty.

445-02535-060　　　　　　　　　　60c

In the tradition of
John Steinbeck's
THE GRAPES OF WRATH

RIVER OF EARTH

by James Still
Winner of the
Guggenheim Fellowship

A powerful novel
of life, love, and the
struggle for existence
in the hills of
Appalachia

"VIVID...
BEAUTIFULLY PHRASED"
—Atlantic Monthly

Cover of the Popular Library edition of *River of Earth*.

Alpha Middleton Baldridge, the boy's mother, is a figure of great significance and importance; the boy's descriptions of her are perhaps the most understated and yet revealing in the novel. *River of Earth* begins, for example, with a description of Mother's intelligence, courage and self-sacrifice in order to sustain her family, the most important thing in her life. The family is near starvation as their supplies run out, diminished even further by the addition of Father's cousins, Harl and Tibb Logan, and his great-uncle Samp, who have come to stay with them during the lean times. Father, as the "code of the hills" demands, cannot turn them away as long as he has anything to share with them. Harl, Tibb and Uncle Samp are shiftless and will not do anything constructive to help provide for the needs of the family. They are greedily taking the last drop of food out of the mouths of their long-suffering kin. Yet Father states, "I can't turn my kin out" (4).

It is Mother who finally takes matters into her own hands. When Father prepares to go into town to see if he can get some groceries at the general store, Mother realizes this plan's futility:

Mother leaned against the wall, clutching the baby. Her voice was like ice. "They won't let you have it on credit. You've tried before. We've got to live small. We've got to start over again, hand to mouth, the way we began." She laid her hands upon the air, marking the words with nervous fingers. "We've got to tie ourselves up in such a knot nobody else can get in." Father got his hat and stalked to the door. "We've got to do hit today," she called. But Father was gone, out of the house and over the hill toward Blackjack. (8-9)

It seems clear that Father can see no way out of the dilemma that faces him—concern for his family and loyalty to his kin. But Mother, realizing she must act, executes a plan she has been formulating.

Just after Father's departure, a brutal attack on the boy by Uncle Samp drives Mother to desperate measures to ensure the family's safety and survival. During the previous night, Harl and Tibb had cut off Uncle Samp's prized mustache as a malicious prank on the old man. When he awakens to discover the trick, Uncle Samp yells out in a rage. The narrator is the first one to enter his room, and Uncle Samp hurls him forcefully against the wall and then runs out of the house. At this point, Mother carries out her desperate act, already conceived, as her talk with Father indicates: she moves all of the family's belongings out of the house and up to the smoke-house, a tiny, cramped building only big enough for her immediate family, and then sets fire to the house. Thus, she is able to make it impossible for Harl, Tibb and Uncle Samp to stay with them any longer:

James Still's Mountain Women   111

When the flames were highest, leaping through the charred rafters, a gun fired repeatedly in the valley. Someone there had noticed the smoke and was arousing the folk along Little Carr Creek. When they arrived, the walls had fallen in, and Mother stood among the scattered furnishings, her face calm and triumphant. (11)

From this first dramatic episode to the very end of the novel, Mother struggles to protect her family and to make their hard lives bearable. Her chief concern throughout is the protection and sustenance of her family, and she will take whatever action is necessary for that, no matter what the personal cost.

The narrator is very much aware of his mother's self-sacrifice for her family. At one point he says: "We had come through to spring, but Mother was the leanest of us all, and the baby cried in the night when there was no milk. Mother ate a little more now than the rest of us, for the baby's sake, eating as though for shame while we were not there to see, fearing we might not understand, that we might think her taking more than her share" (13). Later, he describes Mother's reaction when, as the family is once again on the verge of starvation, Father comes home one afternoon with a big sackful of groceries and announces that he starts work at the mine the next day and has bought the groceries on credit: "A lean hand reached toward the table, blue-veined and bony. It was Mother's, touching the sugar jar, the red-haired meat, the flour sack. Suddenly she threw an apron over her head, turning away from us. She hardly made a sound, no more than a tick-beetle" (70). Mother is often described in the novel as "lean," and the boy is obviously aware of her own starvation in order to sustain the family. This understanding of his mother's self-sacrifice makes a deep and lasting impression on him as he matures into manhood.

The boy's realization of his mother's hard lot prompts him particularly to consider the man's role as provider. Chiefly, he does not want to be a coal miner like his father, barely able to support his family. It is interesting to speculate at this point that it is perhaps the compassion that the mountain man feels for his womenfolk, a feeling begun in childhood, which impels him to wish to provide for his family through money. He feels that the money he earns working helps him to better provide for his family. Brack Baldridge, for example, is obviously driven by this feeling and by his feelings of shame at not being able to provide sufficiently for his family.

When Brack speaks of Taulbee Lovern, Alpha's first beau and a rich man she could have married, for example, Brack's feelings of shame are inherent. Having seen Taulbee Lovern's son, Brack says:

"As bonnie a chap as ever I saw.... Don't reckon he's drawed a sick breath. Fed and clothed proper since he was born." Father's face got dolesome, and his voice lowered into the sound of rain beating the puncheon walls. He looked into all the corners of the room, at the two beds standing in the floor middle, at the empty meat box, at the ball of clothes piled on the table to keep them dry. He looked at Euly standing by the bedboard; he looked at Fletch and me squatting on the floor listening, our heads cocked to one side. "Three hundred acres o land Taulbee has," Father said, "and a passel of that is bottom-flat. Six-room house with two glass windows in every dabbed room. Taulbee's tuck care of his own. They've never gone a-lacking." (45-46)

Brack obviously sees his own accomplishments in contrast with Taulbee Lovern's as sorely lacking, realizing the desperate difficulties his own family has faced.

Brack's own apparent recognition of his weaknesses obviously strengthens his son's resolve that he will give his own family a better kind of life. Thus, he knows early that he does not want to be a miner, struggling for a living at the mercy of the coal operators who are constantly closing down the mines. Just after his seventh birthday, the boy decides: "Sitting there I thought that I would grow up into such a man as Grandpa Middleton had been before he got killed, learning to read and write, and to draw up deeds for land; and I would learn to plow, and have acres of my own. Never would I be a miner digging a darksome hole" (21). Like Tarvin Bushman in Stuart's *Trees of Heaven*, the young narrator is moved by his mother's hardships in life, and his father's struggles, to desire a life different from his father's, one that will better provide for his own family.[4]

Another characteristic of his mother that the boy recognizes and internalizes into his own character is her love of the land and her desire for roots and a place of her own. He wants to own land and become a farmer. Brack is constantly moving from one mine to another seeking work. He is not a farmer; as he says at one point: "I never tuck natural to growing things, planting seeds and sticking plows in the ground like Taulbee Lovern. A furrow I run allus did crook like a blacksnake's back. A sight of farming I've done, but it allus rubbed the grain. But give me a pick, and I'll dig as much coal as the next 'un" (47). Alpha, on the other hand, loves the land and farming; she hates living in a coal camp.

Just before a move back to the Blackjack Mine after a short time on their farm, during which they have planted a garden, Alpha and Brack express their conflicting views on the subject of moving:

"I had a notion of staying on here," Mother said, her voice small and tight. "I'm agin raising chaps in a coal camp. Allus getting lice and scratching the itch. I had a notion you'd walk of a day to the mine."

"A far walking piece, a good two mile. Better to get a house in the camp."

"Can't move a garden, and growing victuals."

"They'll grow without watching. We'll keep them picked and dug."

"I allus had a mind to live on a hill, not sunk in a holler where the fog and dust is damping and blacking. I was raised to like a lonesome place...."

"Notions don't fill your belly nor kiver your back."

Mother was on the rag edge of crying. "Forever moving yon and back, setting down nowhere for good and all, searching for God knows what," she said. "Where air we expecting to draw up to?" Her eyes dampened. "Forever I've wanted to set down in a lone spot, a place certain and enduring, with room to swing arm and elbow, a garden-place for fresh victuals, and a cow to furnish milk for the baby." (51-52)

Throughout the novel Mother's one desire is for a permanent home, a place that she can call her own, a farm and a garden. Her dreams, however, are hopeless. She is, of course, forced to go back to the mining camps with Brack, to leave her permanent, secure place behind.

Alpha's longing for a permanent home is related to her nurturing and maternal quality in the novel through Still's use of maternal symbols and imagery. For example, even though Alpha goes back to the coal camp with Brack just following the conversation described above, it is significant that she refuses to leave the farm until after her guinea eggs have hatched; she will not leave the farm until after this birth takes place, for in the birth of the guinea chicks there is a symbol of the ongoing life of the farm. Elsewhere, Alpha is again associated with eggs and birth. At the beginning of Part II, after the death of her baby Green, Alpha cries at night and grieves over the baby's death. Baby Green's death is significant in the fabric of the novel, suggesting the loss of the "green" world represented by the farm. Symbolically, Alpha turns for consolation to the construction of an egg tree, hanging empty shells of eggs from a tree in the yard. Although the shells are empty and may thus indicate the futility of Alpha's dreams, the egg tree itself is nevertheless symbolic of Alpha's continuing maternal and nurturing instincts.

When Brack again plans to return to the mines, Alpha once more voices her desire to stay on the farm: "'Since I married I've been driv from one coal camp to another,' Mother said, taking her hands out of the bread dough. 'I've lived hard as nails.... I reckon I've lived everywhere on God's green earth. Now I want to set me down and rest. The baby is buried here, and I've earnt a breathing spell. We done right well this crap. We got plenty'" (179). But Alpha must accompany her husband on his restless search for work, for the better life as he sees it for his family. After they have moved into a house in the camp, Brack surprises Alpha by transplanting the whole egg tree in the front yard. The tree is broken and in a shambles from the move, and Alpha calls Brack a "puore fool" (185). Although he has understood her attachment to the tree and has desired to show his love and affection for her, Brack has not understood that it was not the tree itself Alpha wanted, but all it represented. The maternal imagery used in association with Alpha throughout the novel (as well as her name itself, suggesting beginnings) is representative of the cyclical nature of life, the birth and death patterns, and the nurturing quality of the mountain woman.

In this connection, showing that life and death help to define the cyclical nature of existence, and that women are most often associated with this pattern of life/death in Appalachian literature, especially in Still's work, we can also examine the character of Euly, the narrator's thirteen-year-old sister. Two episodes in particular show Euly's growing awareness of the woman's prescribed role in the mountain society and in life, and the imagery associated with these episodes is of the same type as that connected often in the novel with Alpha—eggs and birth. In the first scene, Euly becomes furious with her younger brother Fletch because he has broken the eggs of a nesting partridge: "Euly came down out of the tree to see what Fletch had. He reached one hand into a pocket to show us. It came out filled with partridge eggs, broken and running between his fingers. Euly's face became as white as sycamore bark. She began to cry . . . , then she opened one hand swiftly slapping Fletch on the cheek, and was gone in a moment, running silently as a fox over the hill" (22). In another scene, Euly is deeply affected by the life/death drama when she is asked to skin a rabbit: "Once Father brought a rusty-eared rabbit home, setting Euly to clean it. When she came on four little ones in its warm belly, she cried out in fear for what she had done, flung the bloody knife into the dirt, and ran away into the low pasture. She stayed there all day crying in the stubble, and never ate wild meat again" (13). This scene is very reminiscent of another little girl's reaction to a similar episode in Katherine Anne Porter's "The Grave."

The episode with Alpha's egg tree and the many quarrels over moving to the coal camp between Brack and Alpha suggest a lack of true understanding and real communication between them. Each has a role to fill as he or she sees it and desires for attaining what he or she thinks is the best out of life. Even though their final goals are the same—the preservation of the family and as good a life as possible—they are almost always at odds with each other about how to obtain the goal, and they hardly ever *discuss* their feelings, although these are often asserted in argument. Brack clearly prefers mining to farming and thinks that he can provide the best life for his family as a miner. He does not wish to harm them and genuinely believes that he is doing the best he can. Alpha longs for roots, a place of her own where she can settle down once and for all.

In the end, however, it is Alpha who must always give in, who must follow Brack to the mines. By the end of the novel, the farm they had rented on Little Angus Creek has been sold for taxes and the family must start all over again, this time moving to the Grundy mine in Virginia. Throughout their moves and their many quarrels over them, Alpha and Brack remain isolated within themselves, neither telling the other what is really deepest in her or his heart, except in moments of strife. They do not sit down and talk about what would be the best course of action. Brack simply announces what *he* is going to do, often with no advance notice; Alpha responds with what *she* had hoped to do, what her desires are, but always in the end her wishes are disregarded and she gives in.

Although she is certainly frustrated by the constant moves, the ever-present hunger of the family, the loss of her own dreams, and even Brack's inability to understand what means the most to her, Alpha does not complain. She patiently accepts what she knows she cannot change. In fact, she knows that she had choices and that she has made them, and she does not seem to regret them. For example, following Brack's speech in which he describes all the material wealth and luxuries that Taulbee Lovern, Alpha's first beau, has, in comparison with their own meager existence, "Mother's face reddened. 'I hain't complaining of the way I'm tuck care of,' she said. 'We hain't starved dead or gone naked yet. I hain't complaining. Now hush'" (46). Alpha has not married Brack for material possessions, but for love, knowing what her life with him would be like. And she certainly never thinks of leaving Brack or of wanting anything different in her life except to stop moving and stay in one place. Alpha's courage to face hardship is manifested in her acceptance of the life she has chosen.

Two words have frequently been used in discussions about the kind of uncomplaining acceptance of life's hardships that Alpha (and the other mountain women we have seen) displays in *River of Earth*: fatalism and endurance. Fatalism, as used to describe the mountain people in general, both men and women, connotes a defeated resignation to life. There is no need to complain of things because nothing can be done about them. Jack Weller, for instance, in *Yesterday's People*, lists fatalism as one of the chief characteristics of the mountaineers. Weller explains the mountaineers' fatalism as a result of the loss of confidence in themselves in the face of unyielding nature. This fatalistic attitude, that what will be will be and there is no changing it, allows the mountaineers, Weller asserts, to avoid accepting the guilt or blame for their lots in life (37ff).

Endurance, on the other hand, suggests not a defeated resignation but a triumphant acceptance of the hardships and uncertainties of life. To endure is to accept and survive. Certainly, Alpha Baldridge accepts her life as it is and does not complain about it, yet she does not fatalistically believe that conditions cannot be changed. The fact that the novel begins with her "triumphant" assertion of power over a difficult situation—when she burns down the house in order to rid the family of Harl, Tibb and Uncle Samp—clearly reveals that she does not yield herself to whatever circumstances present. Endurance suggests resiliency and strength, whereas fatalism intimates weakness and defeat. Alpha is by no means defeated in *River of Earth*. At the end of the novel, for example, she bears a new child and bravely faces a new beginning in another coal camp.

It is not a resigned acceptance of life that the boy admires and cherishes in his mother; it is her active involvement in the struggle to survive. Alpha's influence on his life is one of the chief aspects of the narrator's growing-up experience, and her example is not that of a pawn of fate but of an active participant in life. His many references to her actions in the narrative reveal his awareness of her active, not passive, nature. He is aware of her self-sacrifice, her willingness to "go without" for her family; he is aware of her deep love of place and her desire for a permanent home and roots, a dream that she actively and constantly (though futilely) fights for; he is aware of her nurturing, as she plants and reaps and watches over her animals; and he is aware of her silent strength and endurance as she faces the endless moves and struggles of her life.

Alpha is not overt in her demonstrations of affection for her family; she seldom expresses her emotions openly, except through crying. The above "I hain't complaining" is about the closest she ever comes to expressing her love for Brack, and she never tells her children that she loves them. There are no kisses or demonstrations of affection between Alpha and Brack, and little overt affection between the parents and their children. But, nevertheless, the boy knows he is loved for his mother shows it in her every action.

Alpha is not the only female figure in the novel who exerts a great influence on the boy's maturation from childhood into adulthood. His maternal grandmother, Grandma Middleton, is equally important in his journey toward awareness. Grandma Middleton figures prominently in Part II of the novel when the boy is sent to stay with her during the winter; Grandma's only remaining child at home, the practical-joking

Uncle Jolly,[5] has been sent to the penitentiary. And Grandma's death in Part III of *River of Earth*, juxtaposed with the birth of Alpha's new baby, marks perhaps the greatest stage in the boy's growing awareness of the cyclical nature of life.

Grandma Middleton is a grandly realized character, an aged woman full of wisdom and grit accumulated through a lifetime of experience. She is indeed wise and strong. She is also crafty, and courageous, encountering many trials, but never defeated. It is not surprising that Grandma Middleton is much like her daughter Alpha; the connection between mother and daughter reveals the transmission of qualities and values from one generation to the next in the mountains. Nor is it surprising that Grandma exerts an influence on the boy's maturation, for she is another active participant in his world.

Like Alpha, Grandma Middleton has a deep love for her family. She has had eight children, "every one a wanted child" (120), and has seen four of them die in infancy or childhood. She is proud that she has reared her children to be good and honest people. Uncle Jolly, in particular, is an example of her mothering. Uncle Jolly believes in rightness and fairness. He has blown up Pate Horn's dam, for example, in order to protect the spawning fish. And he has obeyed his mother's wishes in never seeking revenge on his father's murderer. He is a fun-loving, gentle and good man. Grandma is proud that no son of hers ever died of a bullet or "pleasured himself with shooting off guns, rim-recking at Hardin Town and in the camps, a-playing at cards and mixing in knife scrapes, traipsing thar and yon, weaving drunk" (120).

Even though her children are grown and all but Jolly have married and left home, Grandma is still concerned for their welfare. Near the beginning of the novel, when Uncle Jolly comes to visit Alpha and Brack, he says he came because Grandma sent him: "'Son,' she says, 'you make a circle round and see how the chaps [her children] are. See Alpha, and Toll, and Luce. 'Tell them their ol' mommy is longing to set eyes on them again. Tell them if'n they get out of something to eat, they's allus a dusting o' meal in my barrel'" (35).

Because her family means so much to her, it is one of Grandma Middleton's greatest sorrows in life that, as she perceives it, they have drifted away from her. Except for Jolly, who lives at home and takes care of his mother, Grandma's children have all been caught up in their own lives, and she feels that they have little time for her. This is true, it seems, especially of her sons Toll and Luce, who have become involved with their own families. Because Grandma is so disappointed that her children seldom come to see her, she doesn't even want them to be notified when she dies. She tells her grandson:

"I'd give a year out o' my life to see all my children and their chaps. . . . A year's breathing I'd give. Never they come to see their mommy. Old, and thrown away now. No good to fotch and carry for a soul." Anger rose in her throat. She struck her elbows against the [bed] tick. "When my dying day comes I'm right willing to be hauled straight to Flat Creek burying ground and put beside my man, buried down and kivvered over against any o' my blood kin was told. My chaps won't come when I'm sick and pindly; they hain't no use in coming to see me lay a corpse." (131)

At the end of the novel, on her dying bed, Grandma makes Uncle Jolly promise to take her straight to the cemetery without telling any of her children. He does, however, take her body to Alpha and Brack's.

There is an irony in Grandma's statement above, however, for even though she feels that her children have not been to see her or help her enough in her old age, she nevertheless so longs to see *them* that she is willing to give a year of her life, and she is ready until the end to help them in any way she can. There are mitigating circumstances that have kept her children away. Alpha is so overwhelmed with the struggles of her own life that it is difficult for her to visit her mother very often. During the course of the novel, however, she often speaks of her mother and longs to see her, and she sends her son, the narrator, to help his grandmother when Uncle Jolly is sent to prison. Grandma's son Luce is married to Pate Horn's daughter Rilla, and there has apparently been some ill feeling between the Middleton and Horn families for some time (Uncle Jolly blew up Pate Horn's dam). Luce also has had to struggle for his subsistence and to support his family of five daughters. Luce visits Grandma once during the novel, but it is only after he has been expected to come and help with the fall harvesting that Grandma and the boy have had to do by themselves. Grandma tells her grandson, "It's Rilla hating me that keeps him from coming. Oh, she'll larn all her children to grow up hating their ol' granny" (104).

When Luce finally does come to see his mother, he is full of excuses: it is near Rilla's time to have a new baby and she has been very sick; the children have had the chicken pox; Luce has had to grub stumps in order to pay for Rilla's medicine. But despite the feelings of neglect that Grandma suffers and the notion that her daughter-in-law hates her, when Luce leaves she gives him a necklace of Job's-tears to give to Rilla, hoping it might please her to have them. And later, the reader learns that Luce and Rilla have named their new baby Cordia after Grandma Middleton. Thus it can be seen that even though Grandma feels frustrated and sad because her children do not pay enough attention to her in her old age, there nevertheless abides a great love between them, and an undying love and concern on Grandma's part. Like Alpha, Grandma is willing to sacrifice for the sake of her children.

As well as sharing a deep feeling for family ties with Alpha, Grandma also shares Alpha's love of the land. When she is telling the boy about his mother's girlhood, courtship and marriage to Brack, for example, Grandma reveals her own attitudes about farming and owning a place of one's own:

"Alpha could o' had rings on her fingers and combs in her hair," Grandma said, "but along come Brack Baldridge from Tribbey Camp, a long, lean, strung-out person. Him she tuck. Married a coal digger, a mole-feller, grubbing his bread underground. For gold and silks, she'd no fancy, and I was right glad for a fact. But allus I'd wanted her to choose one who lived on the land, growing his own victuals, raising sheep and cattle, beholden to nobody.... Now nary a word I'd say agin Brack. He's good to work. Hain't scared to bend his back nor mud his boots.... Only if he'd settle some place and grow roots, I'd not be eternally worrying." (130)

Grandma wishes, in concordance with Alpha's own desires, for a secure, abiding place on the land for Alpha, for it is on the land that one can be "beholden to nobody." The land has provided Grandma with security during her life. She tells her grandson, "[H]it would comfort me to know you'd never be a miner" (130). While he is with her, in fact, the boy fulfills one of his dreams—he learns to plow (133).

In his exceptional discussion of *River of Earth* in "The Hillfolk Tradition and Images of the Hillfolk in American Fiction Since 1926," H.R. Stoneback examines the novel in terms of the conflict between farming and the land and the life of the coal camps. Says Stoneback:

Stretched over the cyclic framework of the novel, which associates spring with the closing of the coal mines and the return to the farm from the grimy coal-camps, and fall with the reopening of the mines and the return to the camps, is the controlling pattern of agrarian-urban contrasts which develops Still's major theme: in this moving world, man needs "a place certain and enduring." (182)

Later, he states, "[T]he primary business of the first part of the novel is to define the conflict between the father and the mother, which is accomplished in repeated scenes involving argument between the two over the relative virtues of farm and town" (184). He follows this statement with a discussion of the many quarrels between Alpha and Brack that have been previously discussed herein. Stoneback then points out that "Alpha gets her motivating desire honestly, for her mother, Grandma Middleton, has never left the farm, and views the coal camps as a strange outland intrusion on the hills" (186). Stoneback's emphasis in this discussion is on the agrarian-urban conflict in the novel, but he does not take this conflict to one of its logical conclusions: the conflict is inherently masculine-feminine.

In *River of Earth*, particularly, the urban-agrarian conflict is embodied in Brack and Alpha, or more specifically Brack on one side and Alpha and Grandma Middleton on the other. Brack believes in the mines and the camps and thus in the urban or town milieu, although it is obviously dirty, darkening and dehumanizing. His name itself—Brack Baldridge—is suggestive of the brackishhess of the town and coal camps, and of the destruction of the mountains. Alpha and Grandma Middleton, on the other hand, believe in the land and *its* power to sustain and nurture its own, just as woman's traditional role is to sustain and nurture. It is clear in the novel that both his mother and grandmother exert an influence on the narrator towards belief in the land and away from the "machine."[6]

Grandma Middleton's life is also like Alpha's, perhaps most importantly, in that she has had a life of hardship but has learned to *endure* and to exert her will over conditions of her life. She has not fatalistically resigned herself to a life over which she has no control, but has instead learned to control that life in her own way. When her son Luce does not arrive in time to help with the fall harvesting, for example, Grandma realizes that she must take matters into her own hands if the crops are to be saved. Although she is seventy-six years old, she and her grandson harvest the crop of corn, cabbages, cushaws and sweet potatoes. The boy reports: "Grandma crawled along the rows on her knees, digging in the baked earth with her hands" (103).

Perhaps Grandma's greatest example of personal strength and endurance, equal to Alpha's burning down the house at the beginning of the novel, is her revenge on Aus Coggins, the man who murdered her husband Boone. Boone had sold Coggins a nag that died of bloats the night after it was sold; Coggins accused Boone of selling him a sick horse and then cold-bloodedly murdered him. Grandma made her sons swear never to take revenge on Coggins. As she says:

"On Boone Middleton's burying day I had my boys promise. They tuck oath on the Book. Tuck it every one except Jolly, he being only twelve, and too young for swearing. I said: 'There's been blood shed aplenty. Let Aus Coggins bide his time out on this earth. Fear will hant his nights. Hit'll be a thorn in his flesh. Let him live in fear. He'll never prosper nor do well. Let him live in sufferance.'" (125)

Terrible things do happen to Aus Coggins: his barn is burned, his fences are cut, his livestock is turned out, and his ground is salted to such a degree that nothing will grow on it. Uncle Jolly—who had been too young to forswear vengeance on Coggins—is usually blamed for these troubles, but at the end of the novel it is discovered that it was actually Grandma Middleton who was responsible. She admits on her deathbed that it was she who thus revenged herself on her husband's murderer. Even in her seventies, she continued to make life miserable for Coggins. In this way she is able to *endure* her grief and loss and to regain control over her life. Like Alpha, she takes matters into *her own* hands.

The cyclical nature of life—its beginnings and endings, springs and winters—is dramatically exemplified at the end of *River of Earth* through Grandma Middleton's death and the coincidental birth of Alpha's new baby. Grandma's death is the most tragic event of the novel, but from it, and as a result of his closeness to her, the narrator learns about life and death and comes closer to adulthood. The closing words of the novel juxtapose life and death:

"Hush," Father said. He lifted a hand to an ear, catching for a sound through the walls. He had heard something. "Hush."

Uncle Jolly stumbled to the porch, smothering his joy. He clumped into the yard. Father stood again at the kitchen door, grasping the knob, waiting; then he went inside. I heard feet walking, walking. The kitchen fire was being shaken and replenished; the yeast smell of morning bread hung on a windy draft. I closed my eyes, being near to sleep. I looked at Grandma in the dark of my head where I could see her living face. "Grandma," I spoke, "where have you gone?"

I waked, trembling with cold, and it was morning. The coffin box had been taken away. The chairs sat empty upon the hearth. I ran outside, and there were only wagon tracks to mark where death had come into our house and gone again. (245)

The fear and knowledge of death has been replaced by the joy and knowledge of life. The tracks of death are "shriveled and dim under the melting frost."[7]

Grandma Middleton has a lasting influence on her grandson. In her article "River of Earth: Mythic Consciousness in the Works of James Still," Rebecca I. Briley discusses the "questing journey," which she sees as the major theme of the novel,[8] and asserts that the narrator learns from Grandma Middleton that the questing journey is inescapable and must be made alone. States Briley:

It is with Grandma that [the narrator] learns that the journey is inevitable. . . . From Grandma the boy learns to take lessons from nature and to count time by the seasons. "'Even come spring,' Grandma said, 'we've got a passel of chills to endure: dogwood winter, redbud, service, foxgrape, blackberry. . . . There must be seven winters, by count. A chilly snap for every time of bloom'" (127), and the boy comes to realize that for every progression on the journey, there must be some sacrifice. (71)

Briley also points out:

[I]t is interesting to note that when the narrator of the novel separates himself for his learning process, he goes to live with his *female* Grandma Middleton. In the traditional mythic processes, the young hero must separate himself from the mothering female influences of his life and become one with the men in order to develop his manliness. (79 n 17)

In *River of Earth* it is indeed the "mothering female influences" that spiritually nourish the narrator and help him to mature into adulthood. In some ways, as with Tarvin's reconciliation with nature through his marriage to Subrinea in *Trees of Heaven*, the narrator is also reconciled to nature and to his place in the world through his understanding of the feminine and maternal as represented by his mother and grandmother.

Alpha Baldridge and Grandma Cordia Middleton are powerfully and sensitively depicted Appalachian women. Alpha and Grandma are courageous, actively involved in life as they fend off hunger or loneliness or strive to protect their own, accepting both the good and bad in the choices they have made. They love their families, the earth, and nature in all its forms. In an interview with Sidney S. Farr, James Still states:

The mountain women have been so far ahead of the men that it is a shame they have been allowed to run the local politics. The women know the ins and outs of things better than the men do. They know all the little facets, the little pieces of things, in a way that a man could never know. . . . If the women had been running things you can be sure we'd have better roads, better schools; everything would be run better. The trouble with the men has been they have not met the challenge of the times. They never do anything first, they only follow. ("The Appalachian Woman" 55)

Certainly, as Farr further states, "This statement is borne out in the way he portrays the women in *River of Earth*" ("The Appalachian Woman" 61). As an Appalachian woman herself, Farr concludes: "I like the way

James Still portrays the mountain woman. He portrays us as we are" ("The Appalachian Woman" 61).

Jesse Stuart and James Still were native Appalachian writers writing with "authenticity"—as insiders depicting their own people. From their perspective they saw the mountain woman in a more balanced, more fully rounded way than the non-native writers who had presented generally superficial portraits based in large part on conventional stereotypes. Stuart and Still were proud of their heritage and their people, and their depictions of mountain women suggest above all else their admiration and respect. They focus on the fullness of family life in their novels; family relationships between husbands and wives, parents and children, grandparents and grandchildren are at the centers of *Trees of Heaven* and *River of Earth*. A chief characteristic of these novels is the initiation of a young man or boy into manhood, and one of the major characteristics of this initiation is often the boy's realization of woman's role and status as helpmeet and sustainer of the heritage of the mountains, a genuine acknowledgment of woman's sacrifices and triumphs.

6

Harriette Simpson Arnow's Mountain Women: Defeated or Triumphant?

In 1948 Isabella D. Harris ended her dissertation with a prophecy:

When a writer born among the hills acquires literary technique and fictional perspective, if he combines with keen psychological insight a vivid memory of winding roads in winter and summer mud before the building of the parkways, as well as an observant ear for the speech of his people, he may produce the great mountaineer novel. If and when a book like this should appear, who knows but that it may not be also one of the great American novels? (229)

Harriette Simpson Arnow's *The Dollmaker* (and her earlier work *Hunter's Horn*) appears to be the fulfillment of this prophecy, both a great mountaineer novel and a great American novel. Among literary scholars today, Arnow is probably the most highly respected novelist of Appalachia. Thus I end my study with an examination of Arnow's mountain women.

Of the three most prominent early native writers who depicted the Appalachian people, Jesse Stuart, James Still, and Harriette Simpson Arnow, Arnow today is probably the most recognized by the general population, mostly through the popular and critical success of her finest work, *The Dollmaker*. The book was a national bestseller in the mid-1950s, won several literary awards and honors, has consistently remained in print, and was made into a television movie. Arnow has achieved prominence as a novelist of the first rank not only among scholars of Appalachian literature but also among feminists during the past twenty years,[1] which has helped to make her one of the best-known authors writing about the Appalachian mountain people.

Arnow is also considered by many critics to be the best of the writers of Appalachia. Cratis Williams, for example, states:

Harriette (Simpson) Arnow has probed more deeply the hidden recesses of the mountaineer's character and represented more faithfully the complexities of his personality than any other native writer to bend his talents to the interpretation of his own people. . . . Acquainted by background with the mountaineer in the flesh, she has apparently done painstaking research in his historical, sociological, and fictional records as well. She has succeeded in keeping a perspective of her subject that has enabled her to avoid on the one hand the excesses of Jesse Stuart and on the other the shy reticence of James Still. ("Southern Mountaineer Part IV" 385)

In her three Appalachian novels, *Mountain Path*, *Hunter's Horn*, and *The Dollmaker*, Arnow has indeed captured the nature of the Appalachian people and their experiences in America. In these novels, Arnow writes skillfully and perceptively about the woman's experience in particular in the Appalachian culture.

Harriette Simpson Arnow began her career as a novelist in 1936, four years before both Stuart and Still published their first novels. But she achieved her greatest popular and critical success with her second and third novels in the 1940s and 1950s, and, with Stuart and Still, she helped to firmly establish a native literary tradition among the Appalachian people. Together, these three writers, in poetry, novels, short stories, histories and autobiographies, have presented a faithful picture of what mountain people and mountain life were really like from the 1920s through the 1950s. This was a time when the Appalachian people, firmly rooted in their past, were yet on the threshold of a new kind of world, if not, in fact, at the beginnings of the extinction of their traditional culture.[2]

Harriette Simpson was not born in the high mountains of eastern Kentucky, but instead on the fringes of the Appalachian region in the rolling knoblands just west of the Appalachian Mountains in Wayne County, Kentucky. She grew up in Burnside in Pulaski County, just north of Wayne County. Her ancestors had lived in this area for generations, having been among the first pioneers and settlers of the Cumberland region. Her parents and both grandfathers had been schoolteachers, and it was expected that Harriette would also be a teacher. After completing two years at Berea College, she did, in fact, teach for two terms in a remote area of Pulaski County, the obvious setting of *Mountain Path*, *Hunter's Horn*, and the Kentucky chapters of *The Dollmaker*. Following this interruption in her education, she continued her schooling at the University of Louisville, where she graduated in 1930 or 1931.[3]

After her graduation, Arnow was determined that she did not want to be a teacher, but a writer. She moved to Cincinnati and embarked on her writing career, first publishing short stories in small literary magazines and then *Mountain Path* in 1936. It was thirteen years later, in

1949, that she published her second novel, *Hunter's Horn*, followed by *The Dollmaker* in 1954. Following these three novels, Arnow wrote two nonfiction books, social histories of the Cumberland region, *Seedtime on the Cumberland* (1960) and *Flowering of the Cumberland* (1963), before returning to fiction. Her two last novels do not deal with the mountaineers as did the first three. *The Weedkiller's Daughter* (1970) is set in suburban Detroit in the 1950s and '60s, and *The Kentucky Trace* (1974) is a historical novel of Kentucky.[4] Her last published book is a history of her hometown, *Old Burnside* (1977), written for the Kentucky Bicentennial Bookshelf Series.

Mountain Path, written before Arnow's marriage under her maiden name Harriette Simpson, is the story of Louisa Sheridan, a young woman from the Kentucky Bluegrass area who takes a teaching position in a remote area of the Cumberland region. Louisa is left by the bus in the middle of nowhere and expects that she will have to walk into the unknown in search of her destination. Instead, she is met by the man who has been sent to get her, handsome Chris Bledsoe, and rides into the Cavecreek community on a mule. In Cavecreek, Louisa learns about the moonshining business that the Calhouns, the family she stays with, are involved in, and becomes aware of the mysterious "trouble" that preoccupies the mountaineers, which we later learn is a feud between the Calhouns and their kin at one end of the valley and the Barnetts and their kin in the opposite end. Louisa falls in love with Chris Bledsoe, one of the Calhoun clan, who is wanted by the authorities for having murdered one of the Barnetts. She leaves Cavecreek after Chris's death in a raid by the Barnetts on the Calhouns' still, just as her seven-months teaching contract is up.

Mountain Path is similar in many of its elements to the kind of literature about the mountain people that had preceded it. "The plot," as "M.G.T." stated in his review of the novel in *Mountain Life and Work*, "is already thread-bare . . . Quantities of popular stories have been written about schoolma'ams and handsome outdoor men, and also about moonshine, family loyalty and mountain killings" (28). Likewise, Cratis Williams states that "*Mountain Path* is linked with traditional undistinguished fiction about mountaineers in its materials" by its motifs, character types and plot elements ("Southern Mountaineer Part IV" 387). Yet the novel's clear-headed realism sets it apart from these earlier works. "M.G.T." admitted that despite its threadbare plot, Arnow makes *Mountain Path* "so much her own and so dominates it with the mood that she has chosen that its age hardly matters" (28). Williams notes that "[a]lthough most of the motifs, character types, and plot elements found in *Mountain Path* have counterparts in earlier mountain fiction, the book possesses a vital quality of reality in spite of its derivativeness" ("Southern Mountaineer Part IV" 387). And Rosamond Milner, in her 1936 review of the novel in the Louisville *Courier-Journal*, stated: "The novel's familiar matter is treated with a difference so decided that it makes such stories as Maristen [sic] Chapman's realistic romance and the abnormal realism of others like 'This Day and Time' seem purely literary" (5). Indeed, there is so much in *Mountain Path*, including its touches of humor, that is different from earlier works, that it seems fresh and vital even today.

Certainly the feud between the Calhouns and the Barnetts, which provides the central plot complication of *Mountain Path*, is not a new development in the genre of mountain literature. The feud had been an element of fiction about the mountaineers almost from the beginning; even in Mary Murfree's stories of *In the Tennessee Mountains*, such as "The Star in the Valley," there had been feuds between mountain families and murders as a result. Nor is the depiction of the making and excessive drinking of moonshine liquor by mountain men new. But these plot devices in *Mountain Path* are really secondary to characterization, which is the real success of the novel.

It is her depiction of the Calhoun family that is Arnow's real achievement, particularly her portrayals of Corie Cal (Calhoun) and her daughter Rie. As Rosamond Milner states:

From the moment Louisa enters Lee Buck's house and comes on Corie in the kitchen with her remarkable apple-butter "stirrer," the reader feels Corie as Corie—not as, however interesting, a type. Corie's 12-year-old daughter, Rie, takes on the same reality at once. One has not known to what extent talented authors have exploited the mountaineer until he recognizes as sheer surprise his feeling about Rie's naturalness. Miss Simpson's power of characterization is at its best in Corie and Rie. (*MP* 5)

Arnow's total lack of condescension or romanticization makes her depictions of Corie and Rie ring true in every way.

Arnow's first description of Corie reveals both her poverty and her innate dignity. Louisa has just arrived at the Cals' and apparently found no one at home. As she wanders through the house, however, she comes upon Corie in the kitchen:

She was large; not hippy after the fashion of well-fed women in cities, but tall and thin and rangy with loosely put together bones, and a long neck set under a long but well-shaped head. Her jaws were long and thin, so was her nose, and her chin long and pointed—almost pretty. Her feet, however, were what caused

Louisa to forget that it was impolite to stare. They were long like the rest of her; narrow heels, long wide-spreading toes with each great toe standing a little apart from its smaller sisters, and seemingly enjoying a much wider range of experience. . . . Corie was a rhapsody in brown, even her blue eyes were flecked with lights the color of brown sand in yellow sunlight. (*MP* 34)

Louisa's surprise at Corie's barefooted state is quickly dispelled in this scene, however, by her equal astonishment and admiration at the woman's obvious ingenuity as she stirs apple-butter with her own invented stirrer. From the very first, Corie commands Louisa's respect.

Louisa's respect for the mountain women, especially Corie, is strengthened as she learns more and more about the lives of these people she has come to live with. Corie is inventive and resourceful. Not only has she invented her apple-butter stirrer, but when no "store-bought" candles can be obtained for Louisa's Christmas tree, the first ever in Cal Valley, Corie makes handmade ones, coloring them red, at Rie's suggestion, with cinnamon drops. When no cookie-cutters are available for the Christmas cookies, Corie cuts out paper patterns for them. Not the least of her resourcefulness is the way in which she gets "even" with one of the community's gossips, Ellie Stigall. On the second night of a revival, Corie knows that Ellie has been filled with the Spirit and will probably make a profession the next night. Under the guise of religious fervor, Corie and her sister-in-law Sally Calhoun beat the daylights out of Ellie in one of the funniest scenes in the novel.

As Arnow presents them, the lives of the mountain women in Cavecreek are hard, with endless chores, including taking care of the children, planting and harvesting the corn and sugar cane crops, making molasses, milking cows and drying food for the winter. But the mountain women's lives are not merely filled with drudgery; they also often have fun and enjoy themselves. Corie, for instance, learns how to play cards, even though it is a "sinful" thing to do and she is always on the lookout in case a neighbor should come by and catch her. And there are parties, where the men play musical instruments and the women sing. However, although they enjoy these bright spots in their lives, the women's hard lives do take their toll, both physically and emotionally.

The lives of the mountain women are harder than those of their men. At the Cal family cemetery, for example, where Louisa takes her class to gather mistletoe for the Christmas program, Louisa thinks:

One thing about the half illegible births and deaths carved on the stones appealed to her with poignant significance. It was the large number of dead babies and young wives. Among the dead were a great many more old men than old women. The women, it seemed, died often in their thirties and forties, and she could understand why this was so. Corie was only thirty-two, yet she had borne six children, and appeared to be in her late forties. The graves, Louisa knew, told not only of the past but of the now. Babies still died, and women grew old and died before their time in years was ended. (*MP* 237)

But, as Louisa comes to realize more fully, the hardships of daily existence age and wear away the women less than the deep loneliness and the emotional trials that result from the feuding and the danger inherent in the men's moonshining.

Fear and lonesomeness are the greatest trials for the mountain women. They live daily with the prospects of their menfolks' deaths or imprisonment, for they know the consequences of the feuding and the moonshining. And in the face of this ever-present anxiety they are unable to share their concerns with their men or with each other. As Louisa learns, the mountain women endure their constant fear alone. For example, when Louisa finally allows a woman from the other end of the valley, Mrs. Gholston, to secretly visit her at the school house to warn her that the men of the other end, including Mrs. Gholston's husband, are planning to attack the Calhoun still, Louisa realizes that she cannot say anything to the Cals about it because they would not want her to have talked to the Gholston woman. She realizes that she must go home and keep silent: "[T]here she would see Corie, and Corie would look at her and say, 'How wuz school tu-day, Teacher?' and she would answer, 'Fine.' And that was all she could ever say. She understood now why most hill women believed so in God. They had to have something. They were so alone" (*MP* 302-03).

Later, when Louisa does, in fact, tell Corie that she has talked with the Gholston woman, she realizes even more the emotional losses that the feud inflicts upon the women, for Corie reveals that Mrs. Gholston is her own sister, with whom she has had no communication since Corie married into the Calhoun clan. Corie says: "Not as long ez Lee Buck's my man cud I listen tu her tawk" (*MP* 317). The fact that the women, even sisters, cannot communicate their fears to each other or to their husbands makes Louisa understand and appreciate their predicament: "Only now did she understand the loneliness of most women. Women who love men, and because of that love must forever be strangers to the men, and alone and cut off though they be in crowds of people" (*MP* 318). Thus Arnow suggests that men and women are strangers to each other in much the same way as Emma Bell Miles described in *The Spirit of the Mountains*.

The mountain women also do not interfere with the affairs of their men, and they have little influence on them. They cannot stop them, and would not even try, from doing what the men want to do. Mrs. Gholston, for instance, would never dream of stopping her husband from trying to kill Lee Buck Cal, his own brother-in-law. And, likewise, Corie would never try to interfere with Lee Buck's affairs. She would not want him to know, for example, that she had had any contact with her sister, Mrs. Gholston, even indirectly, and would not try to stop him from going to his still, even though she knew he was in danger.

When, on the night that the Barnetts actually plan to raid Lee Buck's still, Mrs. Gholston sends Corie a message warning her, Corie cannot warn Lee Buck or beg him to stay at home. She agonizes throughout the day, knowing of the planned attack, but cannot try to keep Lee Buck and Chris from going to the still. After the men have left, Corie reluctantly confides in Louisa about the warning message. Louisa runs out of the house to warn the men:

> She was almost across the road before Corie came to life and ran and caught her shoulders in her strong hard hands. "Teacher, ye know ye cain't. Lee Buck 'ud learn how we knowed."
>
> "But you'd rather have him alive and knowing—and going to the Barnetts —than dead?"
>
> Corie stared down the white valley. "No," she said, "I'd druther see him daid." (*MP* 339)

Corie would rather see her husband killed in the raid on the still than have him know that she had not "kept faith" with her family by communicating with his enemies, and would send him to that death before she would interfere. Thus we can see, as Louisa learns, that it is not the hard work of daily survival but the emotional fears and loneliness that are the mountain woman's greatest trials. It is not surprising that Corie hates guns, for they are the instruments of destruction and the cause of her fear and anxiety.

One scene in particular shows Louisa's growing love and respect for Corie. At Christmas time, Louisa sends her relatives in Lexington a package of holly and mistletoe. Corie decides to send them something, too. In a fruit-jar box she packs a quart jar of molasses, a jar of unstrained honey, some fodder beans, and a peck of sun-dried apples—a veritable feast of her best produce. Louisa ponders Corie's magnanimous charity:

She could not help but picture to herself the reception Corie's miscellany of gifts would receive. However, much to her surprise, a week or so after sending the present Corie received a letter from Mrs. Sheridan together with a quilted silk dressing gown. The dressing gown was one given to the sender a number of years before, and never worn because of an un-suitability of both coloring and size. Corie knew nothing of the antecedents of the gown and was childishly pleased. . . . The woman's deep appreciation of the useless gift irked Louisa. It did not seem fair. Corie had given whole-heartedly of things she could use and might at some time need. Her aunt had reciprocated the homely gift with a fine-appearing thing, given only because the giver had no need of it. (*MP* 233-34)

In many ways this scene sums up Corie's character, her "whole-hearted" generosity, her "childish" delight in kindnesses bestowed. From the beginning Louisa feels nothing but "admiration for [Corie's] directness and simplicity" (*MP* 37) and she comes to respect this woman tremendously.

It is no wonder that Louisa learns to respect and admire Corie. As she becomes aware that there are many things that Corie must keep to herself, Louisa realizes:

Corie might be nothing more than a long brown barefooted woman in an ill-made cotton dress, but she had a natural dignity and reserve that Louisa, accustomed to the dignity that comes of heroic corseting and much learning or money, respected too much to attempt to violate. (*MP* 97)

In many instances throughout the novel there are subtle comparisons such as the above between the mountain women and women of the "outside" world, and the mountain women always come out the better—more honest, more naturally dignified, less materialistic and snobbish. Although Mary Noailles Murfree's works about the mountain people are very different in many respects from Arnow's *Mountain Path*, Arnow's first book shares this interesting similarity with Murfree. Like Murfree in "The Star in the Valley," Arnow attempts in *Mountain Path*, by explicit comparison, to show the differences between the Appalachian mountain people and the outsiders. Whereas Murfree appealed to the "common humanity" between the outsiders and the mountain people, however, Arnow shows the positive qualities of the hill people that outshine those of the outsiders.

The advent of the era of realism in Appalachian fiction in the 1930s brought with it a plea for objectivity toward mountain life. Louisa Sheridan can be seen as a representative of the outside world, who, through contact with the mountain people, learns to appreciate them and see them more clearly. This is the same function that Murfree's Reginald

Chevis performs in "The Star in the Valley." Just as Chevis learns that he must discard many of his preconceived ideas about the mountain people, so must Louisa.

At the beginning of the novel, Louisa's thoughts reflect her preconceived attitude toward the "hillbilly," whom she believes to be poverty-stricken, illiterate, shiftless, bashful, backward and unambitious:

> Would the fathers of her pupils be tall men dressed in blue, eating with jackknives, speaking in soft voices, friendly, laughing little, not boisterous like other men?
> Last night she had watched a group of teamsters from her hotel window and they were like that. Poor people, and ignorant and unambitious, holding in them a curious power to make her feel young and afraid. (*MP* 7)

When she begins to live with these people and comes to know them, however, Louisa finds that she must give up many of her attitudes. At first, Louisa "felt that she and they could never find a common ground on which to meet" (*MP* 54): "In her thoughts she still saw her role among these people as that of a bystander and nothing more. She did not want to be anything else. When ugly painful things such as Aunt Elgie's insanity or Chris's danger and trouble came into her mind she always—sometimes without success—immediately tried to put them away from her, and think of her own life waiting for her in Lexington" (*MP* 98). And yet, against her will sometimes, she does become involved in the lives of the people of Cal Valley.

Louisa learns of the necessity that impels the mountaineers to make moonshine and, although she finds it hard to understand, to feud with each other. She falls in love with Chris Bledsoe, and she comes to understand *why* he has killed a man:

> By all the standards that had been set up for her out there in the world Chris was uncivilized and lawless. Yet to himself and those who knew him he was a lawful man. She caught glimpses of something deeper than words written on paper by other men calling themselves legislators. Chris's laws were of the hill law, older than the modern mechanism of law, rooted in freedom and living in people rather than in books. Chris and Lee Buck and Corie and others of their kind, she knew with the same certainty that she knew her name, would not steal or fail to give a guest the best their place afforded. They would not lie except in connection with such things as moonshining, neither would they be friendly with an enemy or forget to hate one they had determined to hate. They sent their children to school because they wanted to, and not because of a state law they had never heard of.

> Such thoughts were confusing. They left her without a yardstick for measuring people and their conduct. (*MP* 124-25)

Louisa especially learns to judge and measure people as individuals and to value individuality.

While looking upon the gravestones in the Cal cemetery, for example, she has a moment of truth:

> For the first time in her life, perhaps, she saw herself with absolute candor, and the sight was not an inspiring one. Always, though never an egotist, she had owned her share of pride in her mind, that she knew to be better than average; in her body, which was strong and sound and not unbeautiful; in her race; her family, its traditions and culture. Now with the same eye that saw the tragedy of the gravestones she saw herself. She was not an individual, but one of a pattern, like the cheap silk dresses sold in department store basements, differing perhaps in minor details, but in their quality and origin essentially the same.
>
> Seeing herself so, she wanted to wreck the mold of her universe, and make of herself a person, an individual with a place in the world of her choosing. . . . (*MP* 238)

It is through her association with the independent mountain people and their intense individuality that Louisa comes to appreciate the individuality of people, a theme that Arnow similarly explores in *The Dollmaker*.

Hunter's Horn, Arnow's second novel, was both a national bestseller and a critical success. Victor P. Hass, for example, in his review of the novel in *The Saturday Review*, said: "It is possible that 1949 will see the publication of a better novel than 'Hunter's Horn' but I, for one, do not look for literary lightning to strike twice in so short a time. Certainly, to date, this is the strongest contender I have seen for the Pulitzer Prize in fiction" (20). Ray West, Jr., in the *Sewanee Review*, though pointing out the novel's use of many of the typical elements of "rural Southern" fiction, nevertheless praised its vitality, as critics had done with *Mountain Path*:

> The familiar trappings of the rural Southern novel are all represented, including the manufacture of illicit corn whiskey, the struggles in child-birth, the religious revival, the one-room country school, superstition, poverty, and ignorance combined with native intelligence and shrewdness; yet it is to Mrs. Arnow's credit that such details are presented with a freshness that brings them completely to life. (691-92)

Despite the fact that *Mountain Path* and *Hunter's Horn* share many of the familiar descriptions of mountain life, the second novel shows a great leap in Arnow's literary talents. In *Mountain Path* she had used the outmoded technique of the outsider learning firsthand about the mountaineers and the worn plot of the love affair between an outsider and a mountaineer (although, in this case, it is an outsider woman in love with a mountain man). In *Hunter's Horn* Arnow focuses exclusively on the mountain people, especially their inner lives, like the works of Jesse Stuart and James Still.

Hunter's Horn covers a two-and-a-half-year span just prior to the beginnings of World War II in the lives of Nunnely Ballew, a Kentucky mountain farmer, and his family. The Ballews own a farm on Little Smokey Creek on the Big South Fork of the Cumberland River and have tried to make it prosper, with little success. Nunn has become so obsessed with killing a great red fox, whom he calls King Devil, that he lets everything go, runs up debts, sells off livestock and produce to buy pedigreed hounds to chase King Devil and dogfood to feed them, and neglects both the farm and his family.[5] By the end of the novel, Nunn is in debt and his family is torn apart when he disowns his eldest daughter Suse for being pregnant out of wedlock. King Devil is finally killed, but the victory that the fox's death brings to Nunn is clouded by the losses that he and his family have incurred throughout the novel.

As with *Mountain Path*, the vividness of *Hunter's Horn* is chiefly the result of Arnow's characterization. Part of the freshness of the novel, as with her earlier one, comes from Arnow's uncondescending attitude toward the people she writes about and her realistic, if not naturalistic, portrayal of their lives. As Cratis Williams writes:

Essentially a naturalistic determinist in her literary philosophy, Mrs. Arnow has instinctively avoided name calling, labels, caricatures, apologies, smiling condescension to old-fashioned manners and customs, and indulgence in holiday antiquarianism. Stark tragedy and poignant heartbreak stalk the pages of her books, but her characters possess the integrity permitted them within the limitations of their environment. ("Southern Mountaineer Part IV" 385-86)

Especially compelling in *Hunter's Horn* is Arnow's realistic and complex characterization of the women in the novel, from the outspoken old midwife, Sue Annie Tiller, with her salty language full of profanities, to the pathetic Lureenie Cramer, who dies horribly in childbirth after almost starving to death and going insane. The two most important female characters in the novel, however, are again a mother and daughter—like Corie and Rie in *Mountain Path*. In fact, although the novel can be said, on the one hand, to be "about" Nunn Ballew and his obsession with killing King Devil, it can also be seen, perhaps more rightly so, as the story of Nunn's wife and daughter, Milly and Suse Ballew, and how their lives are altered in consequence of Nunn's obsession.

One critic calls Milly Ballew "the most profoundly affecting character" in the novel (Raeschild 56). Another states: "Milly is of the earth, a snaggle-toothed slattern who seems only beautiful" (Hass 20). Although she does sometimes "let herself go" in a slovenly way, loves to chew homegrown tobacco and spit amber juice, and has rotten teeth that often cause the toothache, Milly does indeed possess the inner qualities that make her seem beautiful. "An old married woman nearing thirty" (*HH* 67), as she describes herself, Milly is the mother of six children, two of whom have died (she has a seventh child during the course of the novel), and she is the wife of a man who puts his own needs, particularly his need to be victorious over King Devil, always above those of his family. Like Corie Cal in *Mountain Path*, and later Gertie Nevels in *The Dollmaker*, Milly Ballew finds suffering, hard work and heartache to be the main conditions of her life. But, like them also, Milly endures.

Like other mountain women we have seen in literature, Milly is "of the earth," and this helps to sustain her. The land is her sustenance, both physically and emotionally. Owning a farm has been Milly's dream. She has wanted land of her own so that she would not have to be dependent on others. She remembers having to "work in other people's houses" and "the bitterness of cooking other people's bread" (*HH* 350), and she is willing to make every sacrifice in order to own her own farm. It is Milly who works the hardest and struggles the most to keep the farm going and her family provided for, all of which she does uncomplainingly because the reward is her independence and self-sufficiency.

One of Milly's chief joys in life is delight in her labor and its results. At one point, for example, she surveys her winter store of provisions:

. . . in spite of the dull gray weather and an aching jaw tooth, life to Milly was good.

The fall work was done. The house was so crammed with food against the winter that the old floors in the loft room sagged. . . . Almost half of the big room was taken up with the chewing tobacco. . . . The rest of the room was filled with the things cold couldn't hurt: crocks and lard cans of molasses and honey in the comb, jugs of vinegar and jugs of strained honey, more lard cans of peanuts and hulled black walnuts and hickory nuts, and butternuts; buckets and cans and crocks of shelled cowpeas with a few dried beans . . . meal sacks plump with dried apples or peaches, clusters of little yellow ears of popcorn with their shucks stripped back and braided together. Scattered through everything were bunches of dried herbs—hore-hound and catnip and peppermint and sage and tansy—and from the woods and fields were feverweed and dog fennel and sweet fennel and goldenrod and life everlasting and seneca snakeroot and yellowroot and mayapple root. . . . (*HH* 379-80)

Along with all these crocks and jars of dried produce, there are her dozens of glass jars full of canned vegetables. Arnow devotes three pages to cataloguing Milly's cornucopia of winter supplies and her obvious delight in having canned, dried, cured, and preserved it. Life is good to Milly when she is able to fend off hunger for her family by her labor on her own land. Milly is, above all, capable and industrious, knowing that her family's welfare depends greatly on her efforts.

Nunn, in contrast to Milly, takes little if any pleasure in the earth. He spends his energies tracking King Devil, grooming his hounds (Milly also loves the hounds and babies them outrageously), or going on drunken binges after unsuccessful hunts. Nunn's way of coping with the disappointments of life is obviously to forget them in moonshine. After the good old hound Zing is run to death by King Devil, for example, we are told: "Milly saw Nunn's eyes and forgot to wonder what it was he carried home [the dead Zing], for there was a look in his eyes she had seen before, a look he couldn't live with, and so must try to lose in a long drunk" (*HH* 65). And, despite the great store of provisions that Milly has hoarded for the winter, the family often goes without many of the necessities of life (and certainly the "luxuries," such as new clothes and shoes or sugar), because Nunn spends all the money he can get his hands on chasing King Devil. He even sells the family's winter meat supply, and Milly's struggle to provide for the family often seems to be a losing battle.

Milly, however, never complains about Nunn. When he gets drunk she understands or risks embarrassment to fetch him home. When he buys canned dogfood for the hounds rather than food or shoes for his family, she does not reproach him. During the winter, for example, when they are out of meat and butter and sugar, Milly, in fact, feels sorry for Nunn. When he sells her prized heifer, which could have provided them with either milk or the money for store-bought provisions, in order to buy two pedigreed hounds, Milly is not angry but actually sympathetic toward Nunn: "Nunn, she thought, was maybe so hungry he was thinking about the same thing [his sale of the heifer]. She felt so sorry for him she could have cried. . . . Maybe he thought about the black heifer that would be fresh now; he didn't look mad, more like he felt guilty and

This photograph from Muriel Earley Sheppard's *Cabins in the Laurel* (1935) could easily exemplify any of Arnow's mountain women and their families. Reprinted with the permission of the North Carolina Collection, University of North Carolina at Chapel Hill.

ashamed. She didn't hold it against him" (*HH* 192). Far from condemning Nunn's weaknesses, Milly understands them and seems to sense his guilt and shame, something he would never admit, knowing as she does that he is driven by unknown forces.

As we have also seen with many of the mountain women in Appalachian literature, Milly does not question Nunn's actions. He does what he wants to do at all times and seldom, if ever, consults Milly. This unquestioning acceptance of Nunn's actions by Milly, with its concomitant disregard on Nunn's part for Milly's feelings, is a manifestation of the emotional gulf that exists between them. In many ways, although each feels deeply for the other, Nunn and Milly are strangers to each other. For example, in the scene in which Nunn tells Milly that he has decided to sell the heifer Lizzie, he does it in a roundabout way, first telling her to start feeding Lizzie more corn:

> "Give it some nubbins from now on."
> Milly got up from the milking and looked at him in some perplexity, then reminded him that back last fall he had said there mightn't be corn to run them through crop-making time.
> Nunn met her wondering glance and hastily put his eyes on the spotted calf and kept them there. "I'm wanten that calf in good shape. I'm aimen to sell her—the last Saturday fore Christmas I recken it'll be."
> Milly's troubled "Oh" was more like a weary sigh than a word. "It's got the maken's uv a pretty cow," she said, then quickly added, as if afraid of hurting his feelings, "but then I've allus said if we could have two cows, one to milk while t'other was dry, I'd be satisfied—an Lizzie's due in February." (*HH* 100)

When Nunn tells Milly that he intends to sell Lizzie, what *he's* "aimen" to do, she looks at him, "no anger but a piteous disbelief, a kind of tortured hope in her wide brown eyes, like the eyes of a child about to be whipped, who after he felt the first few blows keeps hoping against his belief that there will be more" (*HH* 100).

Later, Milly does try to make Nunn understand her feelings about the heifer, which she has raised from a calf. Milly is willing to sacrifice or endure anything in order to keep Lizzie: "Nunn—I know we're awful short a money—it takes a lot fer me an th youngens—but, Nunn, I'll do without anything, everything, if'n you can just keep Lizzie till her calf comes" (*HH* 101). But Nunn is adamant in his plans to sell Lizzie—in fact, she is only part of what he intends to sell in order to raise the money to buy his new hounds. Milly's plea is ignored. That night, Milly cries in bed "with a pillow pulled over her head so as not to awaken [Nunn]" (*HH* 101), who, nevertheless, hears her and commands, "Shut up, Milly, you're keepen me awake" (*HH* 101). The next morning at breakfast, the distance between husband and wife is further shown:

Milly was silent, moving between the table and the stove as she brought him biscuit hot from the oven, poured fresh coffee, or sat on the nail keg by the stove, her accustomed seat when he took meals at odd hours like this. Their glances were continually meeting, but they seemed the glances of strangers each too timid to speak to the other. (*HH* 102)

Nunn makes such major decisions as selling Lizzie and the family's winter store of meat without consulting Milly and with only a little guilt for his actions.

Because she has so little say in Nunn's decisions, Milly even wonders at times if he has taken out a mortgage on the farm without her knowledge or if he is in some kind of trouble that he hasn't told her about. But she accepts his decisions and, while he goes about his business without regard for Milly, she keeps her thoughts and feelings to herself. As Victor P. Hass states: ". . . patient, wonderful, tobacco-chewing Milly bore [Nunn's] children and scraped a living from the soil with the help of her cooperative, uncomplaining children. None blamed Nunn and all conspired to overlook his faults when he came home drunk from another unsuccessful hunt" (20). Despite the unhappiness which Nunn causes Milly, she does not wish to add to his pain or grief, and thus she suffers her own in silence.

In her quiet suffering and sufferance, Milly finds her greatest solace in fundamentalist religious acceptance of God's will, a force that helps to sustain her. Like the women about whom Arnow had written in *Mountain Path*, whose loneliness, Louisa understands, contributes to their belief in God, Milly seeks comfort in her religious beliefs. Although she does not always understand and sometimes finds it hard to accept her trials, Milly's belief in the will of God as ultimate justification helps her to accept and endure the hardships she must bear. For example, when she contemplates the approaching birth of her seventh child and considers the possible complications:

At times she was afraid, waking at night in a cold sweat of fear, memories of the long agonies of other births vivid as fresh-dreamed dreams; at other times she was filled with a hot hate and an anger against the dry heat, her weary body, and even the children. But mostly she was resigned and sorrowful: she put her trust in Jesus: He would take her and look out for her children, and nothing else mattered. (*HH* 279)

Later, she wonders, "What if she died like Maisie Martin? . . . She shivered and got up, wiping her wet palms on her apron—God's will was God's will, but it was not always easy to understand" (*HH* 308). And she thinks: "It was God's will that all His children have some bad luck, and it was a sin to fight against it" (*HH* 348). To accept "bad luck" and the struggles of life is to accept God's will, and this acceptance sustains Milly throughout her life. There is in Milly's acceptance of God's will a kinship to Corie Cal's like acceptance in *Mountain Path*: "Without being a pessimist Corie expected the worst of all possible combinations in all things, and as a result was eternally grateful for some little things" (*MP* 215). Both Corie and Milly are able to survive the hardships they must endure because of their acceptance of those hardships as a part of life.

Suse Ballew, Milly's daughter, is the second most important female character in *Hunter's Horn*. As with Corie and Rie Calhoun in *Mountain Path*, Arnow exemplifies through Milly and Suse how generations of mountain women are trapped by their surroundings, as the younger women grow into womanhood in their mothers' shadows. In *Hunter's Horn* more than in *Mountain Path* the tragedies of the lives of mountain women from one generation to the next are manifest, especially in the subplot of the novel involving Suse, whom one critic describes as "hammered from gold—a darling girl wrecked for want of one decent dress" (Hass 20).

Enduring the hardships of mountain life, working uncomplainingly like her mother, Suse Ballew has only two dreams in life, both of which are shattered. First, Suse desires an education. Paradoxically, this is also Nunn's desire for her: he wants almost as much as she does for Suse, a bright, intelligent girl, to go to high school and become a teacher like his own mother, "a smiling, redheaded, gray-eyed schoolteacher" (*HH* 20) who had come into the valley from the outside world. It is ironic that Nunn desires an education for Suse, while Milly feels that it is foolish to give girls much schooling (*HH* 308). Perhaps Milly feels that it is useless for girls to be educated when their lives are so narrowly defined. The real irony, however, is that despite Nunn's wish for Suse, it is he who ultimately thwarts her hopes. He is always "aimen" to do things, but never does them.

Suse does not have decent clothes or even shoes to wear and she could not possibly go to school without them. But Nunn spends all his money on his dogs, never giving Suse what she needs most to go decently to school. Suse also becomes somewhat disillusioned with the idea of education when she discovers that Miss Burdine, the teacher from the outside whom she idolizes, is not the kind of teacher that Suse had always imagined. Miss Burdine refuses to acknowledge that Suse and another student, Andy, who plans also to go to high school, have correctly solved a mathematical problem that she cannot solve; as a result, Suse becomes very disappointed in Miss Burdine and in the idea of schooling.

Suse begins more and more to see the futility of her dreams for furthering her education. At one point she overhears Willie Cooksey telling Nunn about picking tomatoes in Indiana. Willie suggests that Nunn and Suse go to earn some money, that Suse could use for school. After Willie leaves, Suse comes out from hiding and begs Nunn to go: "Please, Pop . . . Couldn't we go—we'd make a sight a money—why, I'd make more'n enough to start me out to high school" (*HH* 355). But Nunn is unwilling to leave his chase of King Devil, or to allow Suse to go alone with the Cookseys. He tells her, "Shut up an quit tellen me what to do. What a you mean, anyhow, sneaken around an eaves-drop-pen in th brush? Git on back to the house where you belong" (*HH* 355).

At this point Suse seems to realize how vain her dream is:

Suse did not flinch or drop her eyes in meek acceptance as Milly would have done, but stood a moment straight-shouldered and high-headed and looked at him and her eyes were older than her dangling braids and small pointed breasts pushing in sharp outline against the outgrown ragged, faded dress. Her face, too, was unchildlike, hard with scorn and anger as she said, "I hid in th bushes because I wasn't decent fer a body to see in these rags, an I ain't got no better—but one ole dress I been saven to wear to meeten if'n I got some shoes." (*HH* 355-56)

Suse stands up to her father, rather than meekly accepting his accusations. But her dream of an education is nevertheless destroyed by Nunn's obsession to kill King Devil, and even he seems to realize this. After Suse has gone back into the house, Nunn thinks back over his life:

He sighed; he wasn't the man who had at many times stood a twelve-hour shift in the mines as car loader, or even the man, young and full of plans and dreams, who had come to the valley five—no, seven years ago now. He stopped, the seven striking him, not in his head or his reason where he knew it, but in his heart. Seven years—. . . Religion! If he had religion he could leave King Devil to go his way, but before a man could get religion he had to give his heart and soul to God and get God's grace to forgive his sins. How could a man be certain God would forgive? How could he know God wanted his soul? How could a man know he hadn't committed the unpardonable sin? What was the unpardonable sin? Why did he think of all that now? Suse? If he lived to be a hundred and caught King Devil and died a millionaire, that wouldn't help Suse now—unpardonable, unforgivable. (*HH* 356-57)

Although he feels in his heart that he has wronged Suse, Nunn realizes that his unpardonable inability to save her because of his own obsession has sealed her destiny.

Suse's second dream is closely tied to her desire for an education, for in her wish for schooling Suse also dreams of escaping the life around her. She longs for the outside world. When Miss Betty Catharine Burdine, the school teacher, first comes to the Little Smokey Creek School, Suse is overjoyed:

... she was a piece—a fine though as yet unknown piece—of the outside world come to Suse; that world she had dreamed about since she was big enough to read in the prime about a policeman, and glimpsed vaguely through schoolbooks and the few other books and newspapers and magazines that had come into her hands.... and Miss Burdine would be her friend and tell her how things were—and some day she too would be like that—a part of the outside world. (*HH* 264)

At the party to welcome Miss Burdine to the school, Suse's thoughts are far away: "The banjos were silent and old Dave and Mark Cramer carried the music alone and the sad wailing of the violins became as one with Suse's thoughts—their wordless yearning cry of hunger, not for food alone or clothes, or shelter—a hunger like a hurt, an ache for things mysterious and unseen, nay, undreamed" (*HH* 264). As she contemplates the other women at the party, Suse knows that she does not want to be like them: "Suse studied them, then shivered and looked away; she would never be like that, dull and dead and uncaring; she thought of Milly sleeping at home; she would fit well with the others on the bench. Had she or any of them ever heard the trains blow far away and sad, calling you to come away, calling so clearly you wanted to cry? Or had they ever wanted to run and run through the woods on a windy moonlight night in spite of what God would think and the neighbors say?" (*HH* 265). Throughout the novel, Suse dreams of going away into a "new fine country" from which "she'd never come back" (*HH* 392). She pities her mother and the other women like Milly and longs to escape their world, their fate. Like her dreams of education, however, Suse's dream of escaping the life of the hills is also shattered.

After realizing the futility of her hopes to go to high school, Suse becomes involved with Mark Cramer, whose family is considered "trashy" by most of the neighborhood, and when Mark goes to Detroit

Harriette Simpson Arnow's Mountain Women   143

for work, Suse hopes that he will later take her with him. They exchange letters and when Mark comes home for a visit he seduces Suse. Mark returns to Detroit and Suse discovers that she is pregnant. Unsure whether Mark will marry her or not, Suse does not know what to do. When old Keg Head Cramer, Mark's father, having heard through gossip of Suse's pregnancy, comes to fetch her to his place as a hired girl—the fate that Milly had so abhorred when she was a girl before she had her own farm—Suse is sure that her father will not make her go. When Milly urges her to go with Keg Head without any fuss, Suse says, "Wait till Pop gits home," feeling certain that he will save her from this fate.

At first, Nunn is torn between his love for his eldest child and his own pride:

> Nunn felt the rough chimney rock with his hand and leaned against it; it was good to feel the rock, so hard and old and firm—Samuel had said to do the decent thing—and Lucy hanging on the gate, crying every day from the gibes of the children at school, "Lucy's sister Suse is a witch, witch; she can have a baby thout a man." And, the AAA boys or Pinkney Deegan or Elias visiting, "That your least un, Nunn?" "No—that's my oldest girl's." And Milly, crying, praying, quarreling. And the child—"come-by-chance; come-by-chance; your long tailed mammy lost her pants." And Lee Roy, sullen and silent and knowing. But Suse—Suse, who'd never lived by God and the neighbors no more than he, to go as Keg Head's hired girl into the never done work of raising Lureenie's children along with her own and waiting on Keg Head and his wife in their old age; Suse, the proud one, to be tolerated and shamed and prayed over. (*HH* 565-66)

Yet her belief in Nunn is once again thwarted when he tells Suse, "I ain't a holden th wrong you've done agin you—but this fire—it's never warmed a bastard" (*HH* 566). Thus Suse's dreams of escaping the valley and a life like her mother's is destroyed: ". . . slowly her bright head drooped lower and lower, like a rain-drenched sunflower at twilight. She never looked at him [Nunn] or anyone, but walked away from the fire and through the middle door" (*HH* 566). Suse is doomed to a life of drudgery and heartache.

The tragedy of Lureenie Cramer in *Hunter's Horn* serves as a parallel to and a foreshadowing of Suse's tragedy. Lureenie is married to Mark Cramer's brother Rans. Like Suse, Lureenie dreams always of getting away from the mountain community. Rans gets a job in Cincinnati, and when he sends for Lureenie and the children to join him, Lureenie says, "It's th onliest thing I've ever wanted that's come to pass—gitten away" (*HH* 302). Lureenie learns, however, that the city is not what can make her happy. The only window in her house in Cincinnati looks out against a wall; the town is smokey and foggy; and she is cooped up inside most of the time. So Lureenie returns home.

Rans sends her money but she uses it to make payments on the radio she bought in Cincinnati. During the winter, Lureenie, too proud to beg, virtually starves herself and her children. She is pregnant again, and the loneliness, hunger and failed dreams drive her to insanity. Lureenie dies a painful death in childbirth. While she is dying, her father-in-law, Keg Head Cramer, begins to chant a prayer for her, which precipitates one of the most emotional scenes in the novel between Nunn and Suse. Responding to what she sees as Keg Head's self-righteousness, Suse at first curses Keg Head for letting Lureenie suffer and starve. When Nunn tells Suse to get home, that he won't beat her for this disrespectful conduct, Suse turns all her frustrated rage on her father:

"You couldn't do no more harm than you've already done me, couldn't hurt me no worse—th meanest thing you've done fer me was bringen me into the world. It's too bad Mom couldn't a had a pair of sheep shears that'd cut my head off when I was borned."

"Shut up, Suse. Talken Sue Annie's dirty talk. You'll end up a bad woman."

"In a Cincinnati whorehouse, you mean. Well, it's a pity Mom couldn't a gone to one when she was my age; she'd a had a sight easier time."

"Aw, Suse," he spoke slowly. He had the sickish feeling that he lied and she spoke the truth. "You know I've done the best I could by your mom an I'll do the best I can by you—" (*HH* 441)

But Nunn's words ring false to Suse and she continues to reject her father's apology:

She forgot the short-cut path and strode on down through the corn swag toward the Cow's Horn gate. "Aw, hell. You've always done th best you could to keep her in th family way. An you do get worried when she ain't able to work an wait on you." She went on striding down the road. "As fer me, you'll marry me off to some little shaved-tail son of a bitch when th rest gets big enough to work. You've not got money to keep me in shoes now."

He spoke in desperation, with no time to think. "Aw, Suse, honey, I'm aimen to send you to high school next—"

"High school, hell! You'll never have enough money to send me in decent clothes to th post office, let alone high school. You're always aimen; never finishen nothen—" (*HH* 441)

After Lureenie's death, Suse literally takes her place, doomed to the same futile and unfulfilled life.

Suse's tragedy is the result of many factors in her life. Her dreams of an education and of escaping the mountains are both destroyed, mostly because of her father's inability to forego his obsession with killing the fox King Devil and provide her with the means and clothes to go to school. But her dream of escape, which ends in such misery for everyone when she becomes pregnant and must go as a hired girl to her seducer's parents, makes her tragedy even more poignant. For, despite her dreams, Suse is forced to accept her life as it is and to realize that she has little if any control over it.

Suse's tragedy was hinted at in the closing scene of *Mountain Path*. As Louisa tells her school children a final story on the last day of school she looks at her pupils and contemplates their futures:

She looked at her girls, Rie and Mable huddled together with arms wrapped each about the waist of the other. For them, too, most probably, it was the last day of their last school term—and they were such babies. Rie's waist would twist yet more when she carried her own children instead of her mother's, and the bend of her shoulders grow as she grew with her children, so that at twenty-five she would be an old woman never having been a young one. She would know trouble too—vigils by the fire while her children slept behind her, and her man was away with other men. But Mable was the weak one. She would always want a green silk dress trimmed with lace, and know she wanted it. Rie would never know. (*MP* 364)

Like Mabel, Suse would always want something she couldn't have, and thus her life would be more tragic than Rie's, or Corie's, or Milly's, who endured because they had no such dreams of anything other than their simple lives and acceptance of them.

The world of women in *Hunter's Horn* is filled with tragedy and hopelessness, with few comforts. Women bear the sorrows and the struggles of life. Foreshadowing Suse's failed dreams and recognizing her own condition, Milly at one point contemplates Suse's future: "poor child, soon enough would come the time when not just her body was tied down by work, but her mind, too, with troubles and worries—it seemed sometimes like God made women for trouble" (*HH* 209). And when Lureenie is on her deathbed and says, "Me, I don't want to last a long time. I think I'd ruther go out like a cedar bush in a brush fire than wear out slow like a doorsill," the worldly-wise Sue Annie Tiller sighs: "Child, th world cain't git along without doorsills to walk on; that's why God made women; but it's allus seemed to me that all women, when they die, they ought to go to heaven; they never have nothen much down here but hell" (*HH* 417).

In this respect in relation to the world of women in the novel, the symbolism of King Devil appears not to have failed, as Ray West, Jr., suggests.[6] For King Devil, the illusory red fox who has plagued Nunn Ballew, is actually a vixen, a female fox, and she is finally killed because she is about to have pups and therefore cannot escape the hounds. Like the women of the novel, King Devil (or as Milly more rightly calls her "Queen Devil") is ultimately destroyed because of her female condition. When Milly, who is the first one to reach the fox after the hounds catch her, discovers that she is a pregnant vixen, she feels only pity for the animal: "'Pore thing,' Milly said, and again, 'Pore thing, if'n she hadn't been a vixen they'd never a caught her'" (545). This scene symbolically comes just before the scene in which Nunn banishes Suse. Like "Queen Devil," Suse has been defeated in her dreams of escape because she is a female creature with child.

Hunter's Horn brought critical and popular attention to Harriette Arnow. As with *Mountain Path*, Arnow's greatest achievement in *Hunter's Horn* is her characterization of the poor hill people as they struggle to survive, especially her portrayals of the women. Arnow's greatest literary achievement, however, is unquestionably *The Dollmaker*, the last of her three novels to present the Appalachian people of Kentucky. Published in 1954, it was a popular bestseller and brought national acclaim to Arnow. It also earned high praise from critics. *The Dollmaker* came in second to Faulkner's *The Fable* for the National Book Award, was voted the best novel of the year by *The Saturday Review's* national critics' poll, and won the Friends of American Literature Award. It is indeed Arnow's masterpiece and one of the most outstanding novels written about the Appalachian people. Of all Appalachian novels it is probably the one most consistently taught in college classes, ranging from literature to sociology, and it has endured for four decades, its reputation steadily growing.

The Dollmaker is the story of the Nevels family, Clovis, Gertie and their five children—Reuben, Clytie, Enoch, Cassie and Amos. At the beginning of the novel the family lives on rented land in the Kentucky hills along the Big South Fork of the Cumberland River (the same location as *Hunter's Horn*; even some of the same names are used). It is 1944 and the Second World War has virtually eliminated men and manpower from the community. Most of the men are in the armed forces, some, like Clovis's brother, prisoners of war, others, like Gertie's brother Henley, killed in action. Clovis is almost the only able-bodied man left in the settlement, and he is preparing for his army physical as the novel begins.

Harriette Simpson Arnow's Mountain Women   147

Although he passes his physical, however, Clovis is not called into duty right away and, therefore, instead of returning home, he goes to Detroit to get a job in one of the war-effort factories. Gertie, whose greatest dream has been to own a farm of her own, is just about to realize this wish by buying the Tipton Place when her mother "forces" her, through an appeal to Gertie's sense of duty, to join Clovis in Detroit. The last two-thirds of the novel traces the family's "adjustment," or lack of it, as they must assimilate into the new urban environment or be broken by it.

At the center of this enormous book is the mountain woman Gertie Nevels, the "dollmaker" of the title, so called because of her talent for whittling and wood carving. Like Arnow's earlier mountain women, Corie Calhoun and Milly Ballew, Gertie Nevels possesses the qualities that we have come to associate with the mountain woman: closeness to nature and place, love of family and community, strength and endurance in the face of life's hardships. Gertie also knows the pains of loneliness, emotional and personal distance from her husband, the loss of children, and personal sacrifice. Gertie's trials are indeed heightened as she must leave the familiar world that she has always known and begin life anew in a strange and alien place.

From Murfree on we have seen the mountain woman's close relationship to nature and the land. Gertie, likewise, constantly finds solace in nature, in the land. In a scene early in the novel, for example, after Clovis has left for his army physical and has been gone for almost a week, his whereabouts unknown to Gertie, she goes to the post office to wait for the mail, hoping for a letter from him. Unable to just sit patiently and wait, Gertie asks the postmistress, "Miz Hull, couldn't I dig yer taters? I'd ruther be doen somethen than visiten—er plain waiten" (*TD* 98). And as she carefully digs the potatoes, Gertie's love of the land and its produce is manifest: "she worked, sending the prongs of the spading fork slowly down with her foot, then pushing gently backward with one hand on the handle so that the hill of potatoes came up with the earth, unscarred and whole" (*TD* 98). Rather than waste time visiting or waiting, Gertie finds comfort in digging in the soil, feeling satisfaction and pride in harvesting its produce. Similarly, when she contemplates the old Tipton Place, which she longs to be able to buy, Gertie sees its natural beauty:

She could see the house, and past the strip of shadow that fell slantwise of the yard, the bluegrass, green as grass in spring. The grass, the golden flowers by the house wall, the moss on the roof, the yellow chrysanthemums by the gray stepping-stones, all glowed warmly as if they, with the house on the sheltered southern hillside, were set in some land that was forever spring. (*TD* 53)

Even Gertie's conception of Christ is closely tied to nature. After the news that her younger brother Henley has been killed in action, for example, Gertie has a vision of what Christ is like. Gertie's mother, Mrs. Kendrick, bewails the fact that Henley was not baptized or "saved," that he was too much like Gertie, whom her mother says has been "stiff-necked an stubborn in th face uv th Almighty God" (*TD* 60). Mrs. Kendrick envisions a wrathful God: "You ought to read yer Bible, Gert. It's all foretold. 'I come not with peace but a sword,' Christ said. . . . Christ is a scourgen th world like he scourged th temple, an in his mighty wrath he—" (*TD* 61). But Gertie sees a different Christ:

> "But, Mom, mebbe," Gertie began in a low hesitant voice, turning to look at her, "mebbe they's another side to Christ. Recollect he went to th wedden feast, an had time to fool with little youngens, an speak to a thief an a bad woman. An Henley was like Christ—he worked an loved his fellowmen an—"
>
> Her mother's rocker gave an angry swish, and Gertie, whose voice had grown even lower and more hesitant, fell silent. She looked past her mother through the open door, her eager glance hunting the hill-pasture path she had walked a few minutes before, then pausing on the brow of the hill where the woods met the bright blue sky; and for an instant it seemed that her Christ, the Christ she had wanted for Henley, was there, ready to come singing down the hill, a laughing Christ uncrowned with thorns and with the scars of the nail holes in his hands all healed away; a Christ who had loved people, had liked to mingle with them and laugh and sing the way Henley had liked people and singing and dancing. (*TD* 60-61)

Gertie's Christ is a loving savior, walking down a hillside laughing.

Gertie also finds comfort in contemplating the vastness of the sky and the stars, another manifestation of her relationship with nature. Gertie finds in the stars, and in all of nature, a sense of permanence and security. Cassie, Gertie's youngest daughter, asks her at one point, "Mom—do them men that ride them airplanes like Lena Gholson's man—do them men ever hit the stars?" (*TD* 117). Gertie's reply shows her reverence for nature:

> "Nobody can hurt th stars, honey—they'll allus be there." Cassie blinked at the sky. "What makes you like to look at th stars, Mom?"
>
> "'Th heavens declare th glory of God; an th firmament showeth his handi-work. Day unto day uttereth speech, and night unto night—'"
>
> "But what do they say, Mom?"
>
> Gertie stared up, considering the Little Dipper.

"Different things to different people; fer one thing they say, 'We never change, an we'll never go away—all the nations on this earth with all their wars, they cain't cut us down like we was trees.' And they say to Cassie Marie, 'Little girl, if'n you lost yet friends an kin you'd still have us an th sun and moon.'" (*TD* 117-18)

The eternal security of nature helps to sustain Gertie. As Wilton Eckley states in his critical biography of Arnow:

Gertie's strength does not derive from a relationship with conventional religion, or with people for that matter, as much as it does from her relationship with nature; for in nature she finds her real sustenance, her point of reference as it were. Gertie constantly looks to the stars, particularly the north star. It symbolizes for her the freedom and beauty of all of nature—elements so important to her that she is relieved to be told by the doctor tending Amos [her son] that her brother Henley, after being mortally wounded in battle, might well have been left by the stretcher bearers to die alone outside rather than in a confining tent. (89-90)

It is part of her own tragedy that Gertie is cut off from nature in the ironically named Merry Hill subdivision where the family lives in Detroit and where Gertie longs for hills and trees.

Like Alpha Baldridge in Still's *River of Earth* and Milly Ballew in *Hunter's Horn*, Gertie's greatest wish is for a farm of her own, a sure and abiding place. Her dream takes the form of the Tipton Place, which, because of the war's having taken away its original owners, is now for sale by old John Ballew. Gertie is a farmer who looks to the land to provide her livelihood. Clovis, with his truck hauling and mechanical tinkering, has struggled to provide for his family, but Gertie desires the independence that a place of her own, not a rented farm, can provide. For fifteen years Gertie has saved every dollar she could toward the realization of this dream. The Tipton Place is Gertie's "Promised Land" (*TD* 103). It is the sure foundation on which all her hopes rest.

As she anticipates owning the Tipton Place, which she will finally be able to buy as a result of her brother Henley's last request that all his cattle money be given to Gertie, Gertie feels that all her earthly wants will be met:

She was somewhere on the graveled road near the schoolhouse before she realized that Cassie was gasping for breath from her efforts to keep up with her, while she herself went with long swift strides and sang at the top of her lungs, joyfully, as if it had been some sinful dance tune, "'How firm a foundation, ye saints of the Lord.'" She slackened her pace but she couldn't stop the song as she smiled at the stars through the pines. Her foundation was not God but what God had promised Moses—land; and she sang on, "'Is laid for your faith in His excellent word! What more can He say than to you He hath said—'" What more, oh, Lord, what more could a woman ask? (*TD* 121)

Owning her own land means freedom to Gertie, just as nature means freedom, the human spirit set free: "It was as if the war and Henley's death had been a plan to help set her and her children free so that she might live and be beholden to no man, not even Clovis. Never again would she have to wait to bake bread till Clovis brought home a sack of meal. 'I've reached th land of corn and wine; an all its riches freely mine; here shines undimmed one blissful day where all my night has passed away'" (*TD* 130-31). One of the most tragic ironies of *The Dollmaker* is that just as she is about to buy the Tipton Place, in fact just after she has already given old John Ballew the money for the farm, circumstances conspire to rob Gertie of her dream and her land.

Clovis finds a job in Detroit and, although Gertie could contentedly wait for him on their farm—her farm, her mother overwhelms Gertie with a sense of her wifely and motherly "duty"; Mrs. Kendrick tells Gertie that she and her children should be with Clovis in Detroit. Gertie's mother has also spoken to Old John Ballew and he dutifully gives Gertie back her money. Gertie goes to Detroit to be with Clovis. A final irony comes when Gertie uses all the money she has saved to buy her farm to buy one small plot of earth in Detroit for Cassie's burial after Cassie dies horribly in a train accident.

The bitterest gall of all, however, comes when Clovis tells Gertie that if he had known she had all that money saved and could have bought the Tipton Place, he would have wanted her to stay in Kentucky on the farm and wait for him to return:

"You've saved onct—we can agin—enough to finish payen fer all this [the hospital bills for Cassie] an git th marker." A look of awe came into his eyes. "Just think, back home when you had all that money saved, an th money yer mom give you from Henley together with all I sent, you must ha had six, seven hunnert dollars. Why, that was enough to buy you a little patch a land like you'd allus wanted. I've heard say," he went on, seeing that she was listening, and glad himself to talk about back home, "that John would ha sold th Tipton Place fer less'n that."

"Why, if I'd ha known you'd ha had all that money, I'd said buy a place an wait fer me." (*TD* 411)

But Clovis's well-intentioned talk hits Gertie like a slap:

> "But you never wanted a farm—Mom didn't want me to—Oh, Lord." After the screaming words she dropped back upon the bed and turned her face to the wall.
>
> He cleared his throat, studied her as she lay with her legs drawn up, her head pulled down as if she would hide herself. "I wanted you to have what you wanted, Gert. It was jist—jist that I didn't see no way a saven up fer a farm, an I hated to see you an th youngens a worken an a heavin', allus a given haf a what you made an—" Her unmoving back silenced him, and he stood a long time looking down at her, but reached at last to pick up her coat.
>
> She turned swiftly, raising her hand as if to strike him, crying: "Git away. I allus thought you'd want my money fer a truck—She'd [Cassie] still been alive." (*TD* 411)

Gertie is shattered not only by the death of her daughter but by the loss of her dream of land, and Clovis's confession just makes the loss even greater.

This devastating scene in which husband and wife wrestle with their deepest emotions throws into stark relief one of the major aspects of their marital relationship, so similar to so many others we have seen: although they do love each other and need each other, and although their ultimate hopes and wishes for their family may be the same—Clovis has honestly desired to provide the best he could for Gertie and his family, as she has—there is nevertheless a great gulf of silence and secrecy between them. Many episodes in the novel illustrate the emotional distance that separates Gertie and Clovis.

At the beginning of the novel, for example, Clovis does not tell Gertie that he intends to go on to Detroit and find a job if the army doesn't take him right away. Instead, after he has already gone there and gotten a job, he writes to Gertie. Later, in Detroit, Clovis hides his involvement with the union from Gertie, shutting her out of this dangerous part of his life. Although he may feel that he is keeping her from worrying and thus sparing her from hurt, Clovis actually causes her greater fear. Likewise, when Clovis buys appliances and other things on credit without consulting Gertie, he is shutting her out of an important part of their life together by denying her right to help make important family decisions. Clovis seems to feel that if he provides materially for Gertie and his family, that will be enough.

Gertie, however, is equally silent and secretive with Clovis, going about her own way without communicating many of her deepest thoughts to him. She, for instance, has secretly saved the money she plans to use to buy the Tipton Place, fearing that Clovis would want to use the money to buy a new truck. In fact, her dream of independence, which the farm symbolizes, is based on the desire for complete freedom and independence, even from Clovis. When she thinks of owning the Tipton Place, she thinks that she "might live and be beholden to no man, not even Clovis" (*TD* 131). Both Gertie and Clovis appear to live in a realm of their own that excludes the other. As we have seen in other Appalachian fiction, this distance between husband and wife creates fear, loneliness and unhappiness.

Reminiscent of Alpha and Brack Baldridge in *River of Earth*, Gertie and Clovis have very different outlooks and appear to want very different things out of life. Whereas Gertie is a farmer who loves the land, Clovis is drawn to machinery and tinkering. Although he tries to make a living through what he loves to do, he is hard pressed to do so. When old John Ballew discusses selling the Tipton Place with Gertie, he puts his finger on Clovis's weakness:

> "Now, Gertie, I know Clovis is gone [to work in Detroit] an you're his wedded wife, an you feel bad an miss him.
> . . . But you ain't no Mamie Childers lost on a little farm 'thout no man. Now, I don't mean a word a harm—an I like Clovis an I hoped they'd leave him. He's got a good turn, an when it comes to tinkeren they ain't nothen on earth he cain't fix. But jist between you an me—an I mean no harm—when he was home he warn't worth a continental to you in th crop maken. His coal haulen wasn't regular, an his tinkeren didn't bring in much. He loved it too well—he'd tear down some feller's old car an set it up agin an mebbe never git paid." (*TD* 105)

Clovis dreams of making money in a factory so that he can support his family, and this is why he goes to Detroit. Gertie, on the other hand, as we have seen, dreams of providing for herself and her family through tilling the soil. When Clovis is gone, Gertie does not for a moment think of joining him in Detroit; that is, until her mother coerces her into doing so through an appeal to her wifely and motherly duty.

Deep down Gertie and Clovis do seem to understand each other. Clovis, for example, knows in his heart that Gertie has always wanted a farm, as illustrated by the excruciating scene in which he tells her he would have wanted her to buy the Tipton Place if he had known she had all the money saved. Gertie also knows that Clovis is driven by different desires. When Clovis writes to her that he has found a job in Detroit, she knows that this is best for Clovis but not for her:

Harriette Simpson Arnow's Mountain Women   153

She felt again the loneliness like an old sorrow. Why couldn't she cry for Clovis the way Sue Annie cried for her daughter? Why couldn't Clovis and she have wanted the same things? He'd wanted Detroit since the beginning of the war. She'd seen it in his eyes when he looked at the signs on the pine trees. He'd made his plans to stay away for true while the war lasted. She couldn't blame him. There wasn't any work here for a man like Clovis—now. (*TD* 120)

Gertie thinks of having her farm and waiting for Clovis to return from Detroit. The great tragedy, however, is that, although they may understand each other's characters on one level, Gertie and Clovis do not understand each other in other ways, nor do they communicate with each other. If Gertie had only told Clovis that she had the money saved to buy the Tipton Place, perhaps many of the tragedies in the novel would have been avoided.

Harriette Arnow herself has spoken of the gulf of secrecy and silence between Gertie and Clovis. States Arnow: "Gertie's big fault, I think, was that she was too secretive. She never told her husband she wanted land or anything else" (Miller interview, 86). Likewise, Wilton Eckley addresses the relationship between Gertie and Clovis when he states:

In the typical hill tradition, Gertie is a dutiful wife to Clovis, and on one level at least he is appreciative enough. Yet it is clear that he really does not know Gertie. Having been exposed to some of the ways of life beyond the hills, he can smile upon her ignorance of coal furnaces and hamburgers and criticize her disheveled condition when he meets her after her trying trip to the doctor with Amos. Not once in the entire novel, however, does he see through with any clarity the crude exterior to the inner strength and sensitivity that is the real Gertie. (*TD* 87)

The difference between Gertie's and Clovis's outlooks is perhaps vividly exemplified in their dreams and hopes. For Gertie the Tipton Place—a farm, land—was heaven, the Promised Land. In Detroit, when Gertie dreams of more than the cramped rooms in which they must live, Clovis angrily responds, "Millions a youngens that has growed up in furnished rooms three floors up ud think a place like this with room fer youngens to play outside an automatic hot water an good furniture was heaven" (*TD* 258).

It seems clear in *The Dollmaker* that Clovis is indeed weaker than Gertie, just as Gertie's father is weaker than her mother. Although Gertie's mother is the sickly one, given to fainting spells and hysteria,

Gertie realized early in her life that her father was the weaker one: "The never spoken knowledge of childhood that her father, not her mother, was the weak and pitiful one, the one who needed help, came back to her, but now as then she could only say nothing of what was in her heart" (*TD* 68). It is perhaps Clovis's weakness that makes him feel that he must provide materially for his family, often overlooking the spiritual and emotional sustenance. As Eckley states:

It is clear from the beginning of the novel that Clovis is not as strong as Gertie. He can, for example, barely look at the hole in Amos's neck—the one cut there by Gertie to save the boy's life—when the danger is past and Amos is recovering. And, indeed, Gertie never tells him that it was she who performed the tracheotomy. In Kentucky, Clovis always demanded more of Gertie than he was able to give in return—and deep down he knows this. There he was nothing but a tinkerer who picked up odd jobs where he could. In Detroit, he was a machine repairman and makes good money! (96)

Gertie's chief characteristics are her endurance and her strength. She is a strong woman who faces everything that comes to her and triumphs. From the first moment at the beginning of the novel when she takes control of the situation and cuts a hole in her son Amos's throat to save his life, to the last moment when, in an act of supreme self-sacrifice, she chops up her prized block of wood that she has been carving,[7] Gertie is the epitome of the mountain woman's strength and courage. In the first scene, after Gertie has ridden her mule into the middle of the road to stop a passing car in order to get Amos, choking with diphtheria, to a doctor, she is forced in perform a tracheotomy in order to save his life. As the two soldiers whose car she has stopped look on, she uses her whittling knife to open Amos's windpipe. When she finally gets Amos to the doctor, one of the soldiers looks at Gertie in awe, and, when she expresses her fear at entering the unfamiliar doctor's office, he says to her, "Lady, you can't be afraid of nothing. Just walk in" (*TD* 27).

Gertie endures tremendous hardships as she must struggle to make a new life for her family in Detroit, from the constant worry of buying things on credit, to the prejudices of her neighbors against "hillbillies," to the death of her daughter Cassie, to her fears for Clovis's involvement in the union. She has also endured disappointment and grief at home in Kentucky—her disappointment at not being able to buy the Tipton Place, and her brother Henley's death. But through it all, she endures. Only once in the novel does she really seem on the verge of defeat—after Cassie's death—but even from this she recovers.

Harriette Simpson Arnow's Mountain Women   155

Most critics of *The Dollmaker* have pointed to Gertie's courage, strength and endurance as major qualities in her character. Dorothy H. Lee states, for example, discussing the final scene in the novel:

What is Arnow's final judgment . . . of Gertie Nevels? If the city is Hell, as has been suggested, its inhabitants are the damned. Myth tells us, however, of an occasional heroic figure who makes the archetypal journey there and returns with a boon. Initially, to consider Gertie, modern protagonist, victim of the mechanized society, in an heroic context appears heretical, but the concept merits consideration. The crucial passage for an interpretation of Gertie's dilemma, stature, and journey is the final sequence in which she fragments the cherry-wood block out of which she has half-carved the face of Christ. She is moved to the act by poverty, by the perception that she can thereby obtain without cost a supply of wood to fulfill an order for numerous mass-produced dolls. Her conversion of her art to commercial purposes has been interpreted as betrayal, a yielding of individualism to mass culture, an evidence of defeat. (96-97)

Lee's answers to these questions affirm her belief that Gertie is not defeated, but instead triumphs through her action of splitting the head of Christ carving: "Harriette Arnow, while relentlessly revealing the physical pain, psychological dissociation, and spiritual void encountered by the mountain woman in urban Hell, pays homage to her moral strength, to her capacity to implement the knowledge she has gained. She is not defeated but has rather taken a step toward spiritual exit from the place of the damned" (98).

Indeed it could be argued that although there are many allusions to Hell in Arnow's descriptions of Detroit, there is also, as Gertie comes to realize, a kind of spiritual bond between the people there which helps to transform the urban Hell into, if not a paradise, at least a world peopled with human beings whom Gertie comes to realize are just like her. Wilton Eckley considers this point:

In Kentucky, Gertie was her own woman; but, more than that, she was the force that held her family together. She knew her husband and each of her children—their strengths, their weaknesses, and their dreams.

Moreover, she knew her own dream—to own the Tipton Place; and, though she might have wondered in Kentucky just as she does in Detroit about the ultimate meaning of life, she always had that dream to sustain her. In Detroit, however, she must find something else for spiritual sustenance; and, when she does, she becomes more than she was in Kentucky. . . . Gertie comes to understand and appreciate people—something that she could never have fully come to in the hills. (99)

Gertie also comes to learn something about the nature of Christ, whose face she has been carving in her block of wood: "In her final symbolic act of splitting the block of wood, she does not destroy her Christ, but brings him alive—for He cannot be abstracted or fixed; He must live in people" (Eckley 100). Gertie's triumph in *The Dollmaker* is a spiritual one as well as a physical one.

Likewise, Lewis A. Lawson sees an affirmative conclusion in Gertie's final action:

> The anticipation of the screaming saw ripping into the block of wood no doubt leaves a lingering image in the minds of many readers. They could be tempted to understand the novel as a naturalistic lament about the destruction of the traditional rural values by the necessary evil of modern technology. Poor, naive, even ignorant Gertie passively awaits her doom in a world in which history has passed her by. But such a reading would be an imposition on the text, for the final tableau is not on the whirling saw, but upon a majestic woman, whose consciousness is beautiful and powerful because of its indebtedness to Biblical imagery, as she stands there, ax in hand, decision made, every bit as forceful as any pioneer who cleared the forests that became the dark fields of the republic....
>
> No wonder that the alley children give a great shout when the block is sundered—it was done for them. (78-79)

Like the symbolism of the red fox, King Devil, in *Hunter's Horn*, the symbolism of the block of wood, from which is emerging at Gertie's hand the head of Christ, has been considered cloudy by some critics.[8] Insofar as Gertie must sacrifice the block of wood, just as she has had to sacrifice her dreams of land by giving up the Tipton Place, the splitting up of the block of wood can be seen as a defeat. But, just as she survives the loss of the Tipton Place and finds in the Detroit alley of Merry Hill another place that becomes her own, so too does she replace the inanimate and enigmatic (Is the head that of Jesus or Judas?) head with real people who become her people. In effect, inanimate art is transformed into animate humanity as Gertie performs her act of sacrifice. Likewise, as Lawson's quotation points out, Gertie is not a passive creature helplessly accepting her fate; she makes an active decision and then never shrinks from it. According to Walter Havighurst, "courage and endurance" characterize Gertie to the very last (12).

Cratis Williams has stated that with her three novels, *Mountain Path*, *Hunter's Horn* and *The Dollmaker*, Harriette Arnow may have written "the finale in fiction of the Southern mountaineer" ("Southern Mountaineer Part IV" 386). As he states,

Other writers attempting to interpret him [the mountaineer] during the past thirty years have dropped without a struggle into historical romance or juvenile fiction after two or three feeble efforts. Although the Southern highlands are dying economically at the present time and are experiencing the most devastating migration in history (nearly four million of a maximum population of eight and a half million in 1940 have migrated), the mountaineer of the 1950s is not readily differentiated as a type from other rural and semirural old-stock Americans. By catching him in the last phases of his older social patterns in *Mountain Path*, presenting him as he wallowed in the agonies of the Great Depression in *Hunter's Horn*, and following him into his social anonymity in *The Dollmaker*, Mrs. Arnow appears to have sounded the death knell at the end of the last act of one of America's most pathetic social tragedies. ("Southern Mountaineer Part IV" 386)

Although Williams may have been premature in sounding the death knell of Appalachian literature (the genre is certainly alive and flourishing today and seems, in fact, to be considerably in vogue), *The Dollmaker* does mark a conclusion to an era of mountain life in literature. The old ways were indeed ending in the 1940s and 1950s. The advent of television democratized American values and ideals and Appalachian America is no longer the isolated region it once was.

As we have seen heretofore in this study, it is the mountain woman who sustains the Appalachian culture, and it is thus fitting that in *The Dollmaker* the emphasis should be on the mountain woman. As Williams states:

Like Murfree, Mrs. Arnow recognizes the woman as the bulwark of mountain society. The symbol of its continuity and the pillar of its support, the woman with her silent suffering, unending toil, enormous strength, and boundless resourcefulness is presented with such strokes of true genius that it is safe to say that no writer of fiction before Mrs. Arnow had ever understood so well the genuine depths of the mountain woman's character nor come so close to rendering a true account of her position at the center of the retarded social order, the burden of which she bears. ("Southern Mountaineer Part IV" 386)

Gertie Nevels is Arnow's major accomplishment—"homely, rawboned, indestructible . . . an embodiment of the mountain folk" (Havighurst 12), a "figure hewn from some matriarchal past" (Baer 26). She emerges from the novel as an almost mythic creature, the epitome of Appalachian womanhood.

Notes

Introduction

1. In more recent fiction, likewise, the woman's bond with the land continues to be a part of her characterization. In Wilma Dykeman's *The Far Family* (1966), for example, the name of the main character, Ivy, suggests, like Anne W. Armstrong's Ivy Ingoldsby, that her strength and resilience come from the earth. Ivy's relationship with the land in Dykeman's book is established at the beginning of the novel:

Always in autumn she [Ivy] thought of the farm. No, she did not think of it; she felt it again. The bitter smell of damp leaves, the cry of the blue jay high in the noon sky—any of these or a dozen other sensations could bring the farm into the present; breathe the land to life again; dim the smell of gasoline, the sound of motors, the gleam of chrome and glass . . . the feel of earth, of woods, of weather in the hills, was part of her and would always be part, as indivisibly as skin, as air she breathed. (*The Far Family* New York: Holt, 1966, 2)

Similarly, the main character in Lee Smith's *Fair and Tender Ladies* (New York: Putnam, 1988) is also named Ivy.

2. Roberta Teague Roy discusses the masculine estrangement from the land in "Land and the Southern Appalachian Woman," cited herein.

3. A new direction in this vein is perhaps exemplified by Lee Smith's *Black Mountain Breakdown* (1980), wherein the heroine, Crystal Spangler, a more modern woman growing up in the 1950s and '60s, actually wills herself into a catatonic mental breakdown. Crystal's emotional breakdown appears to be the result of her inability to find a satisfactory "meaning" in life, but could also result from her life as a "new" kind of mountain woman, her inability to cope with many of the attitudes about and attitudes imposed upon women in this new Appalachian culture.

Chapter 1

1. Arnold Toynbee, for example, describes the Appalachian people thus: "The Appalachian mountain people are the American counterparts of the latter-day white barbarians of the Old World: the Rifis and Kaybles and Tuareg, the

Albanians and Caucasians, the Kurds and the Panthans and the Hairy Anu. . . . They are *ci-devant* heirs of the Western Civilization who have relapsed into barbarism under the depressing effects of a challenge which has been inordinately severe" (*A Study of History, Vol. II*, London: Oxford UP, 311-12).

2. Jay B. Hubble, in his comprehensive study *The South in American Literature, 1607-1900* (Durham: Duke UP, 1954) pays scant if any attention to any works of literature dealing with the Appalachian region. To be sure, the scope of his study ends with 1900, but he barely mentions Mary Noailles Murfree and the local colorists who dealt with the mountain region.

3. See, for example, Dwight Billings and David Walls, "Appalachians," in *Harvard Encyclopedia of American Ethnic Groups*, ed. Stephen Therstrom (Cambridge: Belknap P of Harvard U, 1980), 128.

4. If there were those who saw uniformity of culture as the road to a truly national American civilization, there were also those who saw "nationality" in diversity. The local color movement, for example, which exploited regional differences, seems to have had its genesis in the search for national identity. As Benjamin T. Spencer says in *The Quest for Nationality*:

At first glance the regional or local impulse in American letters might seem antithetical to the national. Yet most nineteenth-century American authors did not so construe it.

During the vogue of romanticism before the Civil War [William Gilmore] Simms championed a national literature, but was explicit in pronouncing sectional materials and themes to be the indispensible media for achieving a national utterance. . . . After the war Howells, Garland, Eggleston, Riley and the host of local colorists similarly found no incompatibility in holding at once to a national literary end and a local means. Since America's vastness precludes a representative imaginative grasp in one work, they argued, American literature can be national only in the aggregate of distinctive localized works. (*The Quest for Nationality*, New York: Syracuse UP, 1957, 252-53)

5. See, for example, Bruce Catton's *Terrible Swift Sword* (the second volume in his *Centennial History of the Civil War*, Garden City: Doubleday, 1961-65).

Chapter 2

1. "The Dancin' Party at Harrison's Cove," which was first published in *The Atlantic Monthly* in May 1878 (and was followed by the seven other stories of *In the Tennessee Mountains* by 1884), was not Murfree's first mountain story. As Edd W. Parks states, "she had written and sold mountain stories by 1876, two years before 'The Dancin' Party at Harrison's Cove' appeared in the *Atlantic Monthly*" (Parks, *Charles Egbert Craddock* [Chapel Hill: U of North Carolina P, 1941], 74-76).

160 Notes to Chapter 2

2. Not only did *The Prophet of the Great Smoky Mountains* produce a "literary sensation" in 1885, but also the revelation that Charles Egbert Craddock, by then a renowned author, was actually Mary Noailles Murfree, a woman.

3. When viewed in the light of local colorism and its presumed relationship to the realistic mode in American literature, the writings of Mary Murfree present a critical problem. There is considerable scholarly disagreement over whether Murfree's works are closer to the realistic or to the romantic mode of literature. Perhaps the question of romance or realism is inherent in the nature of local color writing itself. Local color literature was characterized by an emphasis on the peculiarities of certain sections of the nation, particularly ways of life that were disappearing or had already vanished in America.

4. Plots involving romance between cultured outsiders and mountain girls (always men falling in love with women) had been used before Murfree. John Esten Cooke, for example, had used this device in his story "Owlet" (1878), wherein the narrator, a sophisticated outsider, falls in love with the beautiful, half-wild mountain girl Owlet, and in "Moonshiners" (*Harper's Magazine* 58 [Feb. 1879: 380-90]), wherein New Yorker John Norcross falls in love with Conny Neal, the moonshiner's daughter. Cooke also used this plot in his novel *The Virginia Bohemians* (1880): Mr. Elliott, a city man, falls in love with Nelly Welles, a mountain girl. One of the most notable successors to Murfree to use this plot in mountain fiction was John Fox, Jr., in *The Trail of the Lonesome Pine* (1908).

5. Edd Winfield Parks, notably, sees "The Star in the Valley" and "The Romance of Sunrise Rock" as two of Murfree's weakest stories. Comparing "The Star in the Valley" to "The Dancin' Party at Harrison's Cove," Parks asserts: "'The Star in the Valley' is of weaker stuff"; the story "falls to pieces" with Celia's fifteen-mile journey through the snow and Chevis's inability to forget her. "The story goes nowhere," says Parks: "Presumably Celia had died of a broken heart; perhaps simply from prosaic tuberculosis. All is pathos and that all unreal. One can hardly credit this story with doing much more than living up to the usual formulae of local color" (95-96). In a footnote, however, he states: "It is only fair to note that 'The Star in the Valley' was very popular" (96). "The Romance of Sunrise Rock," says Parks, is "by far the weakest in this series" (98).

6. Murfree's young women are certainly willful and outspoken when the need arises, and they show independence and courage. Clarsie Giles, for example, in "The 'Harnt' That Walks Chilhowie," is described by her father as "a likely enough gal. But she air mighty sot ter hevin' her own way. An' ef 't ain't give ter her peaceable-like, she jes' takes it, whether or no" (*ITM* 286). Likewise, Cynthia Ware is the scandal of the community because of her independent journey into the lowlands in order to secure Vander Price's pardon in "Drifting Down Lost Creek."

7. Isabella D. Harris, for example, speaks of Murfree's long descriptive passages:

Enthusiasm for scenery was both the charm and the curse of Miss Murfree's fiction. Seven of the eight stories in her first book [*In the Tennessee Mountains*] contained long accounts of scenery. In the three hundred pages, there were eighty-nine descriptive passages averaging a paragraph in length. Monotony was un-avoidable.... The author was accused of "hauling the moon over the Tennessee mountains too often and too lingeringly." ... Worse than the length of the descriptions was the pedantic language: words like *amethystine, matutinous, sibilant, saltatory*, and *serpentine*; or a passage such as "the sky of a delicate amber tint with scarlet strata, amongst which incongruous gorgeousness the evening star would shine with a pure, a pensive radiance." (103-04)

8. In addition to the suggested associations of the mountain woman with the positive archetypal mother figure in Hestia, in Murfree's works (and in most later fiction depicting mountain women) the mountain woman is also associated with the goddess Demeter through descriptions that link her with nature and the natural world. Demeter, like Hestia, is a positive maternal figure; she is, in fact, "the Matriarchal mother" (Bernikow 29). Demeter is the embodiment of matriarchal values, and one of her chief characteristics in myth is her alliance with the natural world, particularly agricultural life.

9. Murfree's descriptions of mountain women are always filled with multiple suggestions: associations with nature; descriptions of their eyes, one of the chief ways in which she characterizes them, which are always "opalescent," "luminous," "bright," "shining"; and often suggestions of Arcadian worlds, as in this passage where Cynthia is not only associated with nature through the red-bird imagery, but also with the Indian, the "noble savage."

10. Clarsie can be seen as the prototype of Ellie Mae Clampett of *The Beverly Hillbillies*. Ellie Mae, like Clarsie, is surrounded by her "critters" and is even able to communicate with them, thus showing her affinity with the natural world.

11. I use the word "sentimental" cautiously here. As Joan Schulz has stated regarding the use of the term, particularly as it is used to describe regional women authors: "*Sentimental*—that buzz word used to discredit 19th-century writers. How often it comes up. While 'lady poets and novelists,' as they are called in the later 19th century, 'still drip with sentiment,' in Random House [the Random House *Anthology of American Literature*], the *he's* are 'pioneering' modern literature.... Frankly, I'm puzzled as to what definition of 'sentimental' this author has in mind.... My point is that 'sentimental' is a catchall word, applied somewhat indiscriminately to women and designed to remind us that women don't write 'real' literature—that is, significant, mainstream American, universal literature worthy of canonization" (Fetterley and Schulz 11).

12. H.R. Stoneback devotes a great deal of his chapter on Murfree in his dissertation to a discussion of the comparison between the industrialized world and the mountain world, in connection with the encroachment of the former on the latter—the "machine in the garden" motif. (See particularly 107ff.)

13. The mountaineers' attachment to place can easily be seen in the relationship between urban Appalachians and their mountain homes. Even though they may have lived in the city for most of their lives, first generation Appalachian migrants always refer to their hometowns or home counties in the mountains as "home," and even second- and third-generation Appalachians sometimes refer to these mountain localities as home. Likewise, Appalachians in the cities take every opportunity possible to "go back home."

14. As H.R. Stoneback points out in his excellent discussion of the log cabin as a feature of mountain literature, "Much as Hawthorne had done in 'The Ambitious Guest,' Mary Murfree repeatedly burdens her log-cabin imagery with the task of capsulizing the experience of life in the hills" (104). The log cabin, he says, "becomes in Miss Murfree's works an ideal image of the home and the family, or, in a broader sense an ideal image of community" (104-05). Stoneback also sees Murfree's symbolism of the log cabin as revealing an implicit contrast between life in the mountains, with its stability and security, and the turbulent and insecure life outside. Stoneback suggests, Murfree "half-consciously employed the log-cabin image and the mountain world that went with it as a bulwark against an increasingly fragmented world" and "was grounding herself against an increasingly industrialized and bewildering world outside the mountains, a world more and more resembling what Henry Adams was soon to call a 'multiverse'" (106). Thus, Stoneback sees Murfree's log cabin as a "symbol of rootedness and security amid her own and the nation's dizzying mobility and insecurity" (105-06).

15. Mary Nilles asserts of Murfree's women characters:

Most females in *In the Tennessee Mountains,* and in the body of Miss Murfree's writing, lack psychological complexity, variety and the potential to sustain lasting interest. They represent a type of womanhood popular in Southern fiction during Miss Murfree's era, but remain highly unbelievable as "real" persons. . . . These beautiful, sometimes stubbornly determined, but always resigned females enjoyed no deep emotionally or psychologically realistic relationships with males. Their masculine counterparts hunted, fished, made moonshine, or happily loafed away hours, forgetful of any familial responsibilities. Meanwhile, Murfree's young girls pined for them, defended their name and vowed them fidelity; the older, tired but stoic wives cared for an often shabby house and their brood of children; old crones, almost free of the ravages of overwork and loneliness, made witty but caustic comments about life, love and marriage in the mountains. . . . Most of these women did not develop close relationships with other females either, and lived their sheltered lives secure within the vogue of romanticism. (77)

Chapter 3

1. Murfree was by no means the only author writing about the mountain people during the late nineteenth century. Numerous stories containing mountaineers as characters, whether in major or minor roles, appeared during the last quarter of the century in the new middle-class magazines. Among those local colorists whose stories reached a wide audience through these magazines were: Porte Crayon ("The Mountains," *Harper's New Monthly Magazine* 1872); Rebecca Harding Davis ("The Rose of Carolina," *Scribner's Monthly* 1874) and "Qualla," in *Lippincott's Magazine*, 1875; "Effie," *Peterson's Magazine* 1876; and "His Great Deed," *Lippincott's* 1877); Frances Hodgson Burnett ("Seth," *Lippincott's Magazine* 1877; "Esmeralda" and "Lodusky," *Scribner's Monthly* 1877); John Esten Cooke ("Owlet," *Harper's New Monthly Magazine* 1878); Julia Schayer ("Molly," *Scribner's* 1878); and Constance Fenimore Woolson ("Up in the Blue Ridge," *Appleton's Journal* 1878).

2. Says Henry Shapiro:

It was no accident that the northern churches began work in the southern Appalachian mountains at a time when the popularity of Murfree was at its height, or that *In the Tennessee Mountains* was used as a first mission-study text for those who wished to understand conditions in the region. The interest in Appalachia generated by the descriptions of the local colorists was consciously used by the agents of denominational work in the region to support their claim to attention from the churches' boards and societies, and to financial support from their membership, while the very existence of a substantial body of literature describing a strange land and peculiar people in the southern mountains lent credence to their assertions of "Appalachian otherness." (57)

3. It was also the year that saw the founding of the *Arena*, a muckraking magazine that disseminated reform propaganda and suggested the reform spirit that seized the nation in the last part of the nineteenth century, perhaps one of the chief reasons for the increase in emphasis on the worst aspects of many American regions and institutions.

4. The Tennessee mountains, Murfree's domain, were written about by two other native Tennesseans during this period, though neither was a native mountaineer. Will Allen Dromgoole wrote several stories depicting mountain life. After 1889 and her story "The Double Establishment," most of these showed the worst of mountain life. Sarah Barnwell Elliott's *The Durket Sperret: A Novel* (1897) likewise dealt with the Tennessee mountaineers. Both Dromgoole and

Elliott were reformers, both also concerned with women's suffrage and the conditions of women's lives. Thus, they often painted the lives of Appalachian women as exceedingly bleak in order to gain sympathy for reforms. The mountains of North Carolina, particularly around Asheville, which, as a summer resort, had attracted local color writers, was the setting of Sallie O'Hear Dickson's *The Story of Marthy* (1898) and *Reuben Dalton, Preacher* (1900) and Maria Louise Pool's *In Buncombe County* (1896). Pool was a New England journalist. Will N. Harben, a native of the mountains of northern Georgia, wrote about his region in *Northern Georgia Sketches* (1900). And Waitman Barbe, a professor at West Virginia University, wrote about the West Virginia mountaineers in several stories in *In the Virginias: Stories and Sketches* (1896).

5. Carvel Collins states that this theme "shows the unromantic nature of much mountain fiction in the nineties" (75).

6. Born in Canada in 1884, Edith Summers was the daughter of Scottish immigrants. Following her graduation from the University of Toronto, she went to New York, where, by a chance answering of a newspaper advertisement, she became the secretary for Upton Sinclair. She was his secretary during the Hellicon Hall experimental community days, and met many of the intellectuals, writers and professional women who were members of the community (including Alice McGowan, Grace McGowan Cooke, Anna Noyes, Frances Maule, Helen Montague, and Stella Cominski). Here she also met Sinclair Lewis, to whom she was briefly engaged. In 1908, following the burning of Hellicon Hall, Edith married Allen Updegraff, another member of the Hellicon Hall community. Little is known about their life together, and they were divorced in 1913. At this time Edith was living in Greenwich Village, where socialism and feminism were being promoted by many of the Villagers, including Henrietta Rodman, Margaret Sanger and Susan Glaspell.

In Greenwich Village Edith met Fred C. Kelley, an artist, and after divorcing Updegraff, she and Kelley were married. In 1914 they decided to try tobacco farming in Kentucky. They stayed there for two years but failed to make a profit on their farm, tried farming in New Jersey, and finally in 1920 moved once more, this time to Imperial Valley, California, again as farmers. It was there that Edith wrote *Weeds*, based on her life among the farmers of Scott County, Kentucky. Her friends, Floyd Dell, Sinclair Lewis and Upton Sinclair, helped Kelley get the novel published and then helped to promote it.

7. Although the hardships of women's lives are stressed in *Weeds*, Kelley depicts all mountaineers in a negative way. In a descriptive passage similar to this one of the mountain women, the mountain men are shown:

> The men who swarmed after Obe to the barn looked like a throng of animated scarecrows. Unlike the women, they had not dressed for the occasion; but had come in the clothes in which they had been following the plow or hauling

out manure into the tobacco ground. Their ancient garments, mostly bleached to a common drabness by exposure to rain and sun, were torn and patched in the most unexpected places. Long, straggly hair hung about the filthy necks and ears and over the frayed collars. There were gaunt, gawky bodies, small shriveled, distorted bodies, bent shoulders, slouching legs, and shambling feet. The faces, most of them with weirdly assorted features, were skinny, pinched, and bleary-eyed. Only a few of the young men were straight and shone out healthy and wholesome from their dingy clothes. (108-09)

Likewise, Kelley is able to find some sympathy for the hard work these men must do in order to survive even marginally.

    8. A letter from Kelley to Lewis dated 29 May 1922, courtesy of Patrick Kelley and quoted in Charlotte Goodman's "Afterword" to *Weeds*.

    9. Judith has been compared to Sinclair Lewis's "trapped protagonist" Carol Kennicott in *Main Street*, which was published shortly before *Weeds* (Goodman, "Afterword" to *Weeds* 359). It would also be interesting to compare Judith with Emma Bovary in Flaubert's *Madame Bovary* or Sue Bridehead in Thomas Hardy's *Jude the Obscure*.

    10. Like Edith Summers Kelley, Armstrong was an outsider to the Appalachian region, although she, also like Kelley, lived for some time among the mountain people. Born in Grand Rapids, Michigan, in 1872, Armstrong spent some of her childhood in Knoxville, Tennessee, an urban center in the Appalachian region. She retired in her later years to the Big Creek section of Sullivan County, Tennessee, the setting of *This Day and Time,* following an illustrious career in business. She served as the personnel director of National City Company from 1918-19 and as an assistant manager of industrial relations for the Eastman Kodak Company from 1919-23. She was the first woman to lecture before the Amos Tuck School of Business at Dartmouth College and the Harvard School of Business Administration. She was educated at Mt. Holyoke College in Massachusetts and at the University of Chicago. She also lived in Bristol, Tennessee, Lafayette, Louisiana, and Asheville, North Carolina before finally settling down in the later 1940s at the Barter Inn in Abingdon, Virginia, where she lived until her death in 1958. Also like Kelley, Armstrong has not received the critical attention she deserves, although she too has been rediscovered in recent years. A new edition of *This Day and Time* was published in 1970, and Cratis Williams lists the novel as one of the ten books that those interested in Appalachian literature should read. (Information about Armstrong's life comes from "A Note on the Life and Works of Anne W. Armstrong," in Anne W. Armstrong, *This Day and Time* [1930; rpt. Johnson City, TN: Research Advisory Council, East Tennessee SU, 1970], ix.)

    11. The remarriage of a mountain man shortly after the death of his wife is a recurring pattern in mountain literature. It will be noted, for example, that

Judith Pippinger's father in *Weeds* married a second time within a year of his first wife's death.

12. In her non-fiction article "The Southern Mountaineers," Armstrong speaks of the "general lowering of such none-too-high social standards as [the mountain people] possessed" and then continues:

This charge, along with some others, will be indignantly denied by those who seek persistently to "prettify" the Southern mountaineer at any cost. Yet any real probing of mountain life will uncover by no means rare instances of such crimes as infanticide—of mountain girls burying at the foot of the family chimney babies which they had put out of the way. (546)

13. In this respect the ending of *This Day and Time* can be compared to the ending of Harriette Arnow's *The Dollmaker*. In both cases, the heroine, after enduring great hardship and tragedy, still retains an optimism that is manifested in her belief in the inherent goodness of people.

Chapter 4

1. Williams further states: "Although touches of realism in the newer fiction had been given to the Southern Highlander by Elizabeth Madox Roberts in *The Time of Man* (1926), and in one or two of the more recent novels of Charles Neville Buck, and in T.S. Stribling's *Bright Metal* (1928), realism in the contemporary sense of the word was first introduced into the treatment of Southern hill people by Fiswoode Tarleton in *Bloody Ground: A Cycle of the Hills* in 1928" (347).

2. Perhaps Campbell's and Kephart's works were more widely known and regarded than Miles's because they were more compatible with the general notions of reform current in the 1920s and 1930s.

3. David E. Whisnant states in his introduction to the Tennesseeana edition of *The Spirit of the Mountains*:

Emma Bell Miles's life was lived mainly with her husband and his people, but she was also an intellectual, an artist, and a writer whose need for an audience, a market, and personal support drew her into the lives of quite a different set of people. For years she was the darling of the wealthy and socially prominent of Chattanooga. They displayed her paintings and illustrated books in their homes, paid her to paint murals on the walls of their drawing rooms, lamented what they considered the bad judgment that led her to marry a mountain man from Walden's Ridge, and sheltered her as she made her way back and forth between the intellectually and emotionally impoverished drudgery of life in a tumble-down cabin on the ridge, and the solitary comfort of private homes and spartan rented rooms in town, where she could paint and write and attend concerts and lectures. (xxi)

Other information about Miles's life is also from Whisnant's Introduction.

    4. In his discussion of Stuart as a poet, John Howard Spurlock states:

> With the publication of *Man With a Bull-Tongue Plow* (a collection of 703 sonnets) in 1934, Jesse Stuart achieved instant fame. But, as has been typical with Stuart's work, the reviews were mixed. When Mark Van Doren, for example, praised Stuart as "an American Burns," Louis Untermeyer resented the comparison, maintaining that Stuart's lyricism had none of the careful planning characteristic of Burns. . . . The high, or low, point in this critical tradition was reached when John Gould Fletcher rejected the Burns comparison. Stuart is nothing like Burns, Fletcher maintained, because Burns had behind him "a wealth of folk song, old minstrelsy, and rough ballad-making," whereas the Kentucky poet wrote from no tradition at all and, besides, knew nothing of the poet's craft. Fletcher's appraisal shows an almost complete ignorance about Appalachia and about his subject's life. (129-30)

    5. Ruel E. Foster, in fact, goes so far as to describe the mountains themselves as "masculine" in Stuart's works.

    6. In his essay discussing the characteristic elements of Stuart's novels, for example, John T. Flannagan does not even mention Stuart's women characters, although he does discuss the males, the boy narrators and protagonists (81).

    7. Stuart's mother is described in similar terms in a poem addressed to Stuart's deceased maternal grandmother, Violet Hylton, also showing his awareness of his grandmother's life:

> Violet, your youngest daughter is my mother,
> And same as you she loves the wind and sun and rain;
> Not fair as you, but brown-skinned is my mother
> And she hoes in tobacco, corn and cane.
> She loves music and taste of sweet rich wines;
> She loves the good earth and the fields and brooks;
> She loves the starlight hanging through the pines;
> She does not care for cold stone streets and books.
> She loves to work—get out in fields and work;
> She knows all wild plants growing in the woods;
> She loves to dig her hands into the dirt—
> She loves red evening clouds and solitudes—
> She takes her time and lives close to the soil;
> She finds sweetness in wild labor and toil.
> (Poem 308, 161)
> Reprinted with the permission of the Jesse Stuart Foundation.

This poem reiterates his mother's love of working in the fields and her enjoyment of labor.

8. Anse feels that in order to own the land he must subdue and conquer it, and he spends the greater part of his life, even to old age, doing just that. The Tussies, on the other hand, Boliver especially in contrast to Anse, believe that they own the land through a spiritual communion with it. The novel depicts the struggle between these two opposing forces, and Anse eventually realizes that there *is* something in the squatters' relationship to the land. Following a spiritual and religious conversion resulting from being struck by a falling tree, Anse relents in his hatred of the Tussies and realizes that the Tussies belong to the land as much as (or even more than) he does. As he tells Tarvin: "Boliver belongs to the land. He belongs on this farm. I've just been thinkin it over. Boliver hast his faults but he belongs to the dirt same as I belong to the dirt and same as you belong to the dirt—same as the grass, weeds, corn, cane and terbacker belong to the dirt. And Boliver belongs to this dirt" (333).

9. Leavell also states: "perhaps Fronnie sees salvation only in terms of the hereafter [referring to Fronnie's religious fanaticism] because she has known only dreary toil in this life. . . ." (65).

10. In discussing the patriarchal nature of Appalachian culture, Spurlock sees much violence arising from the "intense emphasis on maleness" (85), the "subculture's emphasis upon the male as a potentially explosive individual—ready at all times to take issue with any slights to his honor" (88).

11. One of Fronnie's greatest pleasures in life is dancing. A scene at a party, for example, is described:

"But when that music starts," says Anse, "your Ma's feet will begin workin like they ust to when she's a pert young gal. I know her."
"Is that right, Ma?" Tarvin hollers to Fronnie.
"Is what right?" Fronnie asks. "What air you talking about?"
"Pa said your feet would start workin when you heerd the music tonight."
"Guess he's right," says Fronnie. "When I hear music, I want to dance. I haf to dance. I can't hep how tired I am. I was born to dance, to bear children and to work, I guess." (59)

Chapter 5

1. For an interesting interpretation and discussion of "Mrs. Razor," see Joyce Hancock, "Fiction and Creative Energy in James Still's 'Mrs. Razor.'"

2. It is an interesting facet of the native writers' works that they appear to contain much more of the universal—perhaps archetypal—in their depictions of the mountain people than the non-native writers. This may be because they were writing from their own experience, going beneath the surface peculiarities that non-native writers observed. It may also arise from their native oral literary tradition. Mildred Haun, a contemporary of Stuart and Still, is an

excellent example of a native writer who utilized the oral tradition in her short story collection *The Hawk's Done Gone and Other Stories* (1940).

3. In this same vein, Cratis Williams has said, "Like many of the characters in the fiction of Robert Penn Warren, Still's boys are young Adams moving from innocence into the knowledge of sin, desperation, and death" ("Southern Mountaineer Part II" 367).

4. This recognition of their mothers' hardships by Tarvin and the narrator of *River of Earth* shows a new awareness on the native writers' part of women's status and roles in the mountains. Women's work is acknowledged and appreciated from the perspective of the "insider."

5. See also G.O. Gunter, "The Archetypal Trickster Figure in James Still's *River of Earth*," and Cratis Williams, "The Southern Mountaineer in Fact and Fiction Part IV," 367, for further discussion of Uncle Jolly as a trickster figure.

6. See also Stoneback, 190-92 for a further discussion of the machine-in-the-garden motif in *River of Earth*.

7. Sidney S. Farr has also commented on the life/death rites in Appalachian literature in relation to *River of Earth*. She says:

What has been called the life/death rites, the closeness to both life and death, the supernatural feelings, can be found in all three characters [Grandma Middleton, Alpha, and Euly]. Grandma Middleton was proud that none of her sons had ever taken a life. Euly had an intense emotional reaction when she found the four baby rabbits in the mother's womb and ran away to weep all day in the stubble and vowed to never eat wild meat again. Alpha grieved for her dead baby and determined that he should have a proper funeral. ("The Appalachian Woman" 61)

8. Briley discusses the "mythic consciousness" in Still's works, and relates the boy narrator's journey to awareness to the "recurrence of mythic movement which pulsates and throbs in the very veins of existence in Appalachia" (45). Her description of the mythic journey, following the pattern of "a separation from the domestic security which [the questor] has known, a penetration into some source of natural or spiritual power of knowledge, and a life-enhancing return to the original world" (66), is closely related to the mythic quest of the Romantic poets and therefore bears some relation to H.R. Stoneback's central premise in his dissertation. The same kind of discussion about the mythic dimensions of the boy's experience is presented in the commentary on *River of Earth* in *Masterplots*:

Still's richly evocative style, particularly the sensuousness of his imagery, brings to stirring life the full range of a young boy's introduction to experience. The anonymity of the boy narrator (we never learn his Christian name) adds to the mythic dimension of his point of view. He recalls Wordsworth's persona in the early books of the poet's famous autobiography in verse, *The Prelude*: raised by the "ministries of beauty and fear," like the young Wordsworth, Brack's "boy" is initiated into the fullness of nature. (Magill 5631)

It is also quite interesting in light of further discussion in the text herein that Briley sees the earth and land itself as "the central core of [the boy's] quest" (67), for the earth is clearly associated with the feminine in the novel.

Chapter 6

1. Arnow dislikes labels. When asked if she felt comfortable being labeled as a regional or ethnic writer, an Appalachian writer, or a women's writer, she replied, "I suppose I'd rather be referred to as a writer" (Miller interview 93).

2. Cratis Williams comments on Arnow's trilogy: "Like Stuart and Still, Mrs. Arnow captures the contemporary mountaineer in his struggle with the vicissitudes and uncertainties of an economy and a social order to which he has but recently been introduced and for which he has not been adequately prepared" (386).

3. There is an apparent discrepancy in the date of Arnow's graduation from the University of Louisville. Glenda Hobbs states that she received her B.S. degree in 1930 (67). Sheila Raeschild states that she received the B.S. in 1931 (55).

4. Both *The Weedkiller's Daughter* and the *Kentucky Trace* received poor reviews. Arnow herself says of the books: "Well, one of them, *Kentucky Trace*, did all right, but *The Weedkiller's Daughter* didn't get many reviews. Nobody seemed to like it" (Miller interview 85).

5. Nunn's obsession with killing King Devil has been compared to Ahab's pursuit of Moby Dick. Glenda Hobbs, for example, states: "The story of a hill farmer's obsessive chase after an elusive red fox, *Hunter's Horn* dramatizes the cost of a compulsion as maniacal and as mythic as Ahab's stalking of Moby Dick" (68).

6. West states: "What a pity then that after developing this motif during the greater portion of the novel (and it is developed with a multitude of amazing and interesting variations) Mrs. Arnow allows the final pages of her book to dwindle into inconclusiveness. The fox is killed, not by Nunn, but ironically and accidentally by his wife [this is not exactly correct] when she has gone to assist an old midwife at the birth of a child; and the fox turns out to be not a *King Devil*, but a vixen with puppies. The threat which had hovered over the narrative is removed. Nunn makes good his promise to give up hunting, sells his dogs for a fabulous sum, enough to stock his farm with many of the things he had needed to make it successful, learns all there is to know of government assistance, and even condemns his daughter to an unhappy marriage.

The failure of the symbolism in *Hunter's Horn* is particularly significant, because one feels that it represents a singular confusion in the mind of the author." (692)

7. Gertie's self-sacrifice here could be compared to Christ's. See Danny Miller, "'For a living dog is better than a dead lion': Harriette Arnow as Religious Writer," *South Atlantic Review* 60.1 (Jan. 1995): 29-42.

8. See, for example, Walter Havighurst's discussion in "Hillbilly D. P.'s," 12.

Works Cited

Armstrong, Anne W. "The Southern Mountaineers." *The Yale Review* ns 24 (1935): 539-54.

——. *This Day and Time*. 1930. Johnson City: Research and Advisory Council, East Tennessee State U, 1970.

Arnow, Harriette Simpson. *The Dollmaker*. 1954. New York: Macmillan, 1970.

——. *Hunter's Horn*. 1949. New York: Avon, 1979.

——. *Mountain Path*. New York: Covici-Friede, 1936.

Baer, Barbara. "Harriette Arnow's Chronicles of Destruction." *Appalachian Heritage* 6.1 (Winter 1978): 23-29.

Barbe, Waitman. *In the Virginias: Stories and Sketches*. Akron: Werner, 1896.

Benet, Stephen Vincent. "Review of *River of Earth*." *Books* 4 Feb. 1940: 4.

Bernikow, Louise. *Among Women*. New York: Harmony, 1980.

Billings, Dwight, and David Walls. "Appalachians." *Harvard Encyclopedia of American Ethnic Groups*. Ed. Stephan Thernstrom. Cambridge: Belknap P of Harvard U, 1980.

Briley, Rebecca. "River of Earth: Mythic Consciousness in the Works of James Still." *Appalachian Heritage* 9.3 (Summer 1981): 51-55.

Burnett, Frances Hodgson. "Esmeralda." *Scribner's Monthly* 14 (May 1877): 80-91.

——. "Lodusky." *Scribner's Monthly* Sept. 1877: 273-87.

——. "Seth." *Lippincott's Magazine* Mar. 1877: 296-307.

Campbell, John C. *The Southern Highlander and His Homeland*. New York: Russell Sage Foundation, 1921.

Cary, Richard. *Mary N. Murfree*. New York: Twayne, 1967.

Catton, Bruce. *Terrible Swift Sword*. Garden City: Doubleday, 1961.

Caudill, Harry M. *Night Comes to the Cumberlands: A Biography of a Depressed Area*. Boston: Little Brown and Co., 1962.

Collins, Carvel. "The Literary Tradition of the Southern Mountaineer, 1824-1900." Diss. U of Chicago, 1944.

Cooke, John Esten. "Owlet." *Harper's New Monthly Magazine* July 1878: 199-211.

Crayon, Porte [pseudonym of David Hunter Strother]. "The Mountains." *Harper's New Monthly Magazine* Apr. 1872: 659-75; May 1872: 801-15; June 1872: 21-34; Aug. 1872: 347-61; Sept. 1872: 502-16; Nov. 1872:

801-15; Apr. 1873: 669-80; Nov. 1873: 821-32; July 1874: 156-67; Sept. 1875: 475-85.

Davis, Rebecca Harding. "Effie." *Peterson's Magazine* Jan. 1876: 61-66.

——. "His Great Deed." *Lippincott's Magazine* Sept. 1878: 343-54.

——. "Qualla." *Lippincott's Magazine* Nov. 1875: 576-80.

——. "The Rose of Carolina." *Scribner's Monthly* May 1874-Oct. 1874: 723-26.

Dickson, Sallie O'Hear. *Reuben Dalton, Preacher* (1900).

——. *The Story of Marthy*. Richmond: Presbyterian Committee of Publications, 1898.

Dromgoole, Will Allen "The Double Establishment." *The Youths Companion* 28 Feb. 1889: 109.

Eckley, Wilton. *Harriette Arnow*. New York: Twayne, 1974.

Elliott, Sarah Barnwell. *The Durket Sperret: A Novel*. New York: Holt, 1898.

Farr, Sidney S. "The Apalachian Woman as Portrayed by James Still in *River of Earth*." *Appalachian Heritage* 4.2 (Spring 1976): 55-61.

Fetterley, Judith, and Joan Schulz. "A MELUS Dialogue: The Status of Women Authors in American Literature Anthologies." MELUS 9.3 (Winter 1982): 3-17.

Flanagan, John T. "Jesse Stuart: Regional Novelist." *Jesse Stuart: Essays on His Work*. Ed. J.R. LeMaster and Mary Washington Clarke. Lexington: UP of Kentucky, 1977. 70-88.

Foster, Ruel E. "The Short Stories of Jesse Stuart." *Jesse Stuart: Essays on His Work*. Ed. J.R. LeMaster and Mary Washington Clarke. Lexington: UP of Kentucky, 1977. 40-53.

Fox, John, Jr. "The Southern Mountaineer." *Scribner's Magazine* Apr.-May 1901: 387-99, 556-70.

Frost, William Goodell. "Our Contemporary Ancestors in the Southern Mountains." *Atlantic* (Mar. 1899): 311-19.

Gold, William Jay. "Annals of the Poor." Rev. of *River of Earth* by James Still. *The Saturday Review* 3 Feb. 1940: 6.

Goodman, Charlotte. Afterword. *Weeds*. By Edith Summers Kelley. 1923. Old Westbury: Feminist Press, 1982.

Griffin, Susan. *Woman and Nature: The Roaring Inside Her*. New York: Harper Colophon, 1978.

Gunter, G.O. "The Archetypal Trickster Figure in James Still's *River of Earth*." *Appalachian Heritage* 7.4 (Fall 1979): 52-55.

Hancock, Joyce. "Fiction and Creative Energy in James Still's 'Mrs. Razor.'" *Appalachian Heritage* 8.12 (Spring 1980): 38-46.

Harben, Will N. *Northern Georgia Sketches*. Chicago: McClung, 1900.

Harris, Isabella D. "The Southern Mountaineer in American Fiction, 1824-1910." Diss. Duke U, 1948.

Hass, Victor P. "A Way of Life Down South." *The Saturday Review* 25 June

1949: 20.

Haun, Mildred. *The Hawk's Done Gone, and Other Stories.* 1940. Nashville: Vanderbilt UP, 1968.

Havighurst, Walter. "Hillbilly D.P.'s." *The Saturday Review* 24 Apr. 1954: 12.

Higgs, Robert J. "Hicks, Hillbillies, Hell-Raisers, and Heroes: Traditional Mythic Types in Southern Appalachia." *Appalachian Literature: Critical Essays.* Ed. Ruel E. Foster. Charleston: MHC [Morris Harvey College], 1976. 1-11.

Hobbs, Glenda. "Harriette Louisa Simpson Arnow." *American Women Writers: A Critical Reference Guide from Colonial Times to the Present.* Ed. Lina Mainiero. 5 vols. New York: Ungar, 1979.

Holman, C. Hugh. *A Handbook to Literature.* 4th ed. Indianapolis: Bobbs-Merrill, 1980.

Hubbell, Jay B. *The South in American Literature, 1607-1900.* Durham: Duke UP, 1954.

Kelley, Edith Summers. *Weeds.* 1923. Old Westbury: Feminist Press, 1982.

Kephart, Horace. *Our Southern Highlanders.* New York: Outing, 1913.

Kohler, Dayton. "Jesse Stuart and James Still: Mountain Regionalists." *College English* 3.6 (1942): 523-33.

Lawson, Lewis A. "The Knife and the Saw in *The Dollmaker*." *Appalachian Heritage* 7.4 (Fall 1979): 69-79.

Leavell, Frank H. "Dualism in Stuart's *Trees of Heaven*." *Jesse Stuart: Essays on His Work.* Ed. J.R. LeMaster and Mary Washington Clarke. Lexington: UP of Kentucky, 1977. 54-69.

Lee, Dorothy H. "Harriette Arnow's *The Dollmaker*: A Journey to Awareness." *Critique: Studies in Modern Fiction* 20 (1978): 92-98.

"M.T.G." "Review of *Mountain Path* by Harriette Simpson." *Mountain Life and Work* Oct. 1936: 28.

Magill, Frank N., ed. "River of Earth." *Masterplots.* Englewood Cliffs: Salem, 1976.

Miles, Emma Bell. *The Spirit of the Mountains.* 1905. Knoxville: U of Tennessee P, 1975.

Miller, Danny. "A MELUS Interview: Harriette Arnow." MELUS 9.2 (Summer 1982): 83-97.

———. "A MELUS Interview: Harriette Dykeman." MELUS 9.3 (Winter 1982): 45-59.

Miller, Jim Wayne. "Appalachian Values/American Values: The Role of Regional Colleges and Universities." *Appalachian Heritage* 5.4 (Fall 1977): 24-32.

Milner, Rosamond. "Harriette Simpson in Her Excellent First Novel Gives New Reality to the Kentucky Mountains." *Louisville (Kentucky) Courier-Journal* 25 Oct. 1936: 5.

Murfree, Mary Noailles (under the pseudonym of Charles Egbert Craddock). *In* the *Tennessee Mountains*. Boston: Houghton, 1884.

—. *The Prophet of the Great Smoky Mountains*. Boston: Houghton, 1885.

Nilles, Mary. "Craddock's Girls: A Look at Some Unliberated Women." *Markham Review* 8 (Oct. 1972): 74-77.

"A Note on the Life and Works of Anne W. Armstrong." *This Day and Time*. By Anne W. Armstrong. 1930. Johnson City: Research and Advisory Council, East Tennessee State U, 1970.

Parks, Edd Winfield. *Charles Egbert Craddock*. Chapel Hill: U of North Carolina P, 1941.

Pool, Maria Louse. *In Buncombe County*. Chicago: Stone, 1896.

Raeschild, Sheila. "Arnow, Harriette (Louisa Simpson)." *Contemporary Novelists*. 2nd ed. Ed. James Vinson. London: St. James, 1976.

Ralph, Julian. "Our Appalachian Americans." *Harper's New Monthly Magazine* June 1903: 32-41.

Roy, Roberta Teague. "Land and the Southern Appalachian Woman: Sensual or Poetic?" *Kentucky Folklore Record* 25.3-4 (July-Dec. 1979): 68-75.

Royall, Anne Newport. *Sketches of History, Life, and Manners in the United States. By a Traveller*. New Haven: privately printed, 1826.

Schayer, Julia. "Molly." *Scribner's Monthly* Sept. 1878: 713-20.

Shapiro, Henry D. *Appalachia On Our Mind: The Southern Mountains and Mountaineers in the American Consciousness, 1870-1900*. Chapel Hill: U of North Carolina P, 1978.

Skaggs, Merrill Maguire. *The Folk of Southern Fiction*. Athens: U of Georgia P, 1972.

Smyth, J.F.S. [John Ferdinand Smyth Stuart]. *A Tour in the United States of America: Containing an Account of the Present Situation of that Country*. 1784. New York: Arno, 1968.

Spence, E.B. "Collected Reminiscences of Mary Noailles Murfree." Masters Thesis Peabody College, 1928.

Spencer, Benjamin T. *The Quest for Nationality: An American Literary Campaign*. New York: Syracuse UP, 1957.

Spurlock, John Howard. *He Sings for Us: A Sociolinguistic Analysis of the Appalachian Subculture and of Jesse Stuart as a Major American Author*. Lanham: UP of America, 1980.

Still, James. "Mrs. Razor." *Pattern of a Man & Other Stories*. Lexington: Gnomon, 1976. 1-6.

—. "The Nest." *Pattern of a Man & Other Stories*. Lexington: Gnomon, 1976. 43-52.

—. *River of Earth*. 1940. Lexington: UP of Kentucky, 1978.

Stoneback, H.R. "The Hillfolk Tradition and Images of the Hillfolk in American Literature Since 1926." Diss. Vanderbilt U, 1970.

Stuart, Jesse. *Man with a Bull-Tongue Plow*. 1934. New York: Dutton, 1959.

—. *Trees of Heaven.* 1940. Lexington: UP of Kentucky, 1980.
Toynbee, Arnold J. *A Study of History. Vol. II.* London: Oxford UP, 1951.
Weller, Jack E. *Yesterday's People: Life in Contemporary Appalachia.* Lexington: U of Kentucky P, 1965.
West, Ray, Jr. "Arts and Letters: Notes on Seven Novels." *Sewanee Review* 57 (1949): 686-97.
Whisnant, David. Introduction. *The Spirit of the Mountains.* By Emma Bell Miles. 1905. Knoxville: U of Tennessee P, 1975.
Williams, Cratis. "The Appalachian Experience." *Appalachian Heritage* 7.2 (Spring 1979): 4-11.
—. "The Southern Mountaineer in Fact and Fiction, Part I." *Appalachian Journal* 3.1 (Autumn 1975): 8-61.
—. The Southern Mountaineer in Fact and Fiction, Part II." *Appalachian Journal* 3.2 (Winter 1976): 100-62.
—. "The Southern Mountaineer in Fact and Fiction, Part IV." *Appalachian Journal* 3.4 (Summer 1976): 334-92.
Williams, Shirley, "Still Writing after All These Years." *Louisville (Kentucky) Courier-Journal* 9 July 1978: 23.
Woolson, Constance Fenimore. "Up in the Blue Ridge." *Appleton's Journal* 5 ns (Aug. 1878): 104-25.

Selected Bibliography

Akers, Donna Gayle. "The Appalachian Woman in Young Adult Literature." BA Thesis James Madison U, 1988.

Chung, Haeja K., ed. *Harriette Simpson Arnow: Critical Essays on Her Work.* Lansing: Michigan State UP, 1995.

Collett, Dexter. *Bibliography of Theses and Dissertations Pertaining to Southern Appalachian Mountain Literature, 1912-1991.* Berea: Appalachian Imprints, 1994.

Day, John F. *Bloody Ground.* With a Foreword by Thomas D. Clark and an Afterword by Harry M. Caudill. 1941. Lexington: UP of Kentucky, 1981.

Dickson, Sallie O'Hear. *The Story of Marthy.* Richmond: Presbyterian Committee of Publications, 1898.

Edwards, Grace Toney. "Emma Bell Miles: Appalachian Author, Artist, and Interpreter of Folk Culture." Diss. U of Virginia, 1981.

Farr, Sidney Saylor. *Appalachian Women: An Annotated Bibliography.* Lexington: UP of Kentucky, 1981.

———. "Appalachian Women in Literature." *Appalachian Heritage* 9.3 (Summer 1981): 10-18.

———. *More Than Moonshine: Appalachian Recipes and Recollections.* Pittsburgh: U of Pittsburgh P, 1983.

Fiene, Judith I. "Snobby People and Just Plain Folks: Social Stratification and Rural, Low-Status, Appalachian Women." *Sociological Spectrum* 10 (Oct.-Dec. 1990): 527-39.

Foster, Ruel E., ed. *Appalachian Literature: Critical Essays.* Charleston: MHC [Morris Harvey College], 1976.

Gagne, Patricia L. "Appalachian Women: Violence and Social Control." *Journal of Contemporary Ethnography* 20 (Jan. 1992): 387-415.

Ganim, Carole. "A Bittersweet Beauty: Mountain Women in the Early Twentieth Century: A Review of *The Spirit of the Mountains* by Emma Bell Miles and *Weeds* by Edith Summers Kelley." *Mountain Review* 2.4 (1976): 46-47.

———. "Herself: Woman and Place in Appalachian Literature." *Appalachian Journal* 13.3 (Spring 1986): 258-74.

Graham, Phyllis Arline. "The Appalachian Woman in Young Adult Literature: A Patchwork." MA Thesis Marshall U, 1991.

Hamm, Mary Margo. *Appalachian Women: An Annotated Bibliography* [S.1.: s.n.] 1994.

Selected Bibliography

Harrison, Elizabeth Jane. *Female Pastoral: Women Writers Re-Visioning the American South*. Knoxville: U of Tennessee P, 1991.

Higgs, Robert J., Ambrose N. Manning, and Jim Wayne Miller, eds. *Appalachia Inside Out: A Sequel to Voices from the Hills*. 2 vols. Knoxville: U of Tennessee P, 1995.

Kahn, Kathy. *Hillbilly Women*. Garden City: Doubleday, 1973.

Kinder, Alice J. *Old-Fashioned Mountain Mothers*. Pikeville: Pikeville College P, 1981.

Lewis, Helen M., and Suzanna O'Donnell, eds. *Telling Our Stories, Sharing Our Lives*. Ivanhoe: Ivanhoe Civic League, 1990.

Lord, Sharon B., and Carolyn Patton-Crowder. *Appalachian Women: A Learning/Teaching Guide*. Newton: Education Development Center, 1979.

Maggard, Sally W. "Will the Real Daisy Mae Please Stand Up? A Methodological Essay on Gender Analysis in Appalachian Research." *Appalachian Journal* 21 (Winter 1994): 136-50.

McCoy, H. Virginia, Diana Trevino, and Clyde B. McCoy. "Appalachian Women: Between Two Cultures." *From Mountain to Metropolis: Appalachian Migrants in American Cities*. Eds. Kathryn M. Borman and Phillip J. Obermiller. Westport: Bergen & Garvey, 1994. 33-48.

McKern, Sharon. *Redneck Mothers, Good Ol' Girls, and Other Southern Belles: A Celebration of the Women of Dixie*. New York: Viking, 1979.

Miller, Danny. "'For a living dog is better than a dead lion': Harriette Arnow as Religious Writer." *South Atlantic Review* 60.1 (Jan. 1995): 29-42.

---. "The Mountain Woman in Fact and Fiction of the Early Twentieth Century." *Appalachian Heritage* (Part I, 6.3 [Summer 1978]: 48-55; Part II, 6.4 [Fall 1978]: 15-21; Part III. 7.1 [Winter 1979]: 66-72).

Miller, Jim Wayne. "Appalachian Literature." *Appalachian Journal* 5.1 (Autumn 1977): 82-91.

---. "A People Waking Up: Appalachian Literature Since 1960." *The Cratis Williams Symposium Proceedings: A Memorial and Examination of the State of Regional Studies in Appalachia*. Boone: Appalachian Consortium, 1990.

Moffitt, Phillip. "The Power of One Woman." *Esquire* Jan. 1985: 11-12.

Morley, Margaret W. *The Carolina Mountains*. Boston: Houghton, 1913.

Pool, Maria Louisa. *Buncombe County*. Chicago: H.S. Stone, 1898.

Raine, James Watt. *The Land of Saddle Bags: A Study of the Mountain People of Appalachia*. 1924. Detroit: Singing Tree, Book Tower, 1969.

Relham, Richard. "Mountain Girls." *Appalachian Heritage* 11.4 (Fall 1983): 4-11.

Sheppard, Muriel Earley. *Cabins in the Laurel*. Chapel Hill: U of North Carolina P, 1935.

Selected Bibliography 179

Shorb, Glenda Norman. "Identity within Nature: Contemporary Women and Their Fictions of Appalachia." MA Thesis Memphis State U, 1987.

Smith, Lee. *Black Mountain Breakdown*. New York: Ballantine, 1980.

Stewart, Kathleen C. "Backtalking the Wilderness: 'Appalachian' Engenderings." *Uncertain Terms: Negotiating Gender in American Culture*. Eds. Faye Ginsburg and Anna Lowenhaupt Tsing. Boston: Beacon, 1990. 43-56.

Still, James. *Sporty Creek*. New York: Putnam, 1977.

Tickamyer, Ann R., and Cecil Tickamyer. "Gender, Family Structure, and Poverty in Central Appalachia." *Appalachia: Social Context Past and Present*. Eds. Bruce Ergood and Bruce E. Kuhre. Dubuque: Kendall/Hunt, 1991. 307-25.

Weatherford, W.D., and Wilma Dykeman. "Literature Since 1900." *The Southern Appalachian Region: A Survey*. Ed. Thomas R. Ford. Lexington: U of Kentucky P, 1962. 259-70.

Welch, Jack. "Maidens, Mothers, and Grannies: Appalachian Women in Literature." *Appalachian Journal* 4.1 (Autumn 1976): 43-44.

Williams, Cratis. "Appalachia in Fiction." *Appalachian Heritage* 4.4 (Fall 1976): 45-56.

Index

affection, demonstrations of 116
Appalachia 15, 17, 31, 38, 51, 55
   definition of 15-17
   independence of people 12, 47
   labels 16
   origins of people 17-19, 54
   paradoxical views toward 14-21
   response to Civil War 19-20
   stereotypes 17, 19
Appalachia Inside Out (Higgs, Manning and Miller) 1
appearance of mountain women
   See physical appearance
Arena 163n. 3
Armstrong, Anne W. 2, 3, 6, 12, 30, 56, 68-77, 95, 158n. 1, 166n. 12, 165n. 10
   This Day and Time 6, 30, 56, 68-76, 95, 127
Arnow, Harriette Simpson 2-3, 6-7, 15, 30, 124-57,
   characterization in works 134, 146
   The Dollmaker 6-8, 10, 12-13, 15, 124-26, 133, 135, 146-58, 166n. 13
   Flowering of the Cumberland 126
   Hunter's Horn 6-8, 10, 12, 30, 124-26, 133-46, 149, 156
   The Kentucky Trace 126, 170n. 4
   Mountain Path 10, 12-13, 125-33, 135-36, 140, 145, 156
   Old Burnside 126
   Seedtime on the Cumberland 126
   The Weedkiller's Daughter 126, 170n. 4

   uncondescending attitude toward Appalachians 134

ballads 19, 87
"baseborn" children
   See illegitimacy
Beersheba Springs Hotel 33
Benet, Stephen Vincent 102
Berea College 16
The Beverly Hillbillies 28, 161n. 10
brutality of mountain men 36, 55, 69, 73-74
Burnett, Frances Hodgson 22, 163n. 1
   Esmeralda (play) 22
   "Esmeralda" (story) 22, 163n. 1
   "Lodusky" 163n. 1
Burns, Robert 89, 167n. 4
Byrd, William, II 28

Campbell, John C. 15, 25, 28-29, 35, 81
   The Southern Highlander and His Homeland 15
canning 12, 70, 136
Caudill, Harry 17-18
   Night Comes to the Cumberlands 17-18
   origins of the mountain people 17-18
Chapman, Maristan 79, 127
children 10, 24, 63, 86, 108, 135
   number of 2, 23, 68, 92, 117
Cincinnati, Ohio 144
city-country contrast 45-48, 52, 70, 74-75, 130-31, 162n. 12

Index 181

city life 3
  See also city-country contrast
Civil War 19-21
class distinctions 95-96, 98
coal mining 6, 108, 111-12, 119
Collins, Carvel 31, 40, 53
communication 8
  See also gulf between men and women
community 11-12, 52
Cooke, John Esten 160n. 4, 163n. 1
  "Owlet" 160n. 4, 163n. 1
corruption by outside world 51, 70
Craddock, Charles Egbert
  See Murfree, Mary Noailles
cyclical patterns of life 11, 100, 107-8, 114, 117, 121, 169n. 7

dancing 19, 99, 168n. 11
"The Dancin' Party at Harrison's Cove" (Murfree) 31, 35, 159n. 1, 160n. 5
Davidson, Donald 79
This Day and Time (Armstrong) 6, 30, 56, 68-76, 95, 127
  city-country contrast 74-75
  drunkenness 73
  encroachment of city 70
  moonshining 73
  self-sufficiency 70
  sexuality 71-73
  squalor 70-71, 75
death, early of mountain women 68-69, 128, 129
Deliverance (Dickey) 59
Dickey, James 59
  Deliverance 59
The Dollmaker (Arnow) 6-8, 10, 12-13, 15, 124-26, 133, 135, 146-58. 166n. 13
  ending 155-56
  Gertie's conception of Christ 148

  gulf between Gertie and Clovis 151-53
  nature and Gertie 148-49
  symbolism of wood carving 156
"Drifting Down Lost Creek" (Murfree) 3, 7, 35, 38, 47-49, 51, 160n. 6
drunkenness of mountain men 26, 32,, 36-37, 41, 73, 96, 136
drudgery 23, 26, 34-36, 52

early deaths
  See death, early of mountain women
Eckley, Wilton 149, 155-56
economic subservience of women 8, 26, 59-60
education 10-11, 46, 55, 132, 140-41
endurance of mountain women 2, 82, 87, 97, 115-16, 120-21, 147, 154
escape, women's desire for 10, 55-56, 96, 98, 142-43
extramarital sex 66, 71

fairy tales 4, 106
family, importance of 2-3, 10, 12, 23, 76, 92, 99, 105, 108, 111, 114, 117, 119, 122, 147, 155
  See also children
farming 6, 12, 70, 112, 119, 149, 152, 161n. 8
Farr, Sidney S. 104, 122-23
fatalism 12, 87, 115-16, 120, 139, 140, 156
  See also passivity
Faulkner, William 16, 146
  The Fable 146
feuding 21, 36, 41, 55, 126-27, 129, 132
folklore 19
Foster, Ruel E. 88
Fox, John, Jr. 28-29, 35, 80, 160n. 4

182 Index

The Trail of the Lonesome Pine
    160n. 4
Foxfore 17, 82
freedom:
    men's 15, 59-60, 61
    women's desire for 7, 61, 64
Frost, William Goodell 16, 20-21, 23-24, 35

gender roles 11, 25-26, 59, 86-88, 94, 101, 106-7
    See also men, and women
gloomy portrayals 3, 53-77
Griffin, Susan 4-5
gulf between men and women 7-8, 10, 65, 86, 95, 101, 114-15, 129, 138-39, 151-54

"The 'Harnt' That Walks Chilhowie" (Murfree) 50, 160n. 6
Harris, Isabella D. 34, 37-38, 54, 124
Hass, Victor P. 133, 139
Hawthorne, Nathaniel 162n. 14
    "The Ambitious Guest" 162n. 14
home 51, 113
hopelessness 57, 60
housework 62
Hubble, Jay B. 159n. 2
Hunter's Horn (Arnow) 6-8, 10, 12, 30, 124-26, 133-46, 149, 156
    Millie's delight in work 135-36
    Millie's self-sacricife 138
    religion 139
    Suse Ballew 140-45
    symbolism of King Devil 134, 146, 156, 170n. 6
hygiene 24, 70

ignorance 29, 45, 54-55
illegitimacy 2, 29-30, 71, 134, 143
immorality
    See morality

inbreeding 2, 58, 60, 95, 97-98
incest 2, 72
independence:
    of mountain people 75, 132-33, 160n. 6
    women's desire for 75, 119
infanticide 71, 166n. 12
insanity 13, 144
    See also mental illness
In the Tennessee Mountains (Murfree) 31, 34-35, 127, 159n. 1
inventiveness 12, 128

Jesse Stuart Foundation 90, 92, 167n. 6

Kahn, Kathy 11, 13
    Hillbilly Women 11, 13
Kelley, Edith Summers 2, 13, 56, 95, 164n. 6
    Weeds 56-68
Kephart, Horace 16, 24-26, 35, 81
Kinder, Alice 13
    Old-Fashioned Mountain Mothers 13
Kohler, Dayton 79, 102
Kroll, Harry Harrison 79
    The Mountainy Singer 79
land:
    men's relationship to 92, 112, 136, 168n. 8
    women's relationship to 5-7, 12, 113-12, 119-20, 135, 147, 149
    See also place, sense of
language 24, 33, 61, 79, 102
Lawson, Lewis A. 156
laziness of mountain men 24, 26, 28, 31, 55, 59, 96, 99, 104-5
Leavell, Frank H. 93
lechery of mountain men 66, 72
Lee, Dorothy H. 155

Index 183

Lewis, Sinclair 60, 164n. 6, 165nn. 8-9
Lincoln Memorial University 79-80, 103
literary landmarks 31, 54, 80
local color 2, 21-22, 30, 34, 53, 55-56, 79-80, 159n. 4, 160nn. 2, 3, 5, 163n. 1
loneliness of mountain women 7, 29, 69-70, 86, 129, 153

marriage 7-8, 23, 26, 28, 62, 65-66, 82-86, 88, 99, 104-5, 151-52
"Martha Hylton Stuart" (Stuart) 89-92
matriarchy 52
medical care 55
media depictions 28, 161n. 10
melancholy 7, 23-24, 35
men, mountain 7-8, 21, 24, 26, 73, 162n. 15, 164n. 7
   aversion to "women's work" 94
   brutality of 2, 36, 55, 69, 73, 74
   comparison with women 26
   coal mining 112
   drunkenness 26, 32, 36-37, 41, 73, 96, 136
   economic control 8
   freedom 59-61
   family relationships 105, 108, 111, 114
   gender roles 25-26, 35, 59, 64, 87-88, 94, 206-7
   laziness of 21, 24, 26, 28, 31, 55, 59, 96, 104-5
   lechery of 72
   land, relationship to 96, 136, 168n. 8
   moonshining 21, 31, 70, 73
   nature, relationship to 5-7
   selfishness 63, 85
   stereotypes 21, 31
   work 6, 26, 119, 152

mental illness 158n. 3
   See also insanity
migration 157
Miles, Emma Bell 7-8, 14, 81-88, 129, 166n. 3
   The Spirit of the Mountains 7-8, 14, 81-88, 129
Miles, Frank G. 81
Miller, Jim Wayne 1, 17
moonshining 21, 31, 70, 73, 126-27, 132-33
morality of mountain people 2, 29-30, 66, 71-72, 98
   See also extramarital sex and pre marital sex
Mountain Path (Arnow) 10, 12-13, 125-33, 135-36, 140, 145, 156
   city-country contrast 131-32
   comparison with Mary Murfree 131
   feuding 127, 129
   moonshining 129
mountain women and outsider men, theme of 39-45, 51, 134, 160n. 4
"Mrs. Razor" (Still) 104, 168n. 1
Murfree, Mary Noailles 1-3, 15, 30-52, 57, 93, 102, 127, 131, 157, 159n. 2, 160nn. 2, 3, 161n. 9, 162nn. 14, 15, 163n. 2
   attitude toward mountain people 32, 34
   brutality of mountain men 36-37, 41-42
   "common humanity" theme 39-45, 131
   "The Dancin' Party at Harrison's Cove" 31, 35, 159n. 1, 160n. 5
   "Drifting Down Lost Creek" 3, 7, 35, 38, 47-49, 51, 160n. 6
   enthusiasm for scenic description 161n. 7
   "The 'Harnt' That Walks Chilhowie" 50, 160n. 6

In the Tennessee Mountains 31, 34-35, 127, 159n. 1
  local color 34
  "Old Sledge at the Settlement" 35
  older women 34, 35-37, 39
  "On Big Injun Mounting" 35-36
  pathetic mountain women 36-37
  physical appearance of mountain women 35-36, 41-42
  The Prophet of the Great Smoky Mountains 31, 39, 160n. 2
  "The Star in the Valley" 3, 36, 40-44, 49, 127, 131, 160n. 5
  women's work 36
  young women 34, 37-52, 160n. 6

national uniformity 20, 159n. 4
native writers 1-2, 14, 78-80, 123-24. 168n. 2
nature:
  men's relationship to 5-7
  women's relationship to 3-6, 49-51, 100, 106, 147-49
"The Nest" (Still) 104-8
Night Comes to the Cumberlands (Caudill) 17-18
non-native writers 23, 32, 54
nurturing of mountain women 11, 107-8, 113-14, 116

"Old Sledge at the Settlement" (Murfree) 35
"On Big Injun Mounting" (Murfree) 35-36
outsiders 1, 23-24, 32, 40, 45, 51
  See also non-native writers
outsider men and mountain women, theme of
  See mountain women and outsider men

Parks, Edd Winfield 33, 160n. 5

passivity, of mountain women 12-13, 57, 59, 61, 110, 116
  See also fatalism
patriarchy 2-4, 8, 14, 25-26, 35, 52, 56, 59, 93, 97, 107, 168n. 10
physical abuse 37, 69, 74
physical appearance, of mountain women 2, 13, 23, 24, 26, 28-29, 32, 35-36, 39, 56-58, 68, 70, 93, 97, 127, 135
place, love of 6-7, 12, 51
Porter, Katherine Anne 107, 114
  "The Grave" 107, 114
poverty 54-55, 70, 96, 155
premarital sex 66, 71, 98, 143
preserver, mountain woman as 10-11, 87, 108
Prohibition 73
The Prophet of the Great Smoky Mountains (Murfree) 31, 39, 160n. 2
Protestant missionary movement 54-55, 163n. 2

quilting 12, 86

Ralph, Julian 23-24, 26, 35
realism 34, 131, 160n. 3, 166n. 1
reform movements 2, 54, 163nn. 2, 3, 4
regionalism 102-3
religion 18, 85, 128-29, 139, 141, 148-49, 156, 168n. 9
River of Earth (Still) 6-8, 10-12, 80, 102, 107-23, 149, 152
  cyclical patterns of life 67, 114, 121
  farming versus mining 112
  gulf between Alpha and Brack 114-15
  initiation theme 108, 116, 121-22
  maternal symbolism 113
Roberts, Elizabeth Madox 16, 166n. 1

The Time of Man 166n. 1
romanticization 2, 34-35, 53, 56, 70, 80, 127, 160n. 3
Roy, Roberta Teague 6
Royall, Anne Newport 29
   Sketches of History, Life and Manners in the United States 29
Russell, Annie 22

sacrifice, women's
   See self-sacrifice of women
Scotch-Irish 18-19
self-sacrifice of women 2, 10, 88, 110-11, 119, 156
selfishness of men 63, 85
sexuality 29, 65-66, 98
   See also extramarital sex; morality; premarital sex
Shapiro, Henry D. 19-20, 163n. 2
Sheppard, Muriel Earley 9, 137
   Cabins in the Laurel 9, 137
shyness of mountain women 23-24, 29, 85
Skaggs, Merrill Maguire 30
Smith, Lee 3, 158nn. 1, 3
   Black Mountain Breakdown 158n. 3
   Fair and Tender Ladies 3
The Southern Highlander and His Homeland (Campbell) 15
Spence, E.B. 33
The Spirit of the Mountains (Miles) 7-8, 14, 81-88, 129
   gender roles 86-88
   marriage 82-86, 88
   relationships between men and women 86-87
Spurlock, John Howard 93, 167n. 4, 168n. 10
squalor 55, 70, 75, 95-96
"The Star in the Valley" (Murfree) 3, 36, 40-44, 49, 127, 131, 160n. 5
stereotypes of mountain people 2, 13, 17, 21, 23-24, 28, 32, 132
Still, James 2-3, 6, 79-80, 102-23
   "Brother to Methuselem" 103
   Hounds on the Mountain 80
   literary production 103
   "Mrs. Razor" 104, 168n 1
   narrative point of view 103-4, 108
   "The Nest" 104-8
   Pattern of a Man & Other Stories 103
   "Pattern of a Man" 103
   "A Ride on the Short Dog" 103
   River of Earth 6-8, 10-12, 80, 102, 107-23, 149, 152
   Sporty Creek 10
strength of mountain women 11-13, 82, 92, 94, 108, 120, 147, 153-54
Stuart, Jesse 2-3, 5, 7, 16, 78-80, 88-103, 166n. 4
   admiration for mountain women 89, 96
   comparison with Robert Burns 89, 167n. 4
   "For Mitchell Stuart" 92
   initiation theme 89
   Man With a Bull-tongue Plow 78, 89, 167n. 4
   "Martha Hylton Stuart" 89-92
   masculinity of works 89
   narrative point of view 89
   patriarchy 93
   Taps for Private Tussie 89
   Trees of Heaven 7-8, 10-11, 80, 89, 92-102, 112, 122
Stuart, Martha Hylton 3, 89-92, 167n. 7
Stoneback, H.R. 16, 39, 79, 102-3, 119
Stribling, T. S. 16, 166n. 1

Toynbee, Arnold 158n. 1
Trees of Heaven (Stuart) 7-8, 10-11, 80, 89, 92-102, 112, 122
  inbreeding 95
  initiation theme 89
  nature and women 100
  sexuality 98
  women's work 94-95
uncomplainingness of mountain women 25, 52, 70, 84, 115, 136, 140

Vanderbilt University 103
victimization of mountain women 2, 14, 24-25, 35, 52, 56, 67

weaving 24, 51, 82, 87
Weeds (Kelley) 56-68
  eyes of heroines 57
  inbreeding 58-59
  Judith's masculinity 61, 64
  language of men and women 61, 64
  marriage 62, 65
  sexuality 66
Weller, Jack 16-17, 115
  Yesterday's People 115
West, Don L. 79-80
  crab-grass 79-80
West, Ray, Jr. 133, 146
Whisnant, David 81, 86, 166n. 3
Williams, Cratis 1, 17-18, 26, 31, 33, 39, 102-3, 124, 126, 134, 156, 165n. 10, 169n. 3
Williams, Shirley 102
work:
  of men 119, 152
  of women 26, 51, 59, 62-64, 70, 92-93, 95, 99, 128, 135, 169n. 4
women, mountain
  affection, demonstrations of 116
  aging 23-24, 26, 28, 35-36, 57-58, 68

children 10, 24, 63, 86, 108, 135
city-country contrast 45-48, 130-31
deaths, early 68-69, 129
drudgery 52
economic subservience 8, 26, 59-60
endurance 2, 82, 87, 97, 115-16, 120-21, 147, 154
escape, desire to 10, 56, 142-43
farming 12, 70, 112, 119, 149, 152, 161n. 8
family, importance of 2-3, 10, 12, 23, 76, 92, 99, 111, 117, 122, 147, 155
freedom, desire for 60-61, 64
gender roles 24-25, 35, 59, 64, 86-88, 101, 107
gulf between men and women 7, 65, 86, 95, 101, 114-15, 129, 138-39, 151-54
home 51-52
hopelessness 57, 60, 68
hygiene 24
ignorance of 29, 45, 54-55
independence, desire for 6-7, 119, 135, 149-50, 152; of spirit 38, 62
inventiveness 128
land, relationship to 5-7, 12, 112-13, 119-20, 135, 147, 149
loneliness of 7, 29, 69-70, 86, 129, 153
marriage 7-8, 23, 26, 28, 62, 65-66, 82-86, 88, 99, 104-5, 151-52
media depictions 28, 161n. 10
melancholy 7, 23-25, 35
morality 2, 29-30, 66, 71-72, 98
nature, relationship to 3-6, 49-50, 100, 106, 147-49
neighborliness 70, 75-76
number of children 2, 23, 68, 92, 117
nurturing 107-8, 113-14, 116
physical abuse 37, 69

place, love of 5-7, 12, 51
preserver, as 87
self-sacrifice 10, 43-44, 88, 11-11, 119, 156
sexuality 29, 65-66, 98
shyness of 23-24, 29, 85
stereotypes of 2, 13, 17, 21, 23-24, 28, 32, 132
subservience of 25-26, 62
strength of 11-13, 82, 92, 94, 108, 120, 147, 153-54
uncomplainingnes of 25, 52, 70, 84, 115, 136, 140
work 24, 26, 51-52, 62-64, 70, 92-93, 95, 99, 128, 135, 169n. 4
"women's work" 26, 59, 94-95